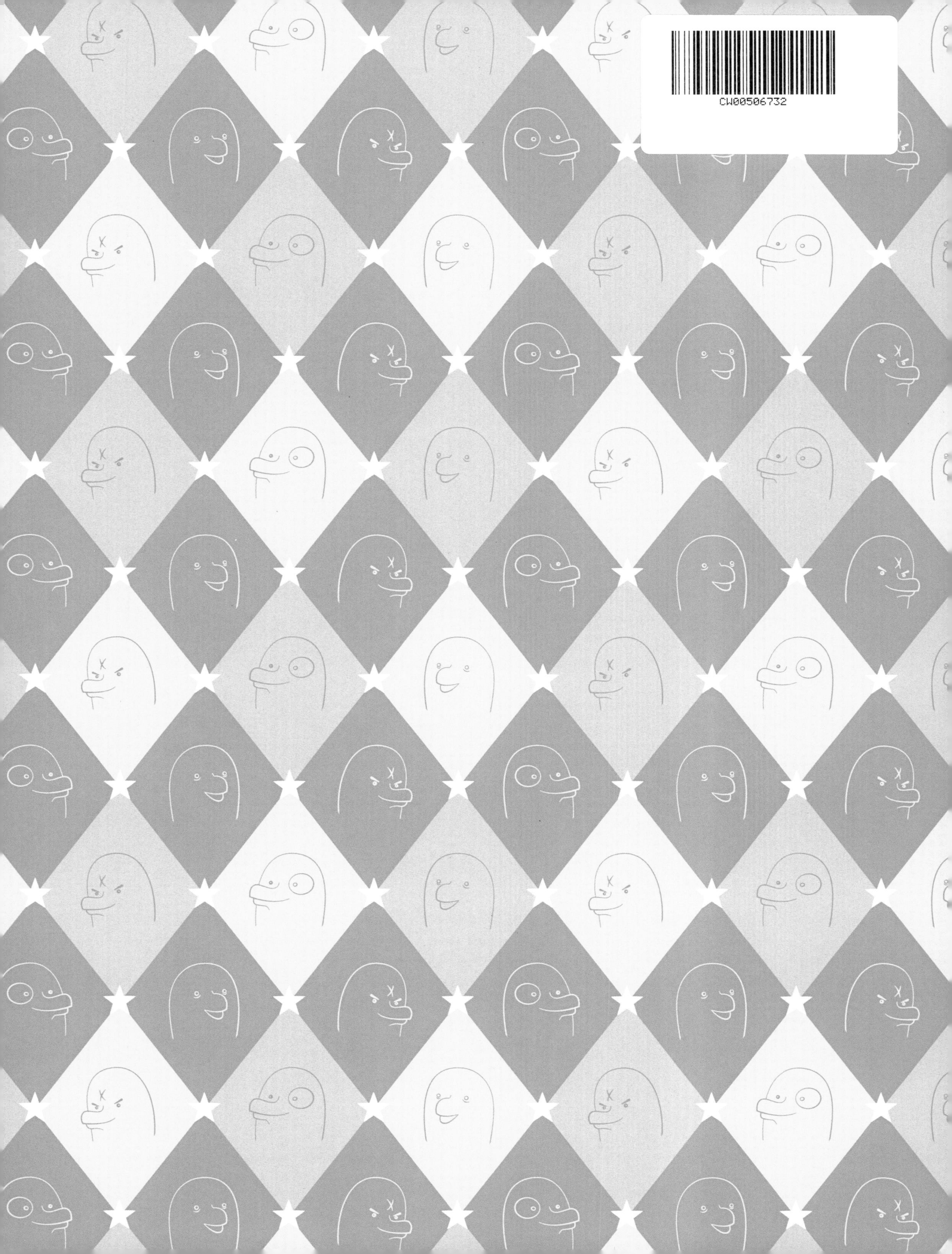

Dolphin Squad II - A Death in the Pod

Agents of S.E.A.W.O.R.L.D

Script   -   Mark Adams
             Matt Warner
Art   -   David Clifford

For Deadstar Publishing

Editor in Chief   -   Kevin Davies
Art Director   -   Danny J. Weston
Junior Editors   -   Becky Garner
                    Kate Kato

No dolphins were harmed in the making of this comic book.

ISBN 978-1-910311-04-2
ISBN 978-1-910311-05-9 (Digital version)

First published 2018 by Deadstar Publishing, Cardiff, Wales
www.deadstarpublishing.co.uk

DOLPHIN SQUAD II
A DEATH IN THE POD
DANNY J. WESTON

JACK + ZOË
BEST
FISHES!

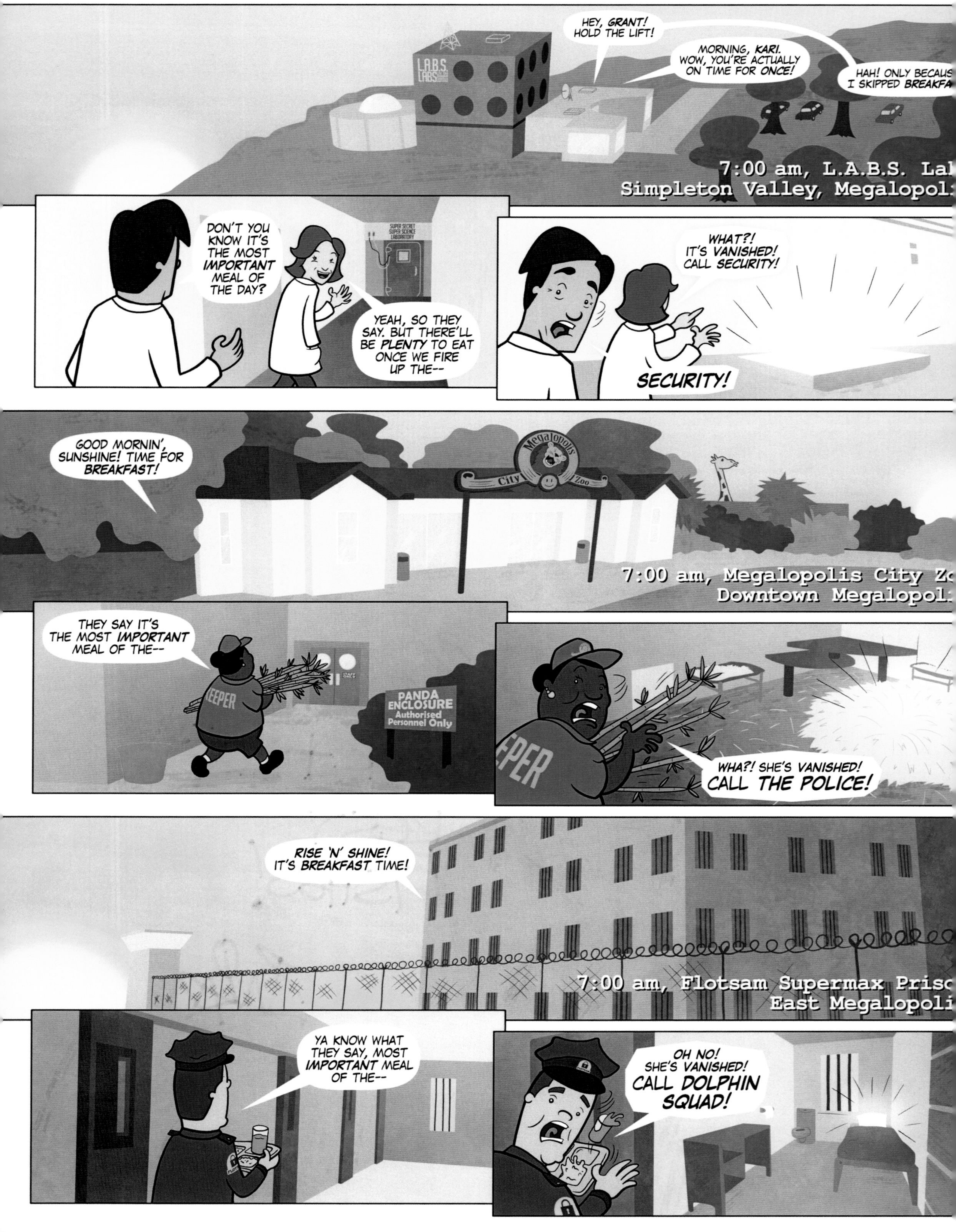

L.A.B.S. LABS
HEY, GRANT! HOLD THE LIFT!
MORNING, KARI. WOW, YOU'RE ACTUALLY ON TIME FOR ONCE!
HAH! ONLY BECAUS I SKIPPED BREAKFA
7:00 am, L.A.B.S. La
Simpleton Valley, Megalopol
DON'T YOU KNOW IT'S THE MOST IMPORTANT MEAL OF THE DAY?
SUPER SECRET SUPER SCIENCE LABORATORY
YEAH, SO THEY SAY. BUT THERE'LL BE PLENTY TO EAT ONCE WE FIRE UP THE--
WHAT?! IT'S VANISHED! CALL SECURITY!
SECURITY!
GOOD MORNIN', SUNSHINE! TIME FOR BREAKFAST!
Megalopolis City Zoo
7:00 am, Megalopolis City Zo
Downtown Megalopol
THEY SAY IT'S THE MOST IMPORTANT MEAL OF THE--
PANDA ENCLOSURE Authorised Personnel Only
WHA?! SHE'S VANISHED! CALL THE POLICE!
RISE 'N' SHINE! IT'S BREAKFAST TIME!
7:00 am, Flotsam Supermax Pris
East Megalopol
YA KNOW WHAT THEY SAY, MOST IMPORTANT MEAL OF THE--
OH NO! SHE'S VANISHED! CALL DOLPHIN SQUAD!

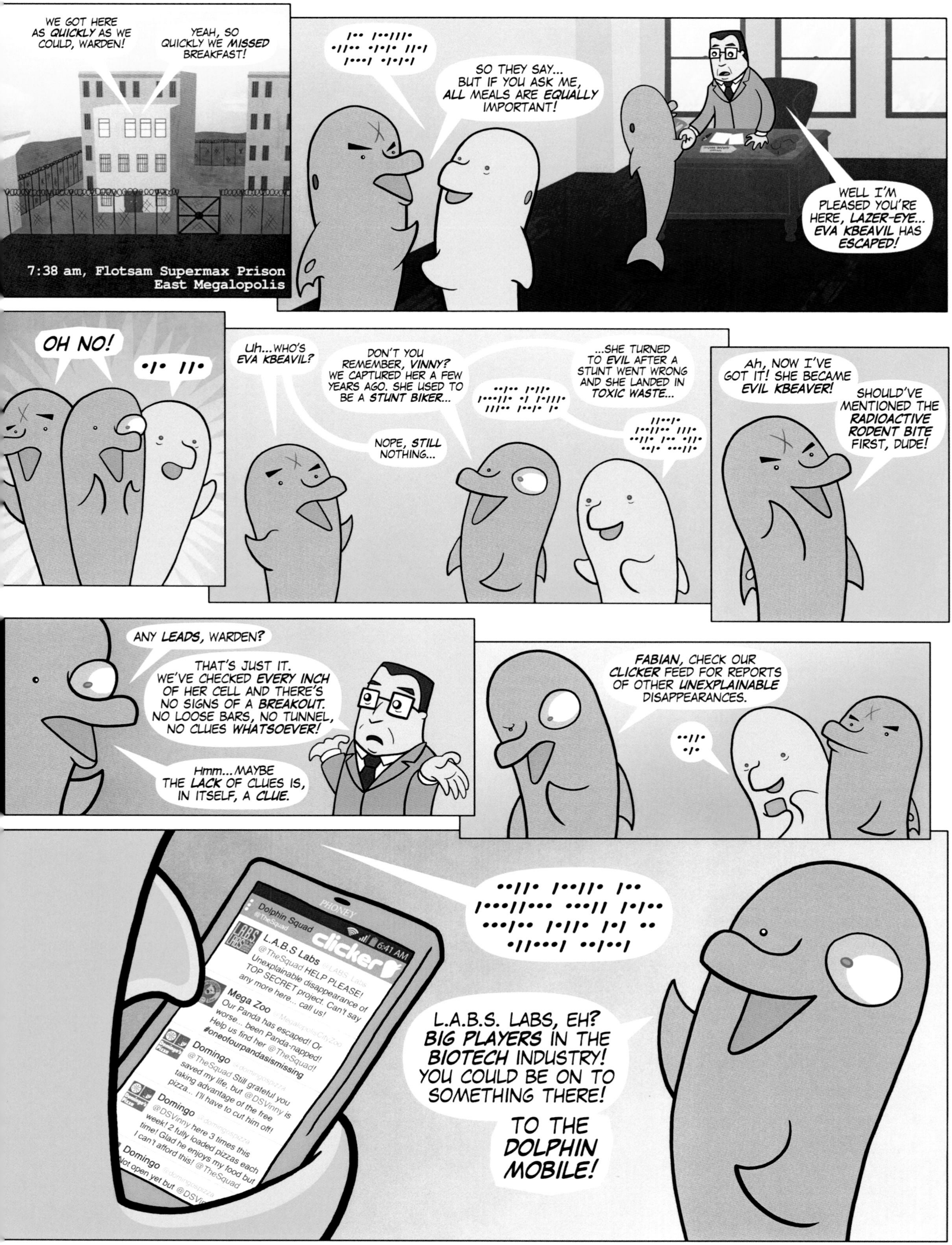

WE GOT HERE AS QUICKLY AS WE COULD, WARDEN!
YEAH, SO QUICKLY WE MISSED BREAKFAST!
7:38 am, Flotsam Supermax Prison
East Megalopolis
SO THEY SAY... BUT IF YOU ASK ME, ALL MEALS ARE EQUALLY IMPORTANT!
WELL I'M PLEASED YOU'RE HERE, LAZER-EYE... EVA KBEAVIL HAS ESCAPED!
OH NO!
Uh...WHO'S EVA KBEAVIL?
DON'T YOU REMEMBER, VINNY? WE CAPTURED HER A FEW YEARS AGO. SHE USED TO BE A STUNT BIKER...
...SHE TURNED TO EVIL AFTER A STUNT WENT WRONG AND SHE LANDED IN TOXIC WASTE...
NOPE, STILL NOTHING...
Ah, NOW I'VE GOT IT! SHE BECAME EVIL KBEAVER!
SHOULD'VE MENTIONED THE RADIOACTIVE RODENT BITE FIRST, DUDE!
ANY LEADS, WARDEN?
THAT'S JUST IT. WE'VE CHECKED EVERY INCH OF HER CELL AND THERE'S NO SIGNS OF A BREAKOUT. NO LOOSE BARS, NO TUNNEL, NO CLUES WHATSOEVER!
Hmm...MAYBE THE LACK OF CLUES IS, IN ITSELF, A CLUE.
FABIAN, CHECK OUR CLICKER FEED FOR REPORTS OF OTHER UNEXPLAINABLE DISAPPEARANCES.
PHONEY
Dolphin Squad
@TheSquad
clicker
6:41 AM
L.A.B.S Labs @LABS_Labs
@TheSquad HELP PLEASE! Unexplainable disappearance of TOP SECRET project. Can't say any more here... call us!
Mega Zoo @MegalopolisCityZoo
Our Panda has escaped! Or worse... been Panda-napped! Help us find her @TheSquad! #oneofourpandasismissing
Domingo @domingospizza
@TheSquad Still grateful you saved my life, but @DSVinny is taking advantage of the free pizza... I'll have to cut him off!
Domingo @domingospizza
@DSVinny here 3 times this week! 2 fully loaded pizzas each time! Glad he enjoys my food but I can't afford this! @TheSquad
Domingo @domingospizza
Not open yet but @DSVi
L.A.B.S. LABS, EH? BIG PLAYERS IN THE BIOTECH INDUSTRY! YOU COULD BE ON TO SOMETHING THERE!
TO THE DOLPHIN MOBILE!

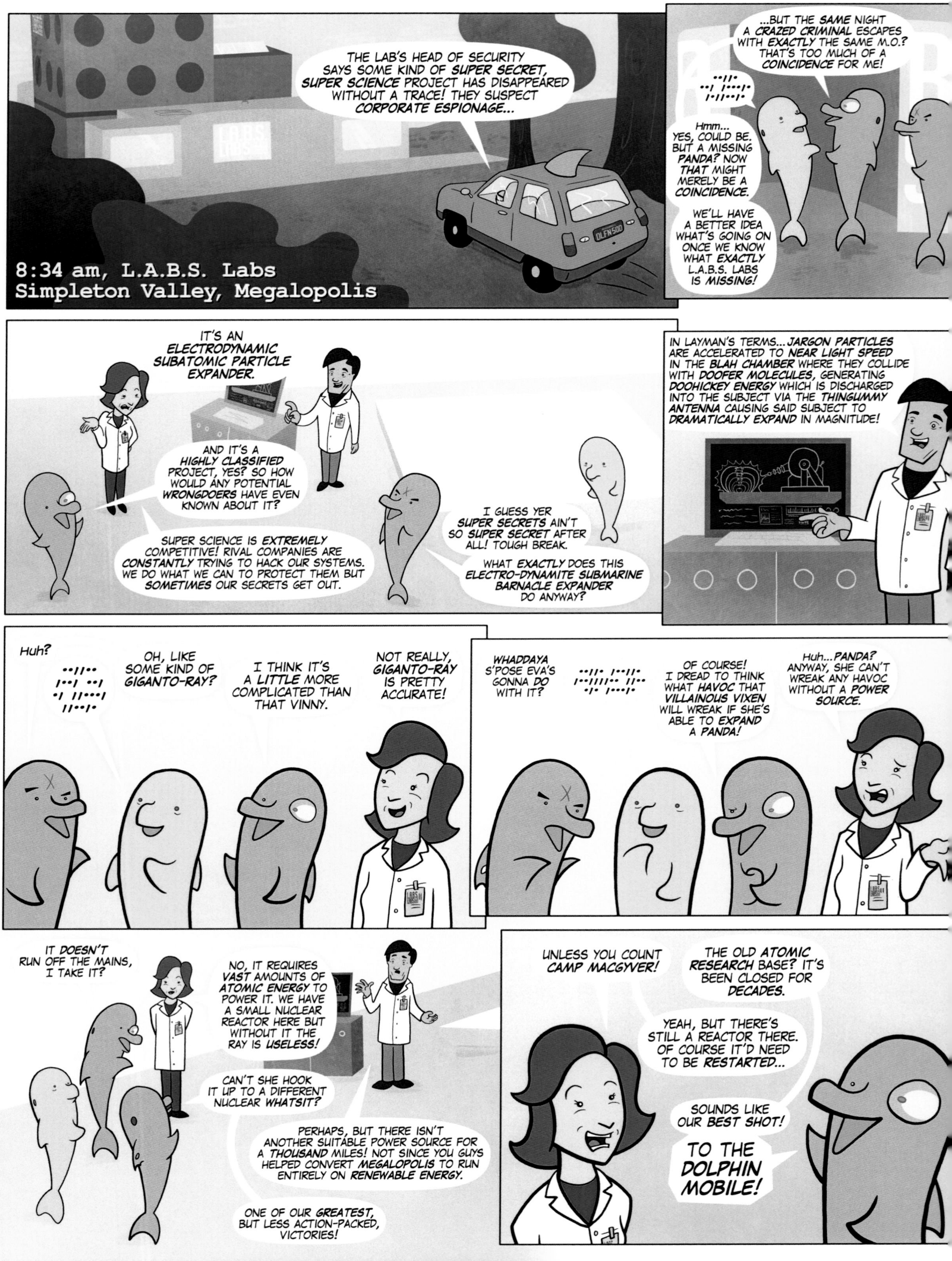
8:34 am, L.A.B.S. Labs
Simpleton Valley, Megalopolis
THE LAB'S HEAD OF SECURITY SAYS SOME KIND OF SUPER SECRET, SUPER SCIENCE PROJECT HAS DISAPPEARED WITHOUT A TRACE! THEY SUSPECT CORPORATE ESPIONAGE...
DLFN500
...BUT THE SAME NIGHT A CRAZED CRIMINAL ESCAPES WITH EXACTLY THE SAME M.O.? THAT'S TOO MUCH OF A COINCIDENCE FOR ME!
Hmm... YES, COULD BE. BUT A MISSING PANDA? NOW THAT MIGHT MERELY BE A COINCIDENCE.
WE'LL HAVE A BETTER IDEA WHAT'S GOING ON ONCE WE KNOW WHAT EXACTLY L.A.B.S. LABS IS MISSING!
IT'S AN ELECTRODYNAMIC SUBATOMIC PARTICLE EXPANDER.
AND IT'S A HIGHLY CLASSIFIED PROJECT, YES? SO HOW WOULD ANY POTENTIAL WRONGDOERS HAVE EVEN KNOWN ABOUT IT?
SUPER SCIENCE IS EXTREMELY COMPETITIVE! RIVAL COMPANIES ARE CONSTANTLY TRYING TO HACK OUR SYSTEMS. WE DO WHAT WE CAN TO PROTECT THEM BUT SOMETIMES OUR SECRETS GET OUT.
I GUESS YER SUPER SECRETS AIN'T SO SUPER SECRET AFTER ALL! TOUGH BREAK.
WHAT EXACTLY DOES THIS ELECTRO-DYNAMITE SUBMARINE BARNACLE EXPANDER DO ANYWAY?
IN LAYMAN'S TERMS... JARGON PARTICLES ARE ACCELERATED TO NEAR LIGHT SPEED IN THE BLAH CHAMBER WHERE THEY COLLIDE WITH DOOFER MOLECULES, GENERATING DOOHICKEY ENERGY WHICH IS DISCHARGED INTO THE SUBJECT VIA THE THINGUMMY ANTENNA CAUSING SAID SUBJECT TO DRAMATICALLY EXPAND IN MAGNITUDE!
Huh?
OH, LIKE SOME KIND OF GIGANTO-RAY?
I THINK IT'S A LITTLE MORE COMPLICATED THAN THAT VINNY.
NOT REALLY, GIGANTO-RAY IS PRETTY ACCURATE!
WHADDAYA S'POSE EVA'S GONNA DO WITH IT?
OF COURSE! I DREAD TO THINK WHAT HAVOC THAT VILLAINOUS VIXEN WILL WREAK IF SHE'S ABLE TO EXPAND A PANDA!
Huh...PANDA? ANYWAY, SHE CAN'T WREAK ANY HAVOC WITHOUT A POWER SOURCE.
IT DOESN'T RUN OFF THE MAINS, I TAKE IT?
NO, IT REQUIRES VAST AMOUNTS OF ATOMIC ENERGY TO POWER IT. WE HAVE A SMALL NUCLEAR REACTOR HERE BUT WITHOUT IT THE RAY IS USELESS!
CAN'T SHE HOOK IT UP TO A DIFFERENT NUCLEAR WHATSIT?
PERHAPS, BUT THERE ISN'T ANOTHER SUITABLE POWER SOURCE FOR A THOUSAND MILES! NOT SINCE YOU GUYS HELPED CONVERT MEGALOPOLIS TO RUN ENTIRELY ON RENEWABLE ENERGY.
ONE OF OUR GREATEST, BUT LESS ACTION-PACKED, VICTORIES!
UNLESS YOU COUNT CAMP MACGYVER!
THE OLD ATOMIC RESEARCH BASE? IT'S BEEN CLOSED FOR DECADES.
YEAH, BUT THERE'S STILL A REACTOR THERE. OF COURSE IT'D NEED TO BE RESTARTED...
SOUNDS LIKE OUR BEST SHOT!
TO THE DOLPHIN MOBILE!

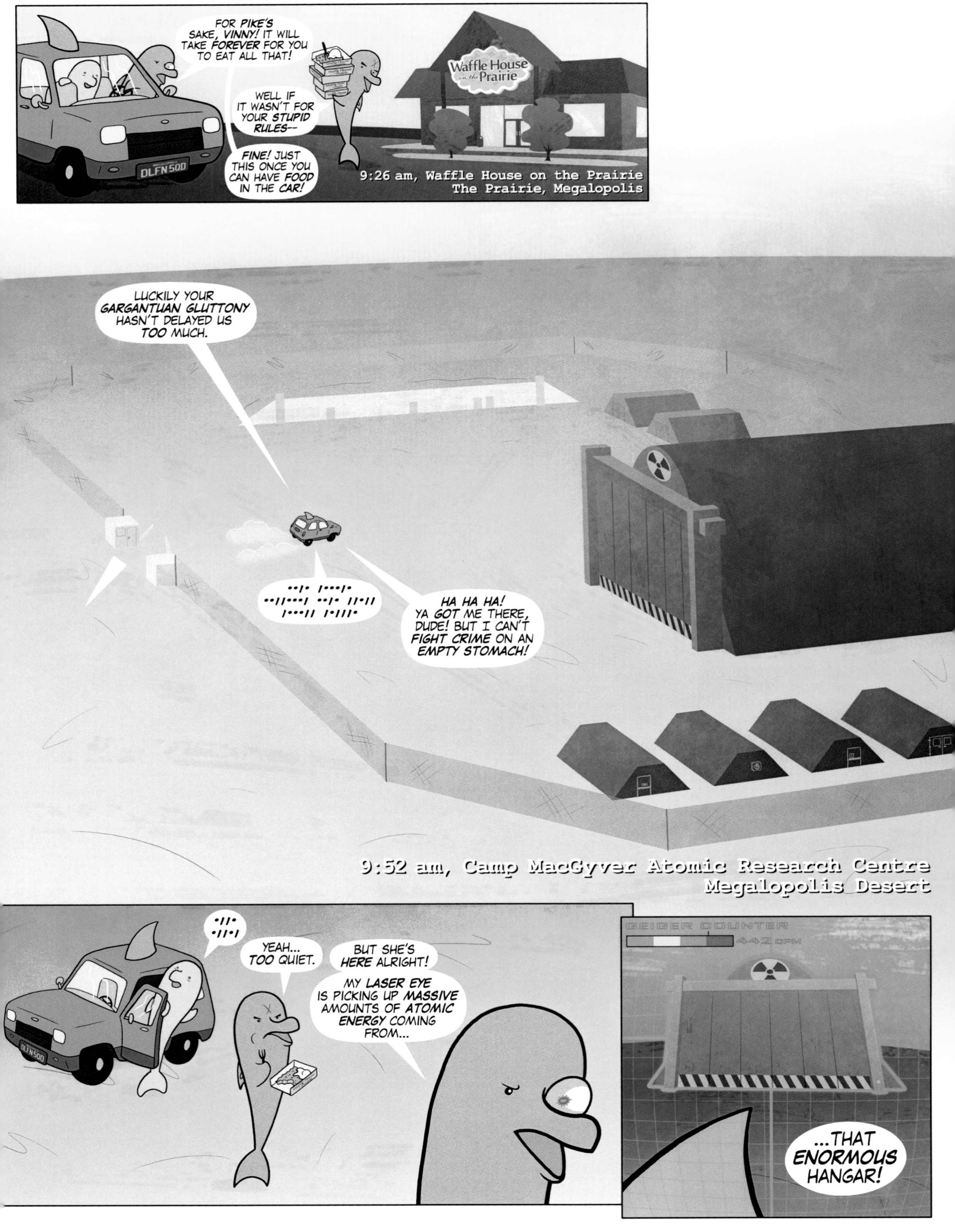
FOR PIKE'S SAKE, VINNY! IT WILL TAKE FOREVER FOR YOU TO EAT ALL THAT!
WELL IF IT WASN'T FOR YOUR STUPID RULES--
FINE! JUST THIS ONCE YOU CAN HAVE FOOD IN THE CAR!
Waffle House on the Prairie
DLFN 50D
9:26 am, Waffle House on the Prairie
The Prairie, Megalopolis
LUCKILY YOUR GARGANTUAN GLUTTONY HASN'T DELAYED US TOO MUCH.
HA HA HA! YA GOT ME THERE, DUDE! BUT I CAN'T FIGHT CRIME ON AN EMPTY STOMACH!
9:52 am, Camp MacGyver Atomic Research Centre
Megalopolis Desert
YEAH... TOO QUIET.
BUT SHE'S HERE ALRIGHT!
MY LASER EYE IS PICKING UP MASSIVE AMOUNTS OF ATOMIC ENERGY COMING FROM...
GEIGER COUNTER
...THAT ENORMOUS HANGAR!

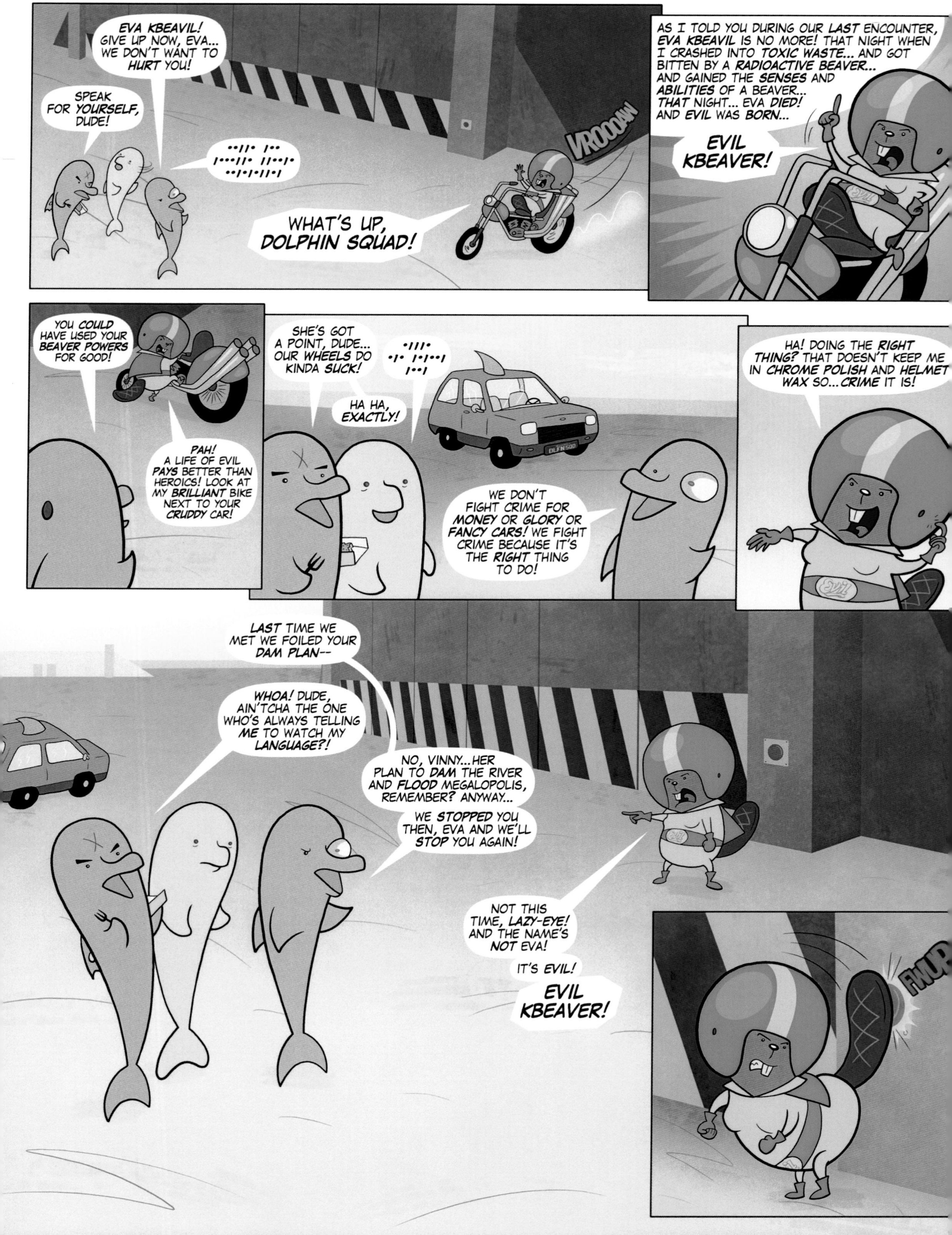
EVA KBEAVIL! GIVE UP NOW, EVA... WE DON'T WANT TO HURT YOU!
SPEAK FOR YOURSELF, DUDE!
VROOOAW
WHAT'S UP, DOLPHIN SQUAD!
AS I TOLD YOU DURING OUR LAST ENCOUNTER, EVA KBEAVIL IS NO MORE! THAT NIGHT WHEN I CRASHED INTO TOXIC WASTE... AND GOT BITTEN BY A RADIOACTIVE BEAVER... AND GAINED THE SENSES AND ABILITIES OF A BEAVER... THAT NIGHT... EVA DIED! AND EVIL WAS BORN...
EVIL KBEAVER!
YOU COULD HAVE USED YOUR BEAVER POWERS FOR GOOD!
PAH! A LIFE OF EVIL PAYS BETTER THAN HEROICS! LOOK AT MY BRILLIANT BIKE NEXT TO YOUR CRUDDY CAR!
SHE'S GOT A POINT, DUDE... OUR WHEELS DO KINDA SUCK!
HA HA, EXACTLY!
WE DON'T FIGHT CRIME FOR MONEY OR GLORY OR FANCY CARS! WE FIGHT CRIME BECAUSE IT'S THE RIGHT THING TO DO!
HA! DOING THE RIGHT THING? THAT DOESN'T KEEP ME IN CHROME POLISH AND HELMET WAX SO... CRIME IT IS!
LAST TIME WE MET WE FOILED YOUR DAM PLAN--
WHOA! DUDE, AIN'TCHA THE ONE WHO'S ALWAYS TELLING ME TO WATCH MY LANGUAGE?!
NO, VINNY... HER PLAN TO DAM THE RIVER AND FLOOD MEGALOPOLIS, REMEMBER? ANYWAY...
WE STOPPED YOU THEN, EVA AND WE'LL STOP YOU AGAIN!
NOT THIS TIME, LAZY-EYE! AND THE NAME'S NOT EVA!
IT'S EVIL!
EVIL KBEAVER!
FWUP

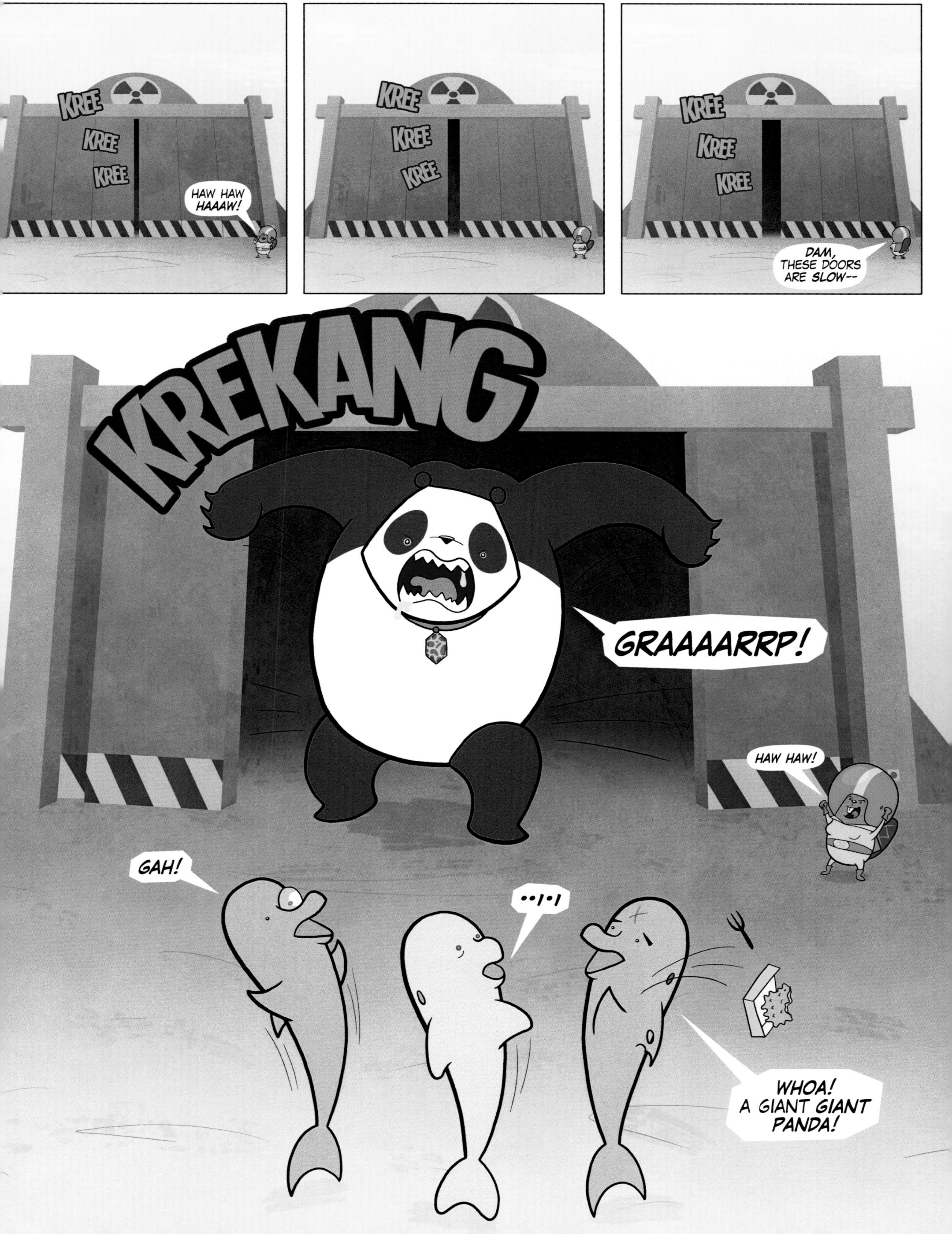
KREE
KREE
KREE
HAW HAW HAAAW!
KREE
KREE
KREE
KREE
KREE
KREE
DAM, THESE DOORS ARE SLOW--
KREKANG
GRAAAARRP!
HAW HAW!
GAH!
••!•!
WHOA! A GIANT GIANT PANDA!

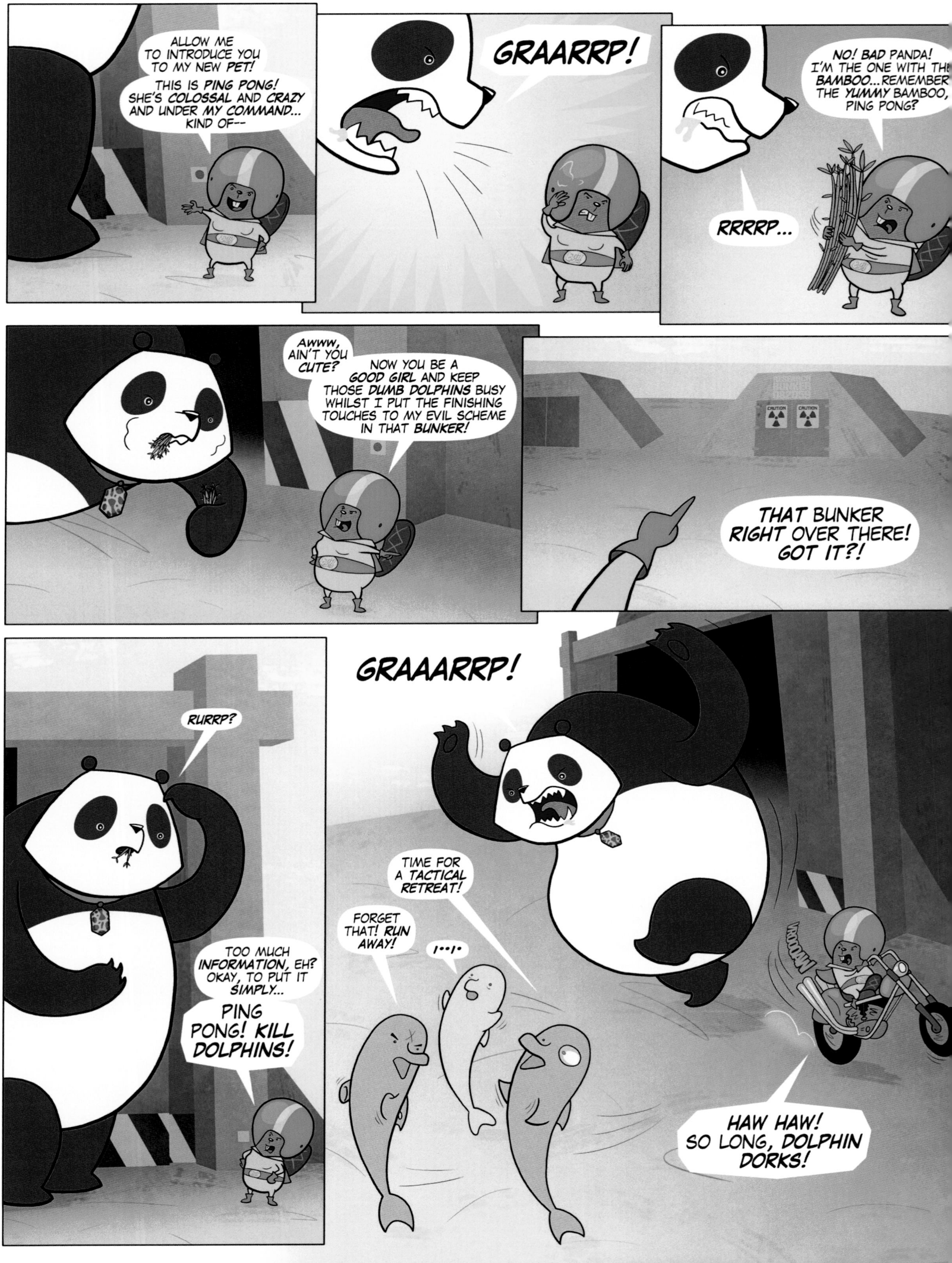

ALLOW ME TO INTRODUCE YOU TO MY NEW PET!
THIS IS PING PONG! SHE'S COLOSSAL AND CRAZY AND UNDER MY COMMAND... KIND OF--
GRAARRP!
NO! BAD PANDA! I'M THE ONE WITH THE BAMBOO...REMEMBER THE YUMMY BAMBOO, PING PONG?
RRRRP...
AWWW, AIN'T YOU CUTE?
NOW YOU BE A GOOD GIRL AND KEEP THOSE DUMB DOLPHINS BUSY WHILST I PUT THE FINISHING TOUCHES TO MY EVIL SCHEME IN THAT BUNKER!
CAUTION
CAUTION
THAT BUNKER RIGHT OVER THERE! GOT IT?!
RURRP?
TOO MUCH INFORMATION, EH? OKAY, TO PUT IT SIMPLY...
PING PONG! KILL DOLPHINS!
GRAAARRP!
TIME FOR A TACTICAL RETREAT!
FORGET THAT! RUN AWAY!
!..!.
VROOOM
HAW HAW! SO LONG, DOLPHIN DORKS!

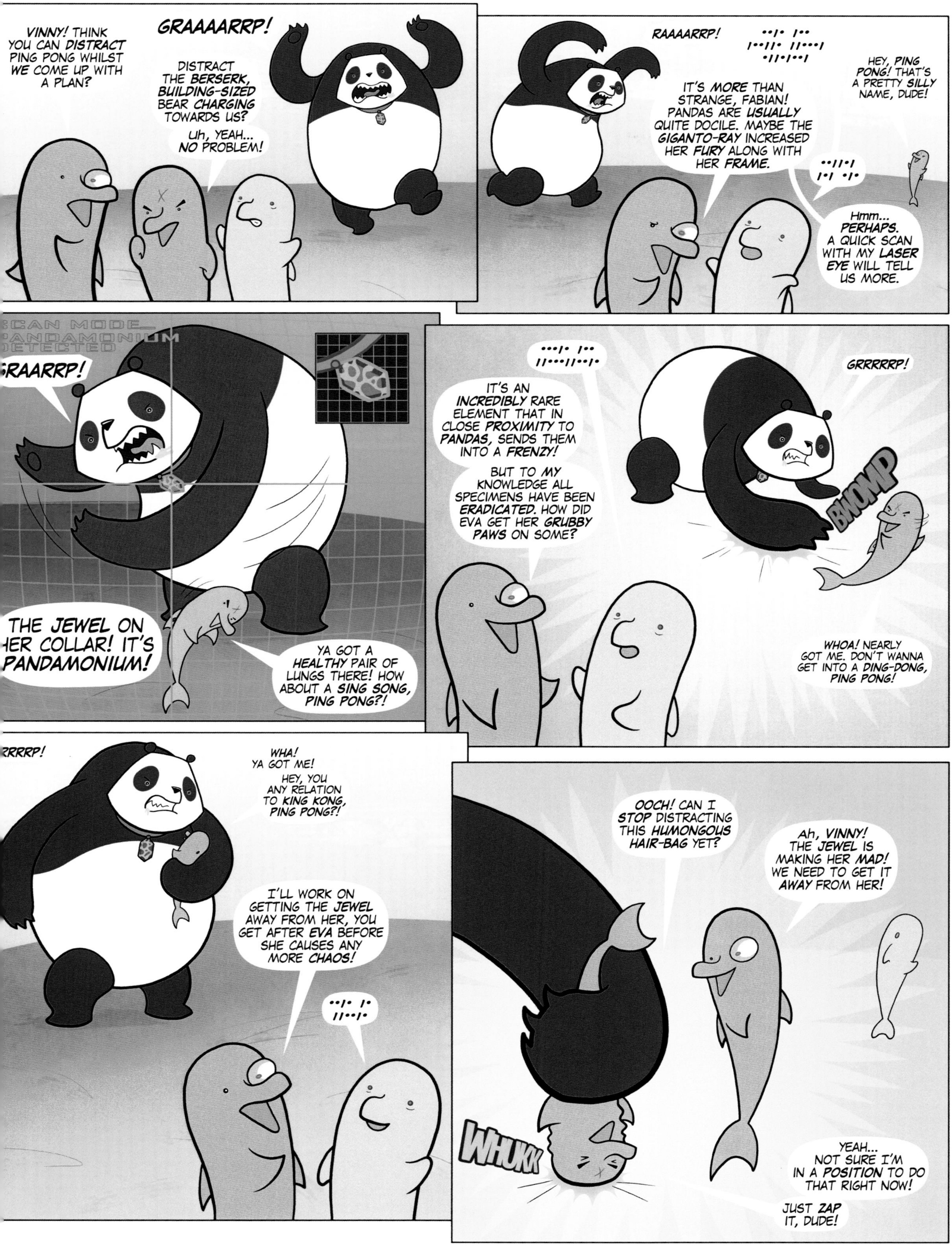
VINNY! THINK YOU CAN DISTRACT PING PONG WHILST WE COME UP WITH A PLAN?
GRAAAARRP!
DISTRACT THE BERSERK, BUILDING-SIZED BEAR CHARGING TOWARDS US?
Uh, YEAH... NO PROBLEM!
RAAAARRP!
IT'S MORE THAN STRANGE, FABIAN! PANDAS ARE USUALLY QUITE DOCILE. MAYBE THE GIGANTO-RAY INCREASED HER FURY ALONG WITH HER FRAME.
HEY, PING PONG! THAT'S A PRETTY SILLY NAME, DUDE!
Hmm... PERHAPS. A QUICK SCAN WITH MY LASER EYE WILL TELL US MORE.
CAN MODE_
ANDAMONIUM
ETECTED
RAARRP!
THE JEWEL ON
ER COLLAR! IT'S
PANDAMONIUM!
YA GOT A HEALTHY PAIR OF LUNGS THERE! HOW ABOUT A SING SONG, PING PONG?!
IT'S AN INCREDIBLY RARE ELEMENT THAT IN CLOSE PROXIMITY TO PANDAS, SENDS THEM INTO A FRENZY!
BUT TO MY KNOWLEDGE ALL SPECIMENS HAVE BEEN ERADICATED. HOW DID EVA GET HER GRUBBY PAWS ON SOME?
GRRRRRP!
BWOMP
WHOA! NEARLY GOT ME. DON'T WANNA GET INTO A DING-DONG, PING PONG!
RRRRP!
WHA! YA GOT ME!
HEY, YOU ANY RELATION TO KING KONG, PING PONG?!
I'LL WORK ON GETTING THE JEWEL AWAY FROM HER, YOU GET AFTER EVA BEFORE SHE CAUSES ANY MORE CHAOS!
OOCH! CAN I STOP DISTRACTING THIS HUMONGOUS HAIR-BAG YET?
Ah, VINNY! THE JEWEL IS MAKING HER MAD! WE NEED TO GET IT AWAY FROM HER!
WHUKK
YEAH... NOT SURE I'M IN A POSITION TO DO THAT RIGHT NOW!
JUST ZAP IT, DUDE!

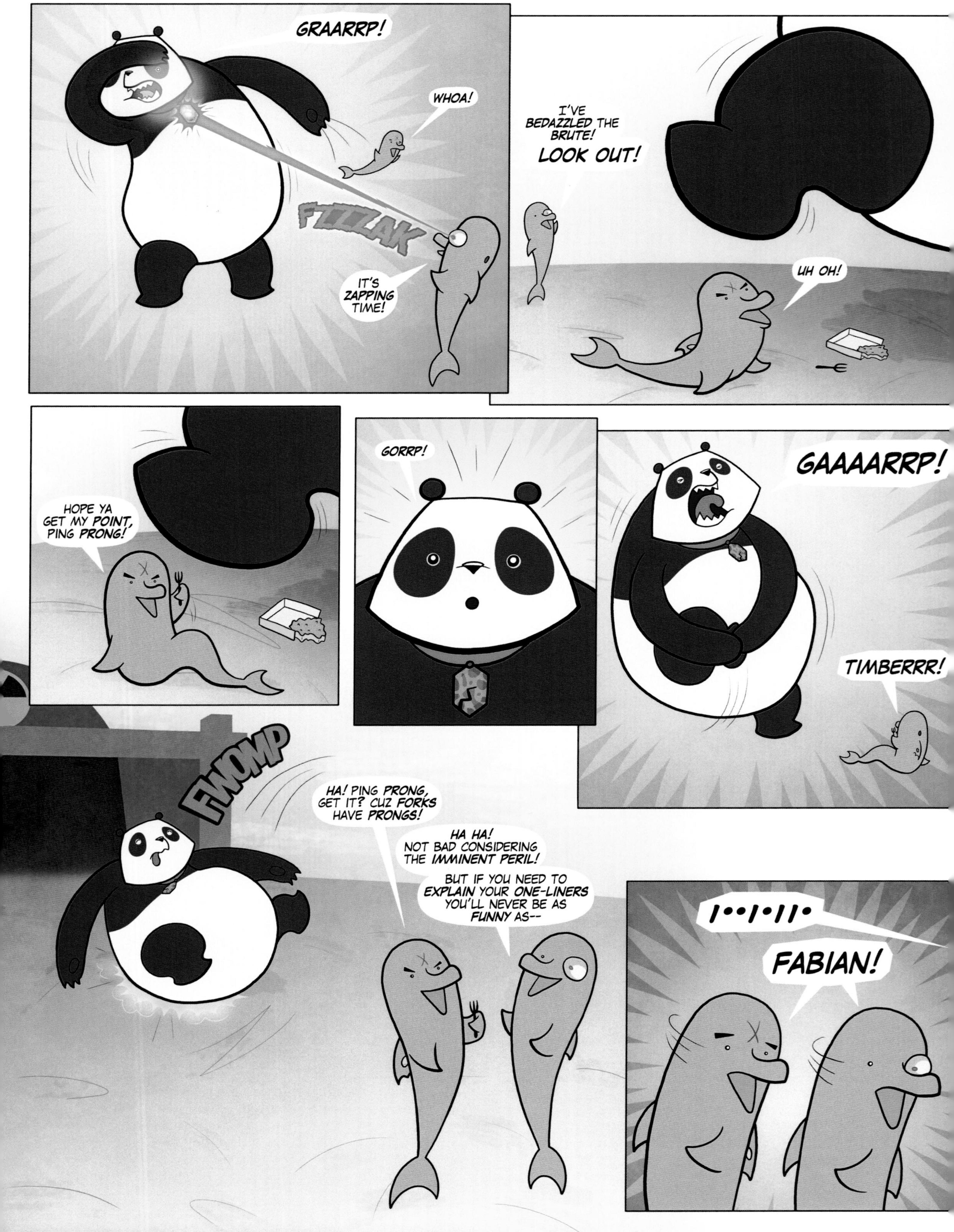
GRAARRP!
WHOA!
FZZZAK
IT'S ZAPPING TIME!
I'VE BEDAZZLED THE BRUTE!
LOOK OUT!
UH OH!
HOPE YA GET MY POINT, PING PRONG!
GORRP!
GAAAARRP!
TIMBERRR!
FWOMP
HA! PING PRONG, GET IT? CUZ FORKS HAVE PRONGS!
HA HA! NOT BAD CONSIDERING THE IMMINENT PERIL!
BUT IF YOU NEED TO EXPLAIN YOUR ONE-LINERS YOU'LL NEVER BE AS FUNNY AS--
FABIAN!

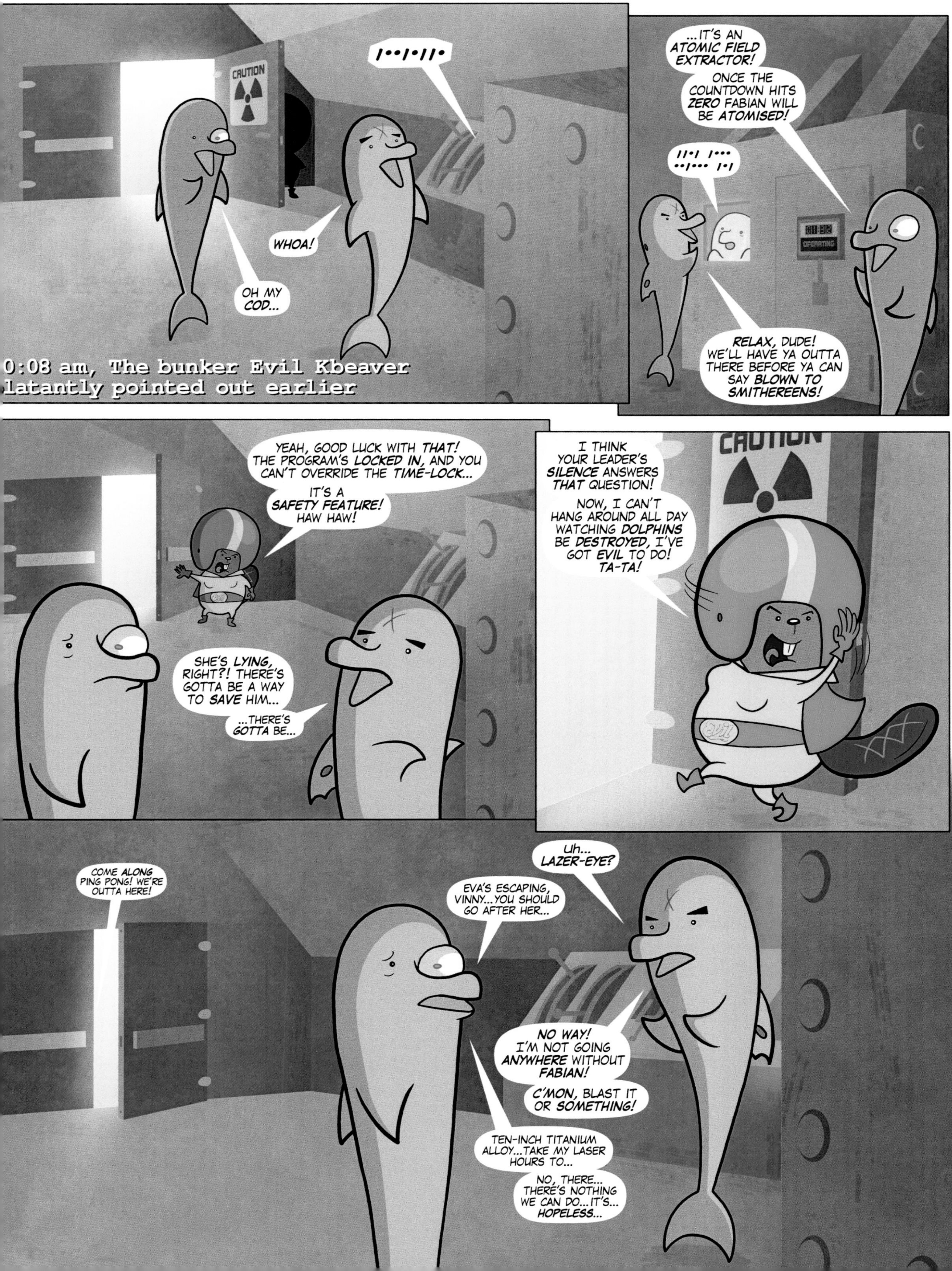
WHOA!
OH MY COD...
0:08 am, The bunker Evil Kbeaver latantly pointed out earlier
...IT'S AN ATOMIC FIELD EXTRACTOR!
ONCE THE COUNTDOWN HITS ZERO FABIAN WILL BE ATOMISED!
RELAX, DUDE! WE'LL HAVE YA OUTTA THERE BEFORE YA CAN SAY BLOWN TO SMITHEREENS!
YEAH, GOOD LUCK WITH THAT! THE PROGRAM'S LOCKED IN, AND YOU CAN'T OVERRIDE THE TIME-LOCK...
IT'S A SAFETY FEATURE! HAW HAW!
SHE'S LYING, RIGHT?! THERE'S GOTTA BE A WAY TO SAVE HIM...
...THERE'S GOTTA BE...
I THINK YOUR LEADER'S SILENCE ANSWERS THAT QUESTION!
NOW, I CAN'T HANG AROUND ALL DAY WATCHING DOLPHINS BE DESTROYED, I'VE GOT EVIL TO DO! TA-TA!
COME ALONG PING PONG! WE'RE OUTTA HERE!
EVA'S ESCAPING, VINNY...YOU SHOULD GO AFTER HER...
Uh... LAZER-EYE?
NO WAY! I'M NOT GOING ANYWHERE WITHOUT FABIAN!
C'MON, BLAST IT OR SOMETHING!
TEN-INCH TITANIUM ALLOY...TAKE MY LASER HOURS TO...
NO, THERE... THERE'S NOTHING WE CAN DO...IT'S... HOPELESS...

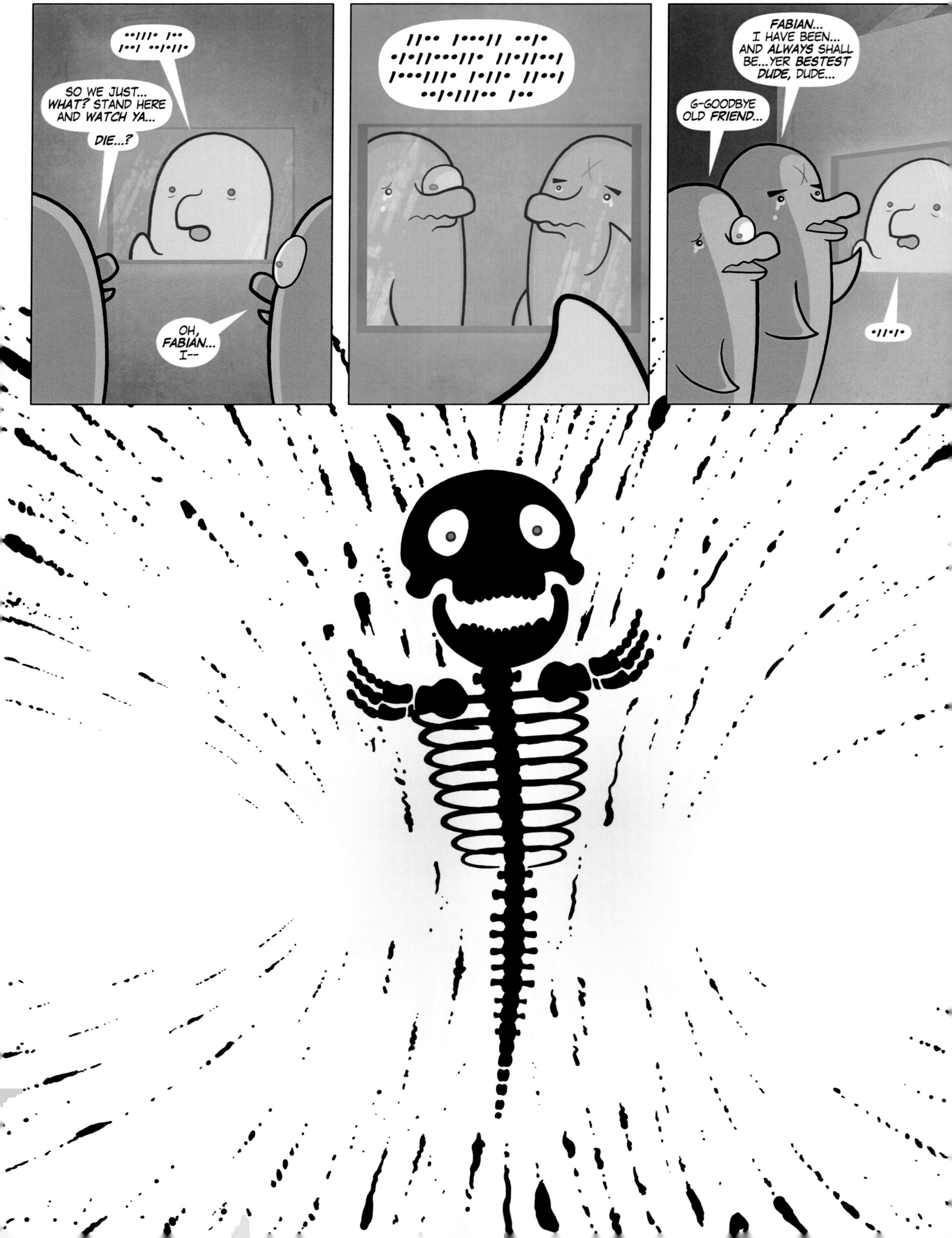
SO WE JUST... WHAT? STAND HERE AND WATCH YA...
DIE...?
OH, FABIAN... I--
G-GOODBYE OLD FRIEND...
FABIAN... I HAVE BEEN... AND ALWAYS SHALL BE...YER BESTEST DUDE, DUDE...

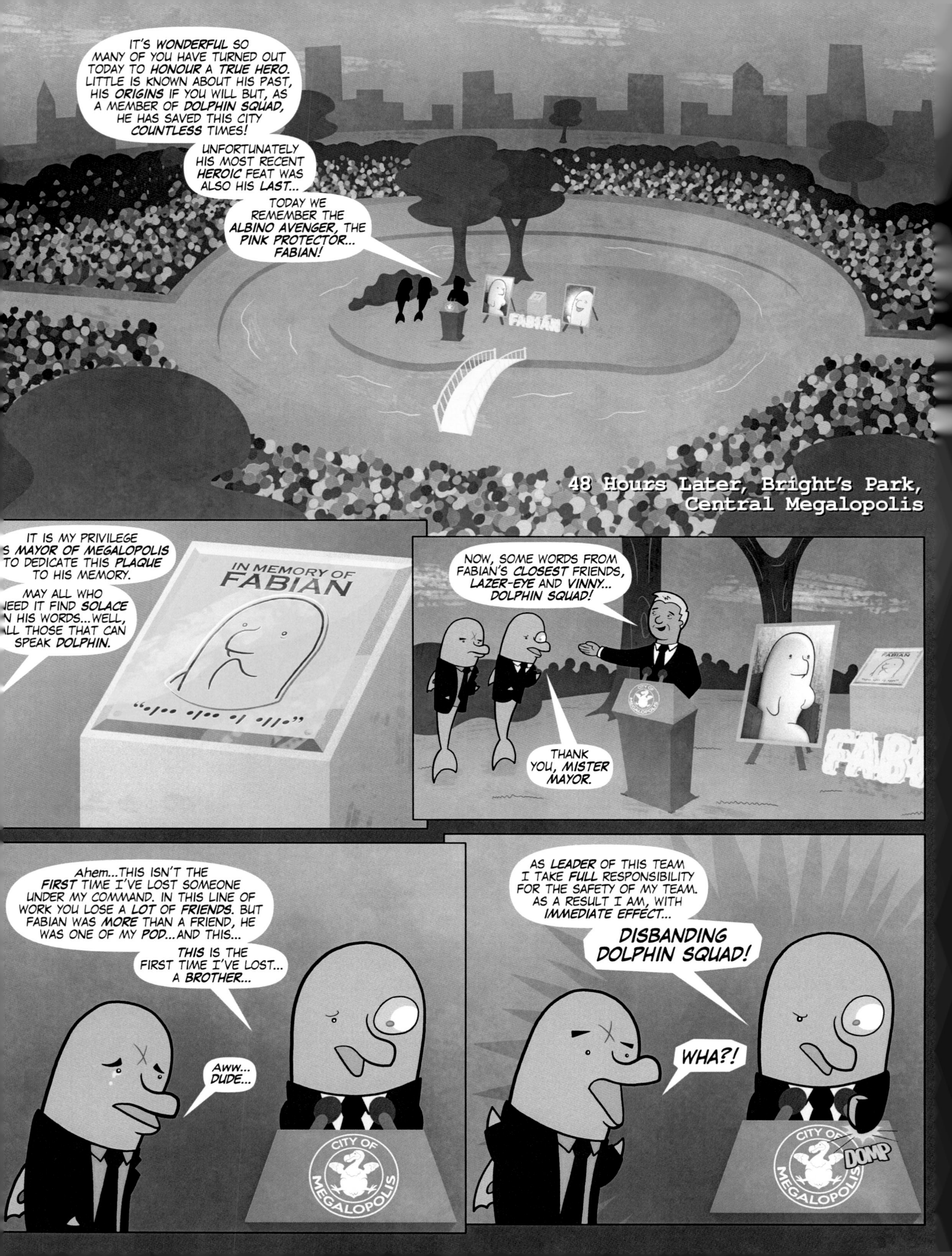
IT'S WONDERFUL SO MANY OF YOU HAVE TURNED OUT TODAY TO HONOUR A TRUE HERO. LITTLE IS KNOWN ABOUT HIS PAST, HIS ORIGINS IF YOU WILL BUT, AS A MEMBER OF DOLPHIN SQUAD, HE HAS SAVED THIS CITY COUNTLESS TIMES!
UNFORTUNATELY HIS MOST RECENT HEROIC FEAT WAS ALSO HIS LAST...
TODAY WE REMEMBER THE ALBINO AVENGER, THE PINK PROTECTOR... FABIAN!
FABIAN
48 Hours Later, Bright's Park, Central Megalopolis
IT IS MY PRIVILEGE S MAYOR OF MEGALOPOLIS TO DEDICATE THIS PLAQUE TO HIS MEMORY.
MAY ALL WHO NEED IT FIND SOLACE N HIS WORDS...WELL, LL THOSE THAT CAN SPEAK DOLPHIN.
IN MEMORY OF FABIAN
NOW, SOME WORDS FROM FABIAN'S CLOSEST FRIENDS, LAZER-EYE AND VINNY... DOLPHIN SQUAD!
CITY OF MEGALOPOLIS
THANK YOU, MISTER MAYOR.
Ahem...THIS ISN'T THE FIRST TIME I'VE LOST SOMEONE UNDER MY COMMAND. IN THIS LINE OF WORK YOU LOSE A LOT OF FRIENDS. BUT FABIAN WAS MORE THAN A FRIEND, HE WAS ONE OF MY POD...AND THIS...
THIS IS THE FIRST TIME I'VE LOST... A BROTHER...
AWW... DUDE...
CITY OF MEGALOPOLIS
AS LEADER OF THIS TEAM I TAKE FULL RESPONSIBILITY FOR THE SAFETY OF MY TEAM. AS A RESULT I AM, WITH IMMEDIATE EFFECT...
DISBANDING DOLPHIN SQUAD!
WHA?!
CITY OF MEGALOPOLIS
DOMP

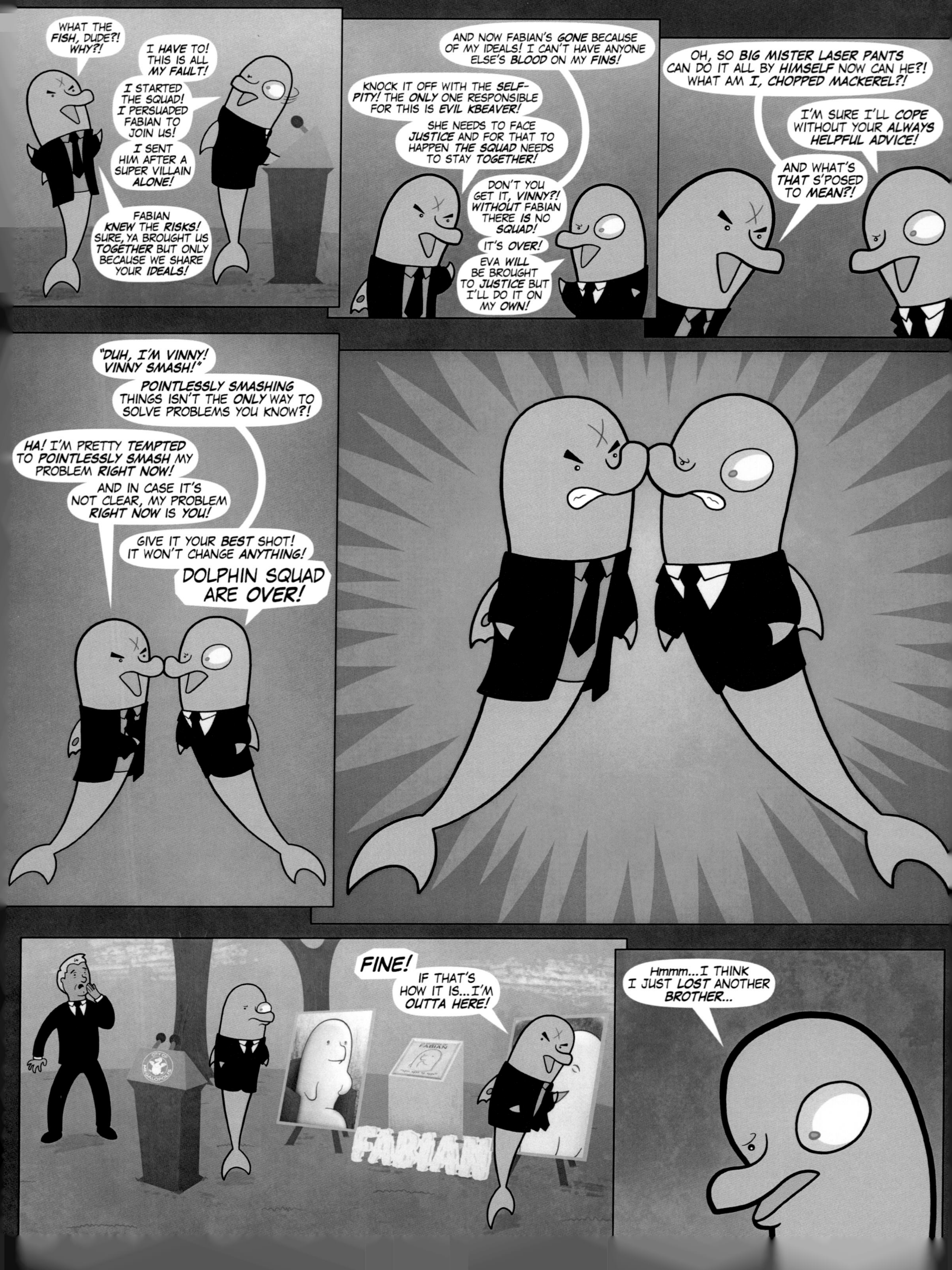

WHAT THE FISH, DUDE?! WHY?!
I HAVE TO! THIS IS ALL MY FAULT!
I STARTED THE SQUAD! I PERSUADED FABIAN TO JOIN US!
I SENT HIM AFTER A SUPER VILLAIN ALONE!
FABIAN KNEW THE RISKS! SURE, YA BROUGHT US TOGETHER BUT ONLY BECAUSE WE SHARE YOUR IDEALS!
AND NOW FABIAN'S GONE BECAUSE OF MY IDEALS! I CAN'T HAVE ANYONE ELSE'S BLOOD ON MY FINS!
KNOCK IT OFF WITH THE SELF-PITY! THE ONLY ONE RESPONSIBLE FOR THIS IS EVIL KBEAVER!
SHE NEEDS TO FACE JUSTICE AND FOR THAT TO HAPPEN THE SQUAD NEEDS TO STAY TOGETHER!
DON'T YOU GET IT, VINNY?! WITHOUT FABIAN THERE IS NO SQUAD!
IT'S OVER!
EVA WILL BE BROUGHT TO JUSTICE BUT I'LL DO IT ON MY OWN!
OH, SO BIG MISTER LASER PANTS CAN DO IT ALL BY HIMSELF NOW CAN HE?! WHAT AM I, CHOPPED MACKEREL?!
I'M SURE I'LL COPE WITHOUT YOUR ALWAYS HELPFUL ADVICE!
AND WHAT'S THAT S'POSED TO MEAN?!
"DUH, I'M VINNY! VINNY SMASH!"
POINTLESSLY SMASHING THINGS ISN'T THE ONLY WAY TO SOLVE PROBLEMS YOU KNOW?!
HA! I'M PRETTY TEMPTED TO POINTLESSLY SMASH MY PROBLEM RIGHT NOW!
AND IN CASE IT'S NOT CLEAR, MY PROBLEM RIGHT NOW IS YOU!
GIVE IT YOUR BEST SHOT! IT WON'T CHANGE ANYTHING!
DOLPHIN SQUAD ARE OVER!
CITY OF MEGALOPOLIS
FABIAN
FABIAN
FINE!
IF THAT'S HOW IT IS...I'M OUTTA HERE!
Hmmm...I THINK I JUST LOST ANOTHER BROTHER...

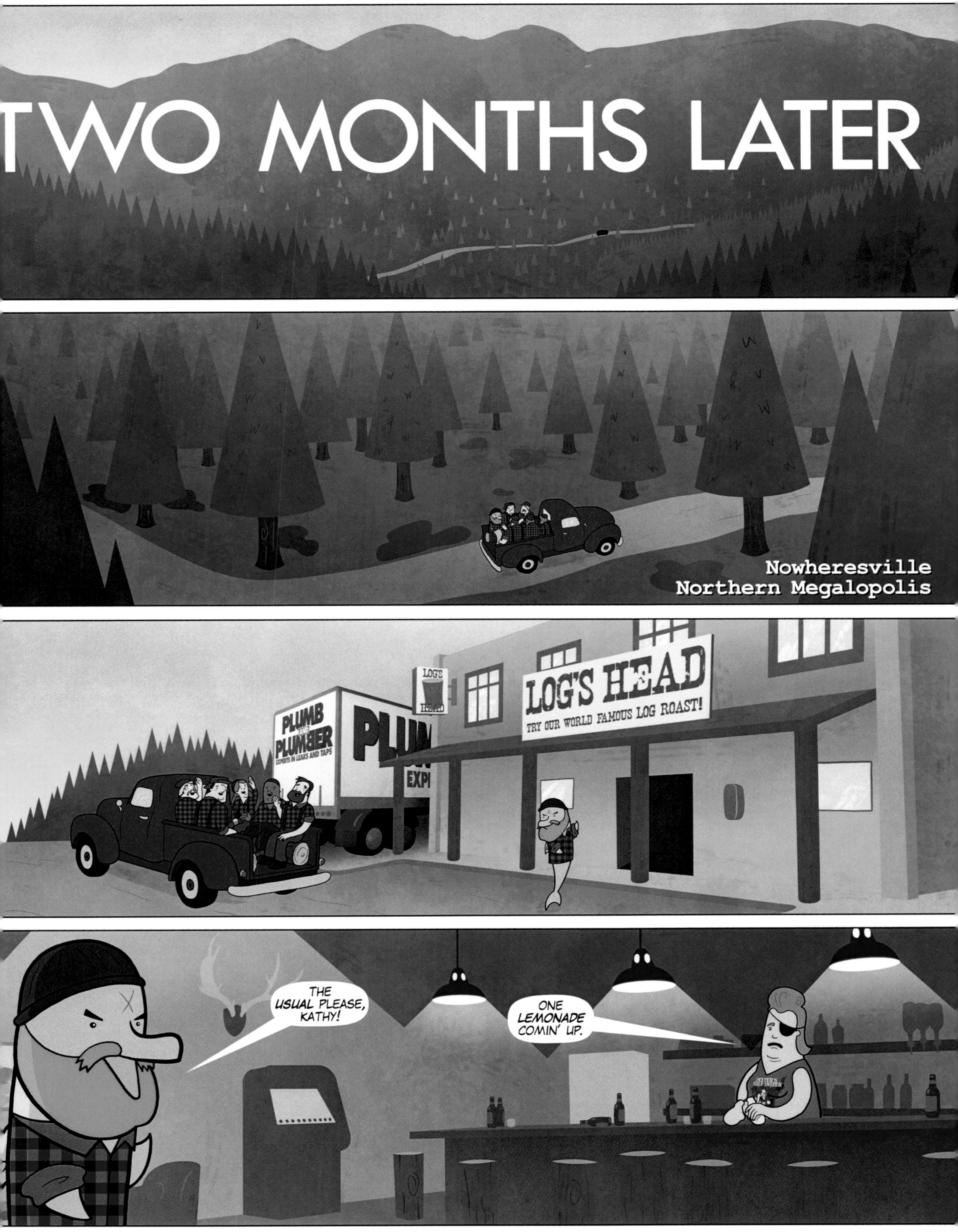

TWO MONTHS LATER
Nowheresville
Northern Megalopolis
LOG'S HEAD
PLUMB AND PLUMBER
EXPERTS IN LEAKS AND TAPS
PLUM
EXP
LOG'S HEAD
TRY OUR WORLD FAMOUS LOG ROAST!
THE USUAL PLEASE, KATHY!
ONE LEMONADE COMIN' UP.

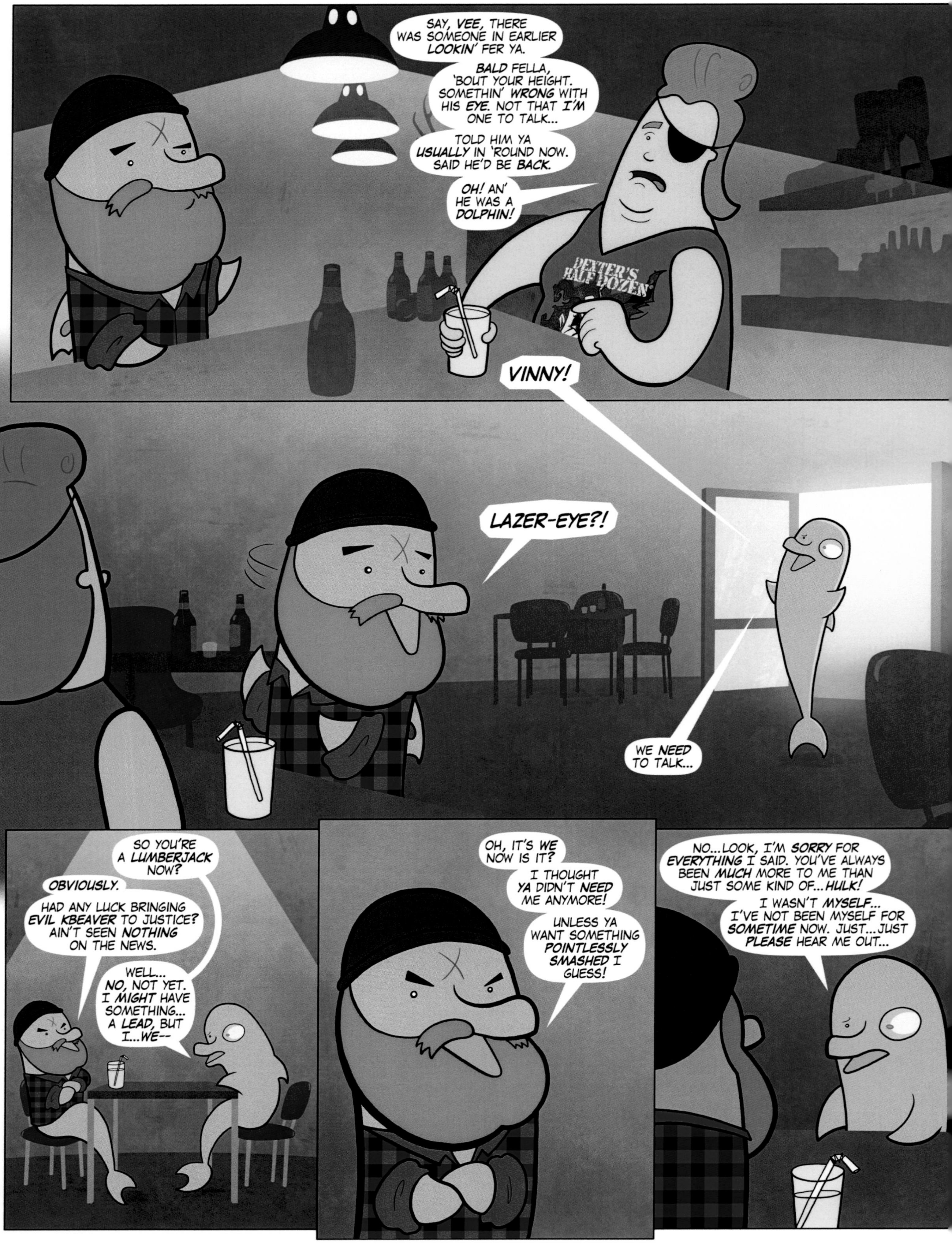
SAY, VEE, THERE WAS SOMEONE IN EARLIER LOOKIN' FER YA.
BALD FELLA, 'BOUT YOUR HEIGHT. SOMETHIN' WRONG WITH HIS EYE. NOT THAT I'M ONE TO TALK...
TOLD HIM YA USUALLY IN 'ROUND NOW. SAID HE'D BE BACK.
OH! AN' HE WAS A DOLPHIN!
DEXTER'S HALF DOZEN
VINNY!
LAZER-EYE?!
WE NEED TO TALK...
SO YOU'RE A LUMBERJACK NOW?
OBVIOUSLY.
HAD ANY LUCK BRINGING EVIL KBEAVER TO JUSTICE? AIN'T SEEN NOTHING ON THE NEWS.
WELL... NO, NOT YET. I MIGHT HAVE SOMETHING... A LEAD, BUT I...WE--
OH, IT'S WE NOW IS IT?
I THOUGHT YA DIDN'T NEED ME ANYMORE!
UNLESS YA WANT SOMETHING POINTLESSLY SMASHED I GUESS!
NO...LOOK, I'M SORRY FOR EVERYTHING I SAID. YOU'VE ALWAYS BEEN MUCH MORE TO ME THAN JUST SOME KIND OF...HULK!
I WASN'T MYSELF... I'VE NOT BEEN MYSELF FOR SOMETIME NOW. JUST...JUST PLEASE HEAR ME OUT...

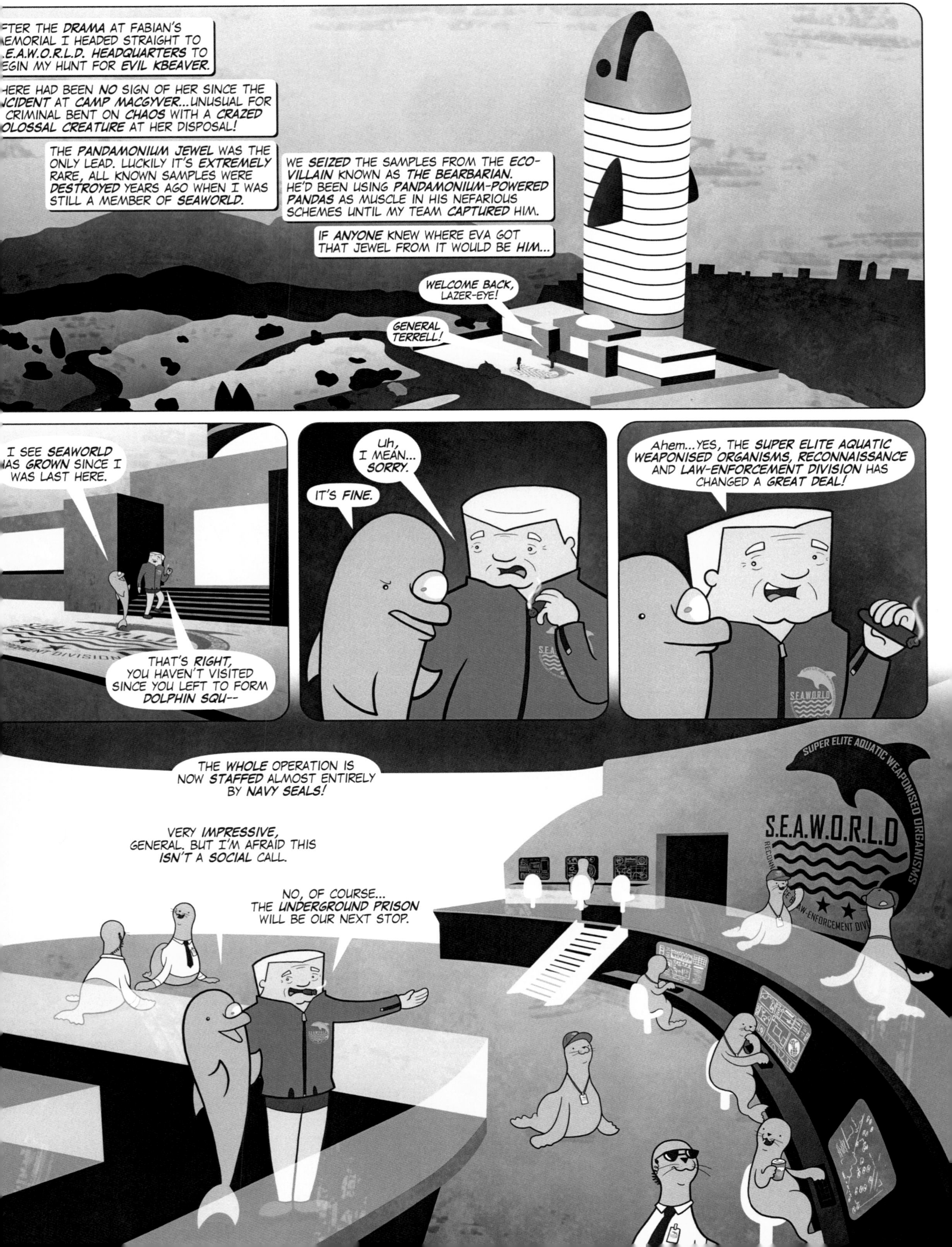
FTER THE DRAMA AT FABIAN'S EMORIAL I HEADED STRAIGHT TO .E.A.W.O.R.L.D. HEADQUARTERS TO EGIN MY HUNT FOR EVIL KBEAVER.
HERE HAD BEEN NO SIGN OF HER SINCE THE ICIDENT AT CAMP MACGYVER...UNUSUAL FOR CRIMINAL BENT ON CHAOS WITH A CRAZED OLOSSAL CREATURE AT HER DISPOSAL!
THE PANDAMONIUM JEWEL WAS THE ONLY LEAD. LUCKILY IT'S EXTREMELY RARE, ALL KNOWN SAMPLES WERE DESTROYED YEARS AGO WHEN I WAS STILL A MEMBER OF SEAWORLD.
WE SEIZED THE SAMPLES FROM THE ECO-VILLAIN KNOWN AS THE BEARBARIAN. HE'D BEEN USING PANDAMONIUM-POWERED PANDAS AS MUSCLE IN HIS NEFARIOUS SCHEMES UNTIL MY TEAM CAPTURED HIM.
IF ANYONE KNEW WHERE EVA GOT THAT JEWEL FROM IT WOULD BE HIM...
WELCOME BACK, LAZER-EYE!
GENERAL TERRELL!
I SEE SEAWORLD IAS GROWN SINCE I WAS LAST HERE.
THAT'S RIGHT, YOU HAVEN'T VISITED SINCE YOU LEFT TO FORM DOLPHIN SQU--
Uh, I MEAN... SORRY.
IT'S FINE.
Ahem...YES, THE SUPER ELITE AQUATIC WEAPONISED ORGANISMS, RECONNAISSANCE AND LAW-ENFORCEMENT DIVISION HAS CHANGED A GREAT DEAL!
THE WHOLE OPERATION IS NOW STAFFED ALMOST ENTIRELY BY NAVY SEALS!
VERY IMPRESSIVE, GENERAL. BUT I'M AFRAID THIS ISN'T A SOCIAL CALL.
NO, OF COURSE... THE UNDERGROUND PRISON WILL BE OUR NEXT STOP.
SUPER ELITE AQUATIC WEAPONISED ORGANISMS
S.E.A.W.O.R.L.D
LAW-ENFORCEMENT DIVI

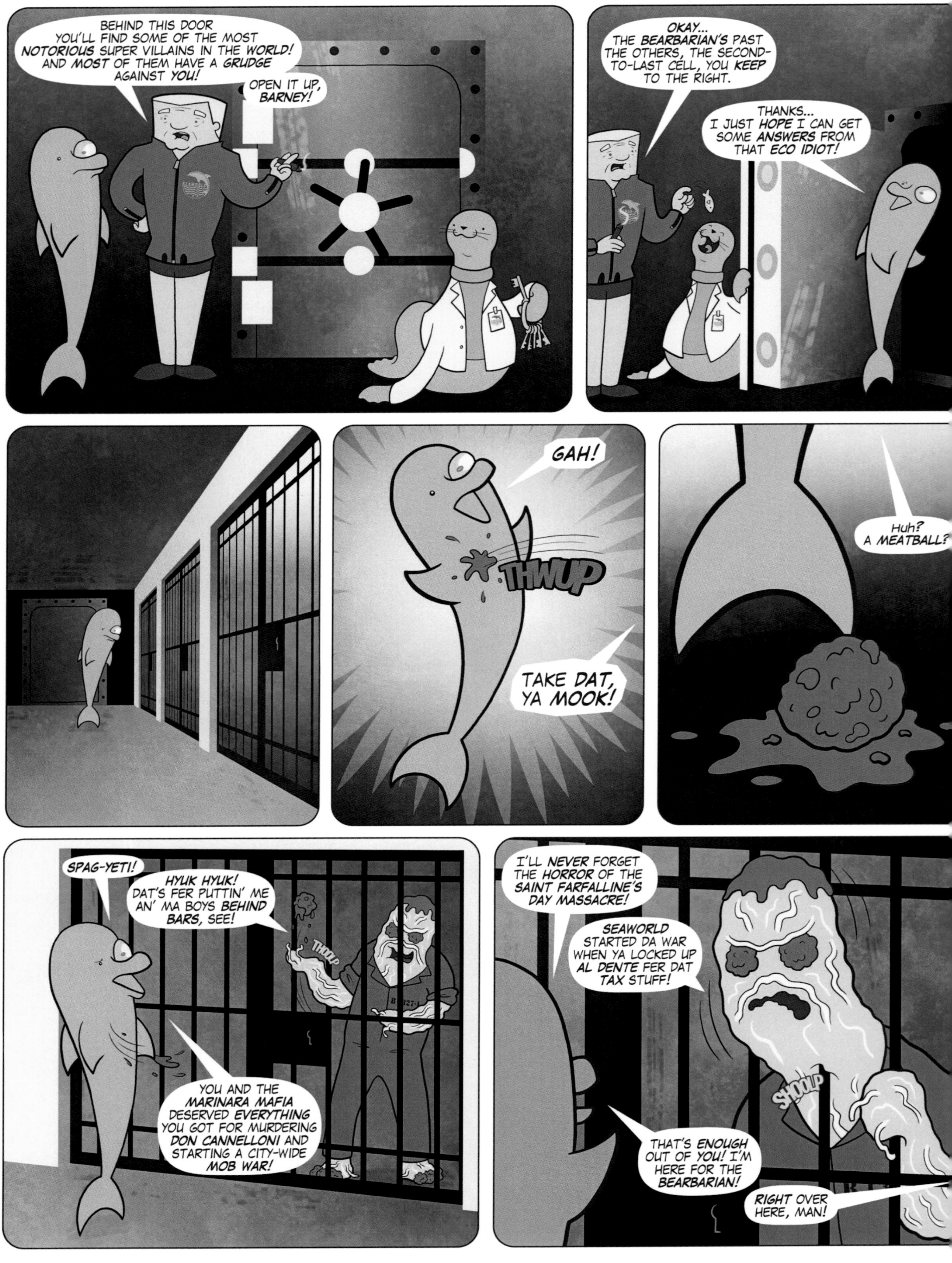
BEHIND THIS DOOR YOU'LL FIND SOME OF THE MOST NOTORIOUS SUPER VILLAINS IN THE WORLD! AND MOST OF THEM HAVE A GRUDGE AGAINST YOU!
OPEN IT UP, BARNEY!
OKAY... THE BEARBARIAN'S PAST THE OTHERS, THE SECOND-TO-LAST CELL, YOU KEEP TO THE RIGHT.
THANKS... I JUST HOPE I CAN GET SOME ANSWERS FROM THAT ECO IDIOT!
GAH!
THWUP
TAKE DAT, YA MOOK!
Huh? A MEATBALL?
SPAG-YETI!
HYUK HYUK! DAT'S FER PUTTIN' ME AN' MA BOYS BEHIND BARS, SEE!
THOOLP
YOU AND THE MARINARA MAFIA DESERVED EVERYTHING YOU GOT FOR MURDERING DON CANNELLONI AND STARTING A CITY-WIDE MOB WAR!
I'LL NEVER FORGET THE HORROR OF THE SAINT FARFALLINE'S DAY MASSACRE!
SEAWORLD STARTED DA WAR WHEN YA LOCKED UP AL DENTE FER DAT TAX STUFF!
SHOOLP
THAT'S ENOUGH OUT OF YOU! I'M HERE FOR THE BEARBARIAN!
RIGHT OVER HERE, MAN!

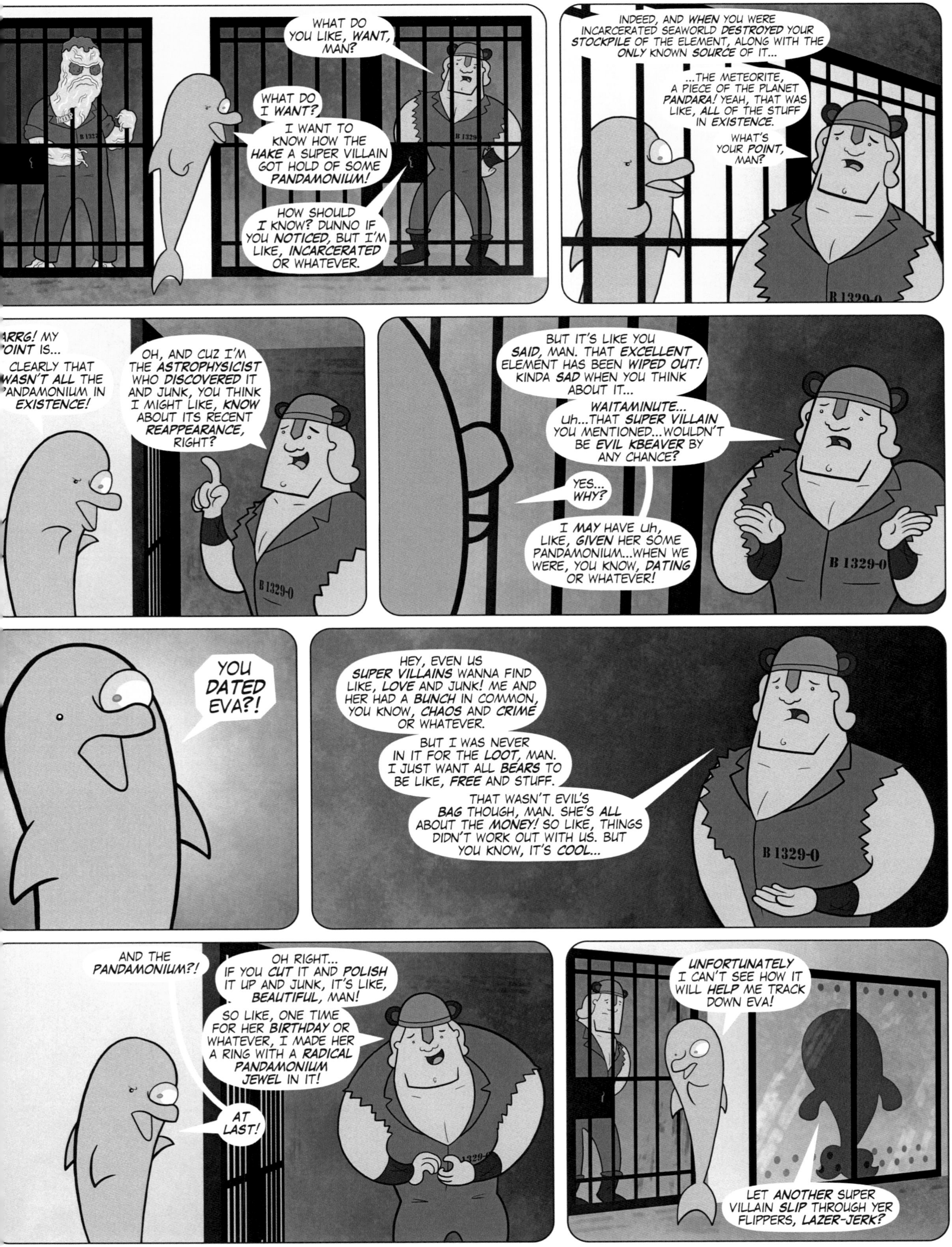
WHAT DO YOU LIKE, WANT, MAN?
WHAT DO I WANT? I WANT TO KNOW HOW THE HAKE A SUPER VILLAIN GOT HOLD OF SOME PANDAMONIUM!
HOW SHOULD I KNOW? DUNNO IF YOU NOTICED, BUT I'M LIKE, INCARCERATED OR WHATEVER.
B 1327
B 1329
INDEED, AND WHEN YOU WERE INCARCERATED SEAWORLD DESTROYED YOUR STOCKPILE OF THE ELEMENT, ALONG WITH THE ONLY KNOWN SOURCE OF IT...
...THE METEORITE, A PIECE OF THE PLANET PANDARA! YEAH, THAT WAS LIKE, ALL OF THE STUFF IN EXISTENCE.
WHAT'S YOUR POINT, MAN?
B 1329-0
ARRG! MY POINT IS... CLEARLY THAT WASN'T ALL THE PANDAMONIUM IN EXISTENCE!
OH, AND CUZ I'M THE ASTROPHYSICIST WHO DISCOVERED IT AND JUNK, YOU THINK I MIGHT LIKE, KNOW ABOUT ITS RECENT REAPPEARANCE, RIGHT?
B 1329-0
BUT IT'S LIKE YOU SAID, MAN. THAT EXCELLENT ELEMENT HAS BEEN WIPED OUT! KINDA SAD WHEN YOU THINK ABOUT IT...
WAITAMINUTE... UH...THAT SUPER VILLAIN YOU MENTIONED...WOULDN'T BE EVIL KBEAVER BY ANY CHANCE?
YES... WHY?
I MAY HAVE UH, LIKE, GIVEN HER SOME PANDAMONIUM...WHEN WE WERE, YOU KNOW, DATING OR WHATEVER!
B 1329-0
YOU DATED EVA?!
HEY, EVEN US SUPER VILLAINS WANNA FIND LIKE, LOVE AND JUNK! ME AND HER HAD A BUNCH IN COMMON, YOU KNOW, CHAOS AND CRIME OR WHATEVER.
BUT I WAS NEVER IN IT FOR THE LOOT, MAN. I JUST WANT ALL BEARS TO BE LIKE, FREE AND STUFF.
THAT WASN'T EVIL'S BAG THOUGH, MAN. SHE'S ALL ABOUT THE MONEY! SO LIKE, THINGS DIDN'T WORK OUT WITH US. BUT YOU KNOW, IT'S COOL...
B 1329-0
AND THE PANDAMONIUM?!
OH RIGHT... IF YOU CUT IT AND POLISH IT UP AND JUNK, IT'S LIKE, BEAUTIFUL, MAN!
SO LIKE, ONE TIME FOR HER BIRTHDAY OR WHATEVER, I MADE HER A RING WITH A RADICAL PANDAMONIUM JEWEL IN IT!
AT LAST!
UNFORTUNATELY I CAN'T SEE HOW IT WILL HELP ME TRACK DOWN EVA!
LET ANOTHER SUPER VILLAIN SLIP THROUGH YER FLIPPERS, LAZER-JERK?

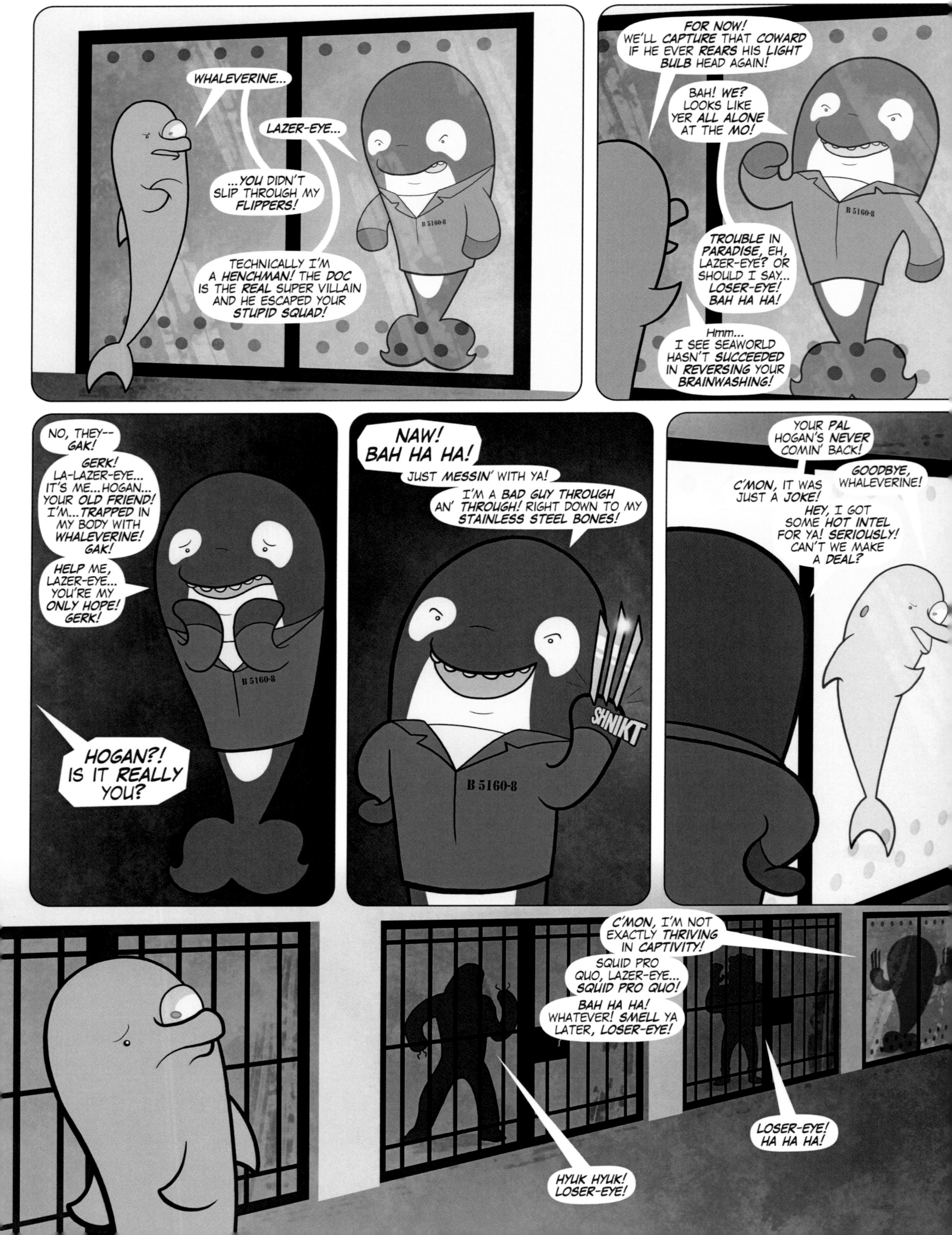

WHALEVERINE...
LAZER-EYE...
...YOU DIDN'T SLIP THROUGH MY FLIPPERS!
TECHNICALLY I'M A HENCHMAN! THE DOC IS THE REAL SUPER VILLAIN AND HE ESCAPED YOUR STUPID SQUAD!
FOR NOW! WE'LL CAPTURE THAT COWARD IF HE EVER REARS HIS LIGHT BULB HEAD AGAIN!
BAH! WE? LOOKS LIKE YER ALL ALONE AT THE MO!
TROUBLE IN PARADISE, EH, LAZER-EYE? OR SHOULD I SAY... LOSER-EYE! BAH HA HA!
Hmm... I SEE SEAWORLD HASN'T SUCCEEDED IN REVERSING YOUR BRAINWASHING!
B 5160-8
NO, THEY-- GAK!
GERK! LA-LAZER-EYE... IT'S ME...HOGAN... YOUR OLD FRIEND! I'M...TRAPPED IN MY BODY WITH WHALEVERINE! GAK!
HELP ME, LAZER-EYE... YOU'RE MY ONLY HOPE! GERK!
HOGAN?! IS IT REALLY YOU?
NAW! BAH HA HA!
JUST MESSIN' WITH YA!
I'M A BAD GUY THROUGH AN' THROUGH! RIGHT DOWN TO MY STAINLESS STEEL BONES!
SHNIKT
YOUR PAL HOGAN'S NEVER COMIN' BACK!
GOODBYE, WHALEVERINE!
C'MON, IT WAS JUST A JOKE!
HEY, I GOT SOME HOT INTEL FOR YA! SERIOUSLY! CAN'T WE MAKE A DEAL?
C'MON, I'M NOT EXACTLY THRIVING IN CAPTIVITY!
SQUID PRO QUO, LAZER-EYE... SQUID PRO QUO!
BAH HA HA! WHATEVER! SMELL YA LATER, LOSER-EYE!
HYUK HYUK! LOSER-EYE!
LOSER-EYE! HA HA HA!

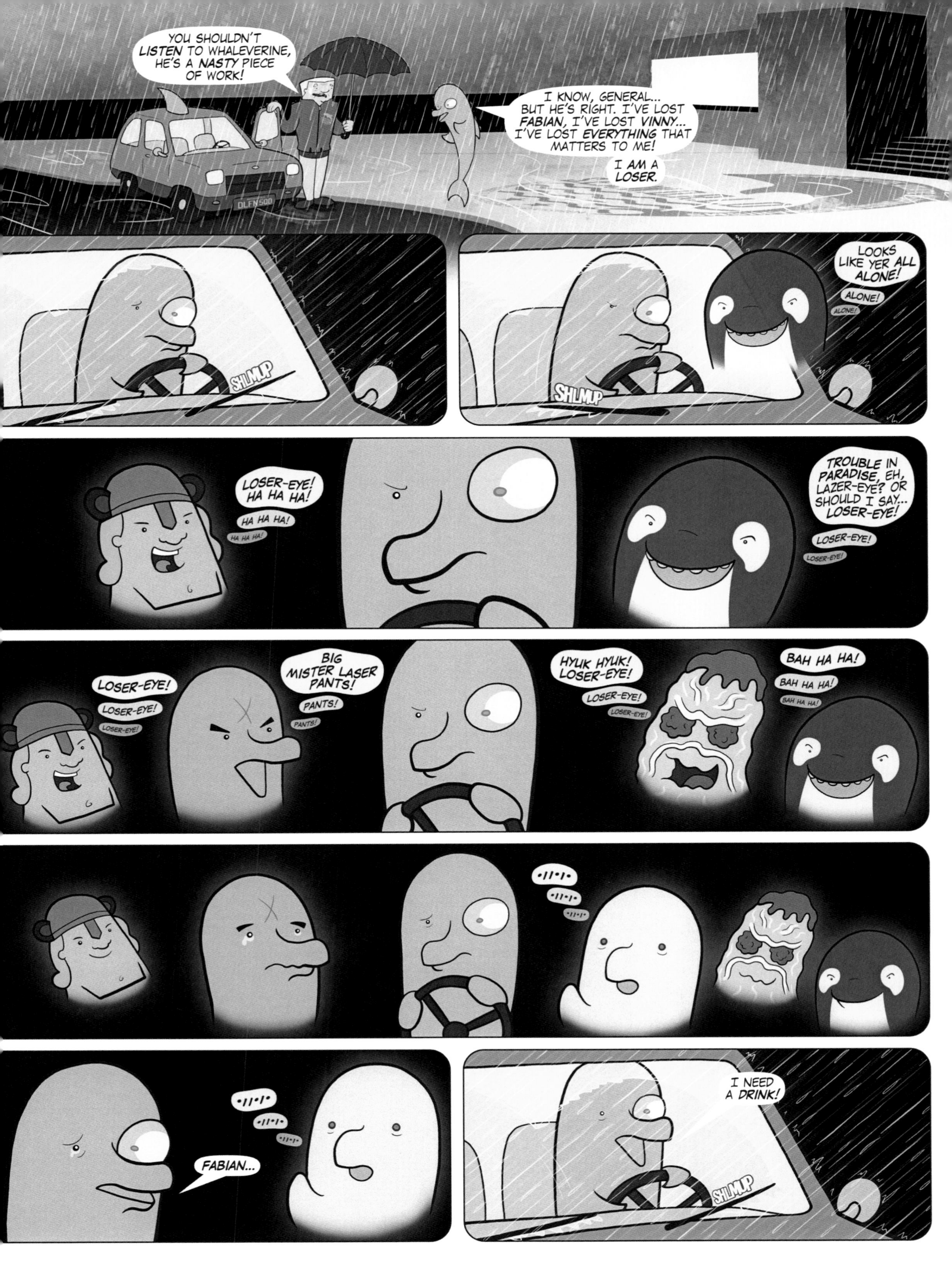

YOU SHOULDN'T LISTEN TO WHALEVERINE, HE'S A NASTY PIECE OF WORK!
I KNOW, GENERAL... BUT HE'S RIGHT. I'VE LOST FABIAN, I'VE LOST VINNY... I'VE LOST EVERYTHING THAT MATTERS TO ME!
I AM A LOSER.
DLFN500
SHLMUP
SHLMUP
LOOKS LIKE YER ALL ALONE!
ALONE!
ALONE!
LOSER-EYE! HA HA HA!
HA HA HA!
HA HA HA!
TROUBLE IN PARADISE, EH, LAZER-EYE? OR SHOULD I SAY... LOSER-EYE!
LOSER-EYE!
LOSER-EYE!
LOSER-EYE!
LOSER-EYE!
LOSER-EYE!
BIG MISTER LASER PANTS!
PANTS!
PANTS!
HYUK HYUK! LOSER-EYE!
LOSER-EYE!
LOSER-EYE!
BAH HA HA!
BAH HA HA!
BAH HA HA!
FABIAN...
I NEED A DRINK!
SHLMUP

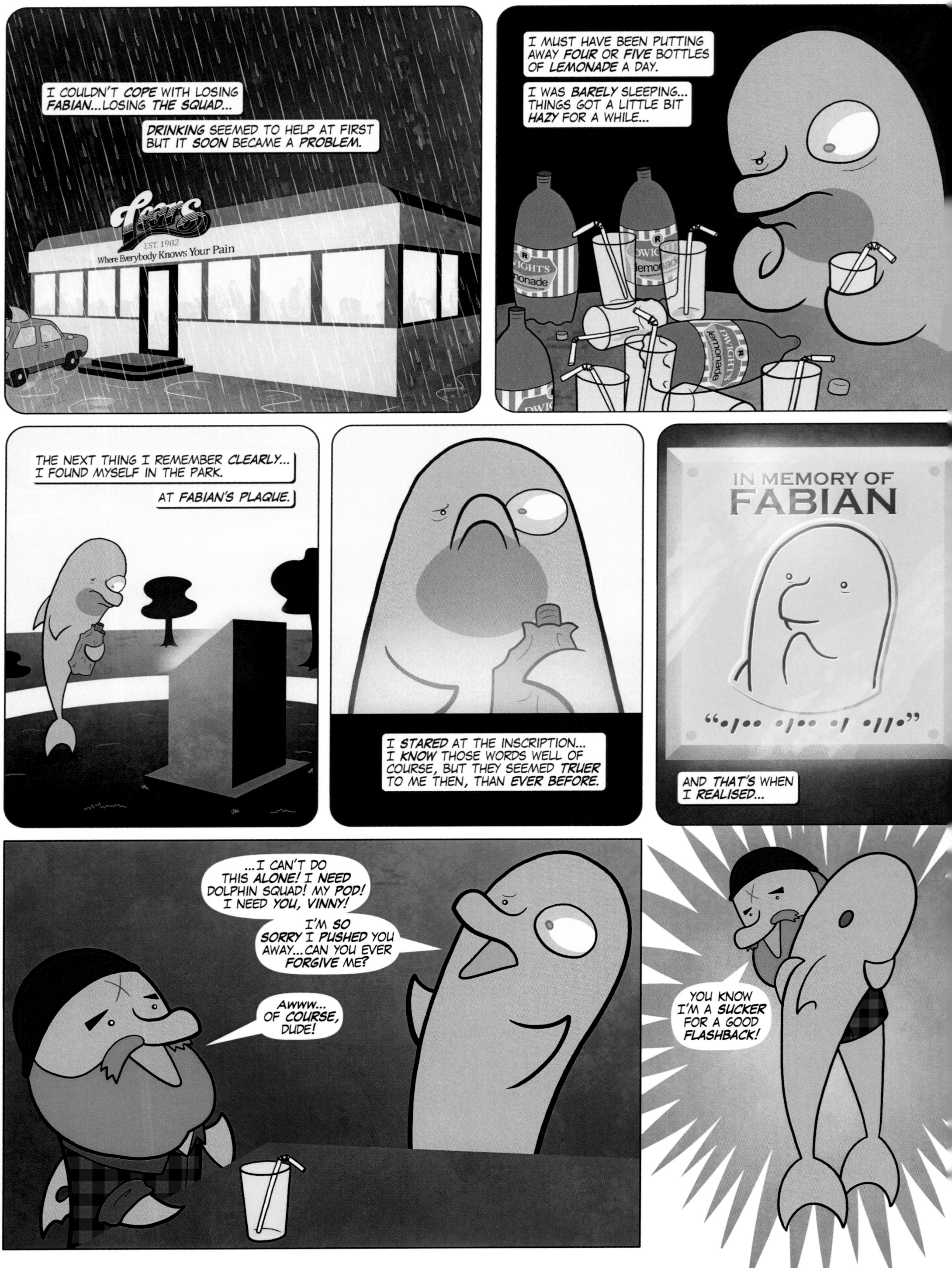
I COULDN'T COPE WITH LOSING FABIAN...LOSING THE SQUAD...
DRINKING SEEMED TO HELP AT FIRST BUT IT SOON BECAME A PROBLEM.
Lears
EST. 1982
Where Everybody Knows Your Pain
I MUST HAVE BEEN PUTTING AWAY FOUR OR FIVE BOTTLES OF LEMONADE A DAY.
I WAS BARELY SLEEPING... THINGS GOT A LITTLE BIT HAZY FOR A WHILE...
DWIGHT'S lemonade
THE NEXT THING I REMEMBER CLEARLY... I FOUND MYSELF IN THE PARK.
AT FABIAN'S PLAQUE.
I STARED AT THE INSCRIPTION... I KNOW THOSE WORDS WELL OF COURSE, BUT THEY SEEMED TRUER TO ME THEN, THAN EVER BEFORE.
IN MEMORY OF FABIAN
AND THAT'S WHEN I REALISED...
...I CAN'T DO THIS ALONE! I NEED DOLPHIN SQUAD! MY POD! I NEED YOU, VINNY!
I'M SO SORRY I PUSHED YOU AWAY...CAN YOU EVER FORGIVE ME?
AWWW... OF COURSE, DUDE!
YOU KNOW I'M A SUCKER FOR A GOOD FLASHBACK!

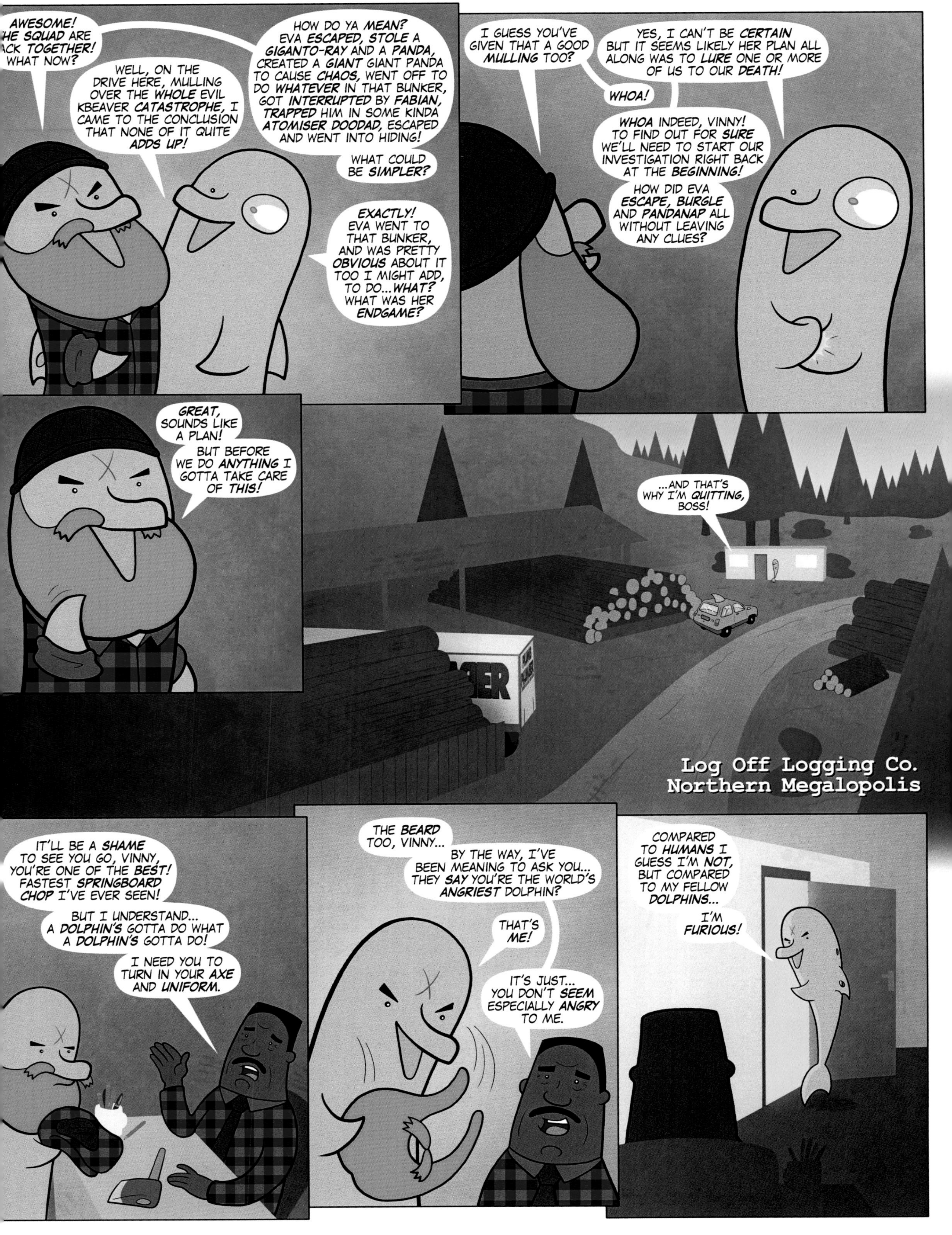

AWESOME! THE SQUAD ARE BACK TOGETHER! WHAT NOW?
WELL, ON THE DRIVE HERE, MULLING OVER THE WHOLE EVIL KBEAVER CATASTROPHE, I CAME TO THE CONCLUSION THAT NONE OF IT QUITE ADDS UP!
HOW DO YA MEAN? EVA ESCAPED, STOLE A GIGANTO-RAY AND A PANDA, CREATED A GIANT GIANT PANDA TO CAUSE CHAOS, WENT OFF TO DO WHATEVER IN THAT BUNKER, GOT INTERRUPTED BY FABIAN, TRAPPED HIM IN SOME KINDA ATOMISER DOODAD, ESCAPED AND WENT INTO HIDING!
WHAT COULD BE SIMPLER?
EXACTLY! EVA WENT TO THAT BUNKER, AND WAS PRETTY OBVIOUS ABOUT IT TOO I MIGHT ADD, TO DO...WHAT? WHAT WAS HER ENDGAME?
I GUESS YOU'VE GIVEN THAT A GOOD MULLING TOO?
YES, I CAN'T BE CERTAIN BUT IT SEEMS LIKELY HER PLAN ALL ALONG WAS TO LURE ONE OR MORE OF US TO OUR DEATH!
WHOA!
WHOA INDEED, VINNY! TO FIND OUT FOR SURE WE'LL NEED TO START OUR INVESTIGATION RIGHT BACK AT THE BEGINNING!
HOW DID EVA ESCAPE, BURGLE AND PANDANAP ALL WITHOUT LEAVING ANY CLUES?
GREAT, SOUNDS LIKE A PLAN!
BUT BEFORE WE DO ANYTHING I GOTTA TAKE CARE OF THIS!
...AND THAT'S WHY I'M QUITTING, BOSS!
Log Off Logging Co.
Northern Megalopolis
IT'LL BE A SHAME TO SEE YOU GO, VINNY, YOU'RE ONE OF THE BEST! FASTEST SPRINGBOARD CHOP I'VE EVER SEEN!
BUT I UNDERSTAND... A DOLPHIN'S GOTTA DO WHAT A DOLPHIN'S GOTTA DO!
I NEED YOU TO TURN IN YOUR AXE AND UNIFORM.
THE BEARD TOO, VINNY...
BY THE WAY, I'VE BEEN MEANING TO ASK YOU... THEY SAY YOU'RE THE WORLD'S ANGRIEST DOLPHIN?
THAT'S ME!
IT'S JUST... YOU DON'T SEEM ESPECIALLY ANGRY TO ME.
COMPARED TO HUMANS I GUESS I'M NOT, BUT COMPARED TO MY FELLOW DOLPHINS...
I'M FURIOUS!

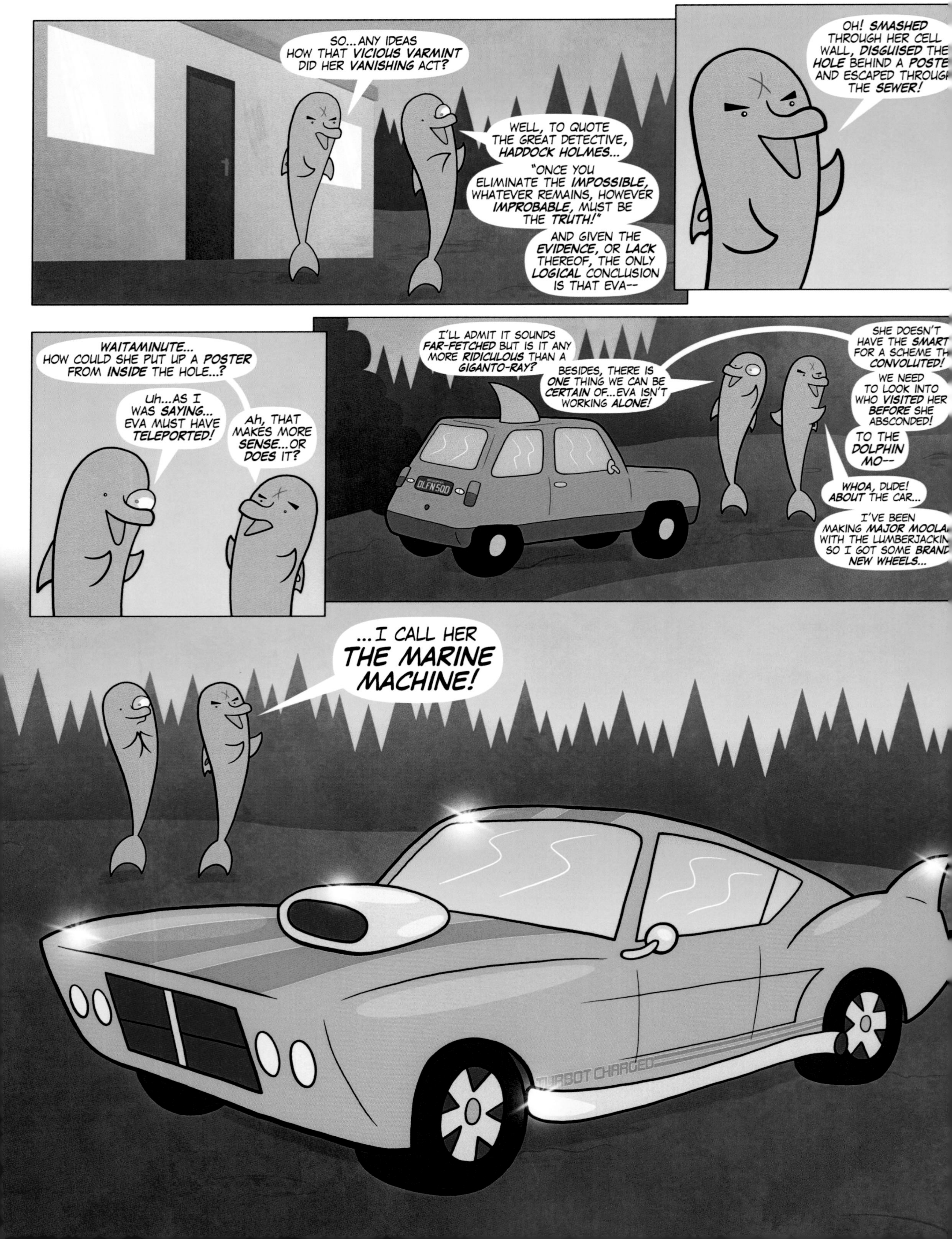

SO...ANY IDEAS HOW THAT VICIOUS VARMINT DID HER VANISHING ACT?
WELL, TO QUOTE THE GREAT DETECTIVE, HADDOCK HOLMES...
"ONCE YOU ELIMINATE THE IMPOSSIBLE, WHATEVER REMAINS, HOWEVER IMPROBABLE, MUST BE THE TRUTH!"
AND GIVEN THE EVIDENCE, OR LACK THEREOF, THE ONLY LOGICAL CONCLUSION IS THAT EVA--
OH! SMASHED THROUGH HER CELL WALL, DISGUISED THE HOLE BEHIND A POSTE AND ESCAPED THROUGH THE SEWER!
WAITAMINUTE... HOW COULD SHE PUT UP A POSTER FROM INSIDE THE HOLE...?
UH...AS I WAS SAYING... EVA MUST HAVE TELEPORTED!
AH, THAT MAKES MORE SENSE...OR DOES IT?
I'LL ADMIT IT SOUNDS FAR-FETCHED BUT IS IT ANY MORE RIDICULOUS THAN A GIGANTO-RAY?
BESIDES, THERE IS ONE THING WE CAN BE CERTAIN OF...EVA ISN'T WORKING ALONE!
SHE DOESN'T HAVE THE SMART FOR A SCHEME TH CONVOLUTED!
WE NEED TO LOOK INTO WHO VISITED HER BEFORE SHE ABSCONDED!
TO THE DOLPHIN MO--
WHOA, DUDE! ABOUT THE CAR...
I'VE BEEN MAKING MAJOR MOOLA WITH THE LUMBERJACKIN SO I GOT SOME BRAND NEW WHEELS...
DLFN 500
...I CALL HER THE MARINE MACHINE!
TURBOT CHARGED

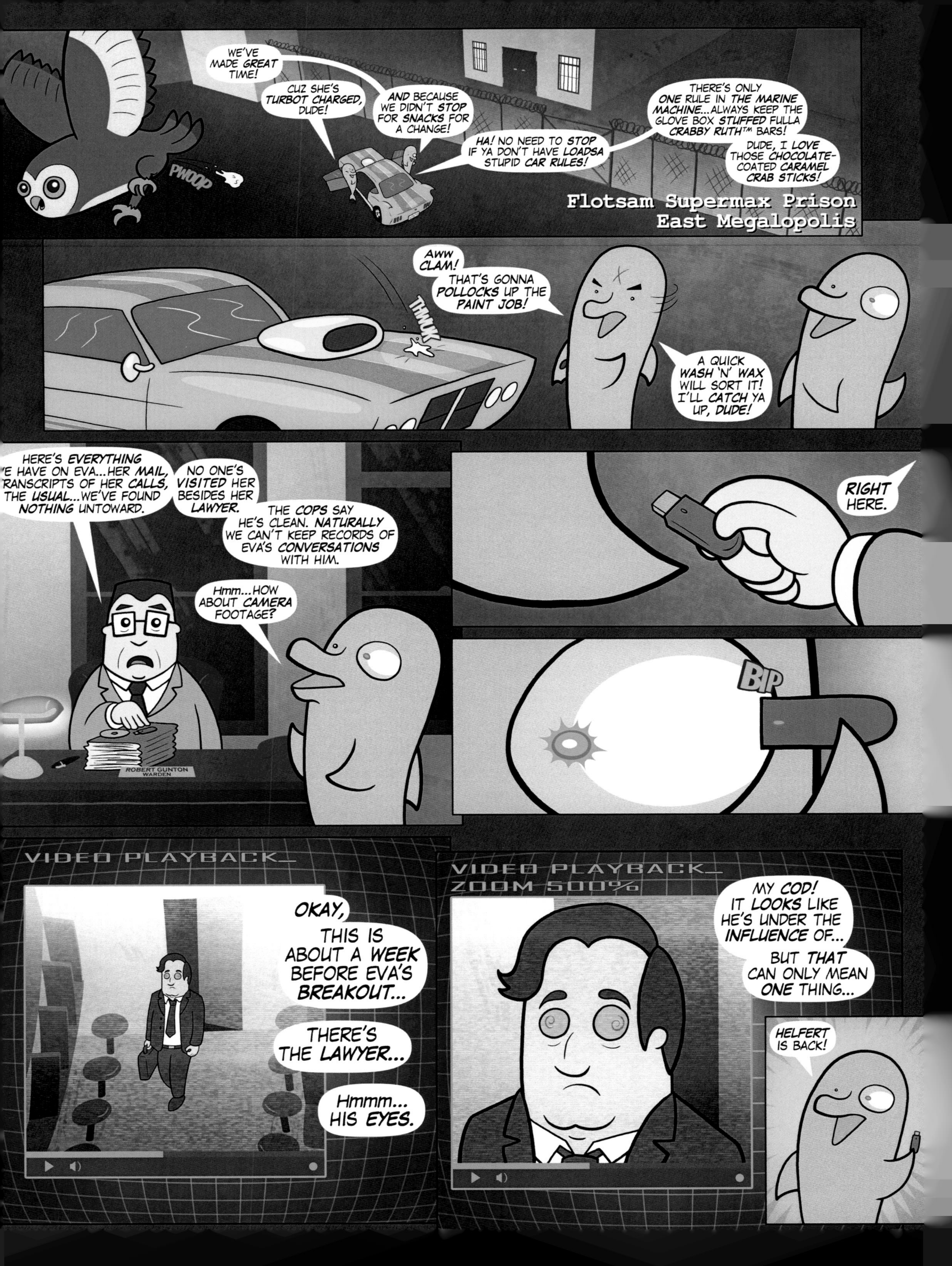
WE'VE MADE GREAT TIME!
CUZ SHE'S TURBOT CHARGED, DUDE!
AND BECAUSE WE DIDN'T STOP FOR SNACKS FOR A CHANGE!
HA! NO NEED TO STOP IF YA DON'T HAVE LOADSA STUPID CAR RULES!
THERE'S ONLY ONE RULE IN THE MARINE MACHINE...ALWAYS KEEP THE GLOVE BOX STUFFED FULLA CRABBY RUTH™ BARS!
DUDE, I LOVE THOSE CHOCOLATE-COATED CARAMEL CRAB STICKS!
PWOOP
Flotsam Supermax Prison
East Megalopolis
AWW CLAM! THAT'S GONNA POLLOCKS UP THE PAINT JOB!
THWUK
A QUICK WASH 'N' WAX WILL SORT IT! I'LL CATCH YA UP, DUDE!
HERE'S EVERYTHING 'E HAVE ON EVA...HER MAIL, 'RANSCRIPTS OF HER CALLS, THE USUAL...WE'VE FOUND NOTHING UNTOWARD.
NO ONE'S VISITED HER BESIDES HER LAWYER.
THE COPS SAY HE'S CLEAN. NATURALLY WE CAN'T KEEP RECORDS OF EVA'S CONVERSATIONS WITH HIM.
Hmm...HOW ABOUT CAMERA FOOTAGE?
ROBERT GUNTON
WARDEN
RIGHT HERE.
BIP
VIDEO PLAYBACK_
OKAY, THIS IS ABOUT A WEEK BEFORE EVA'S BREAKOUT...
THERE'S THE LAWYER...
Hmmm... HIS EYES.
VIDEO PLAYBACK_
ZOOM 500%
MY COD! IT LOOKS LIKE HE'S UNDER THE INFLUENCE OF...
BUT THAT CAN ONLY MEAN ONE THING...
HELFERT IS BACK!

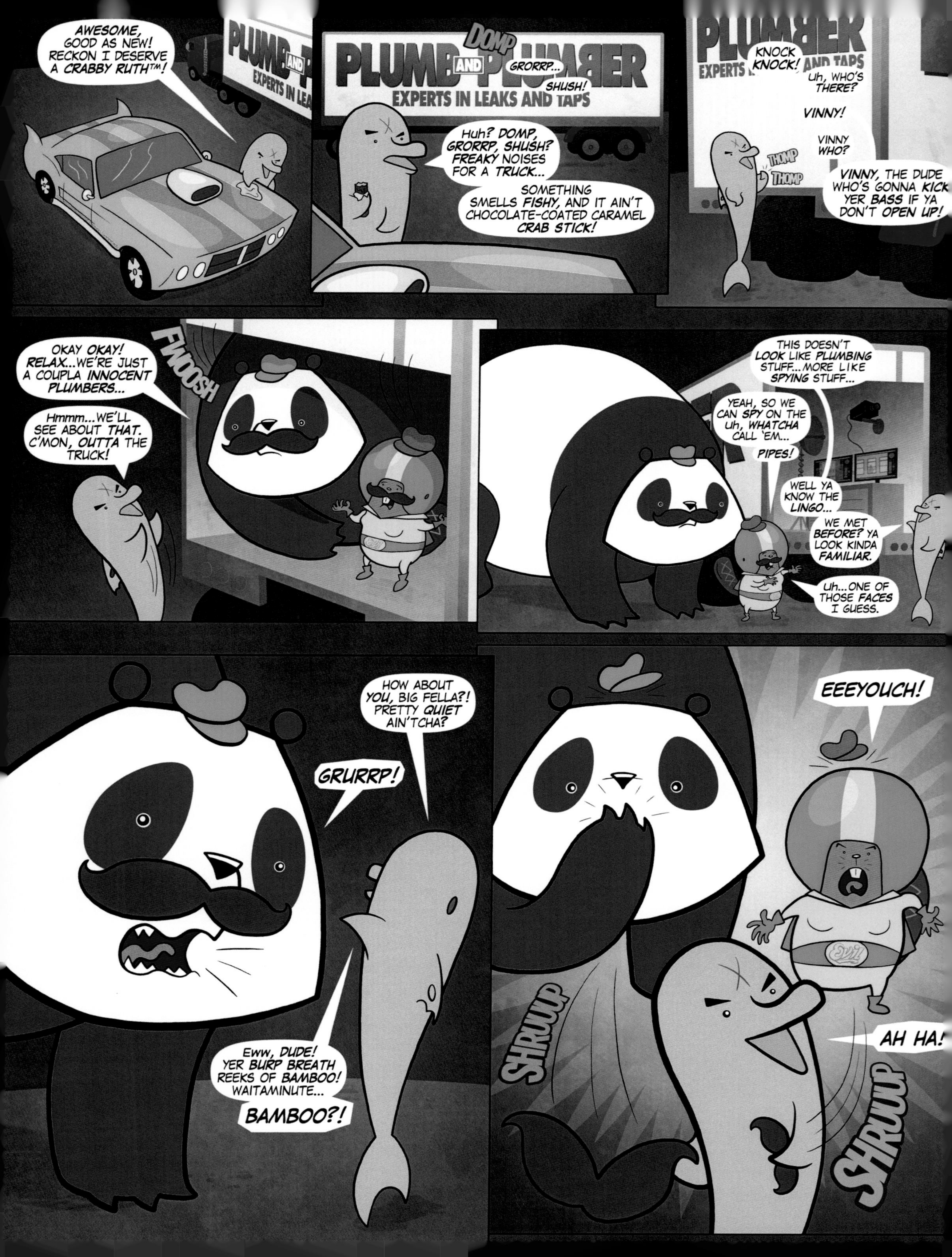
AWESOME, GOOD AS NEW! RECKON I DESERVE A CRABBY RUTH™!
PLUMB AND PLUMBER
EXPERTS IN LEAKS AND TAPS
DOMP
GRORRP...
SHUSH!
Huh? DOMP, GRORRP, SHUSH? FREAKY NOISES FOR A TRUCK...
SOMETHING SMELLS FISHY, AND IT AIN'T CHOCOLATE-COATED CARAMEL CRAB STICK!
KNOCK KNOCK!
Uh, WHO'S THERE?
VINNY!
VINNY WHO?
THOMP
THOMP
VINNY, THE DUDE WHO'S GONNA KICK YER BASS IF YA DON'T OPEN UP!
OKAY OKAY! RELAX...WE'RE JUST A COUPLA INNOCENT PLUMBERS...
FWOOOSH
Hmmm...WE'LL SEE ABOUT THAT. C'MON, OUTTA THE TRUCK!
THIS DOESN'T LOOK LIKE PLUMBING STUFF...MORE LIKE SPYING STUFF...
YEAH, SO WE CAN SPY ON THE Uh, WHATCHA CALL 'EM...
PIPES!
WELL YA KNOW THE LINGO...
WE MET BEFORE? YA LOOK KINDA FAMILIAR.
Uh...ONE OF THOSE FACES I GUESS.
HOW ABOUT YOU, BIG FELLA?! PRETTY QUIET AIN'TCHA?
GRURRP!
Eww, DUDE! YER BURP BREATH REEKS OF BAMBOO! WAITAMINUTE...
BAMBOO?!
EEEYOUCH!
SHRUUUP
AH HA!
SHRUUUP

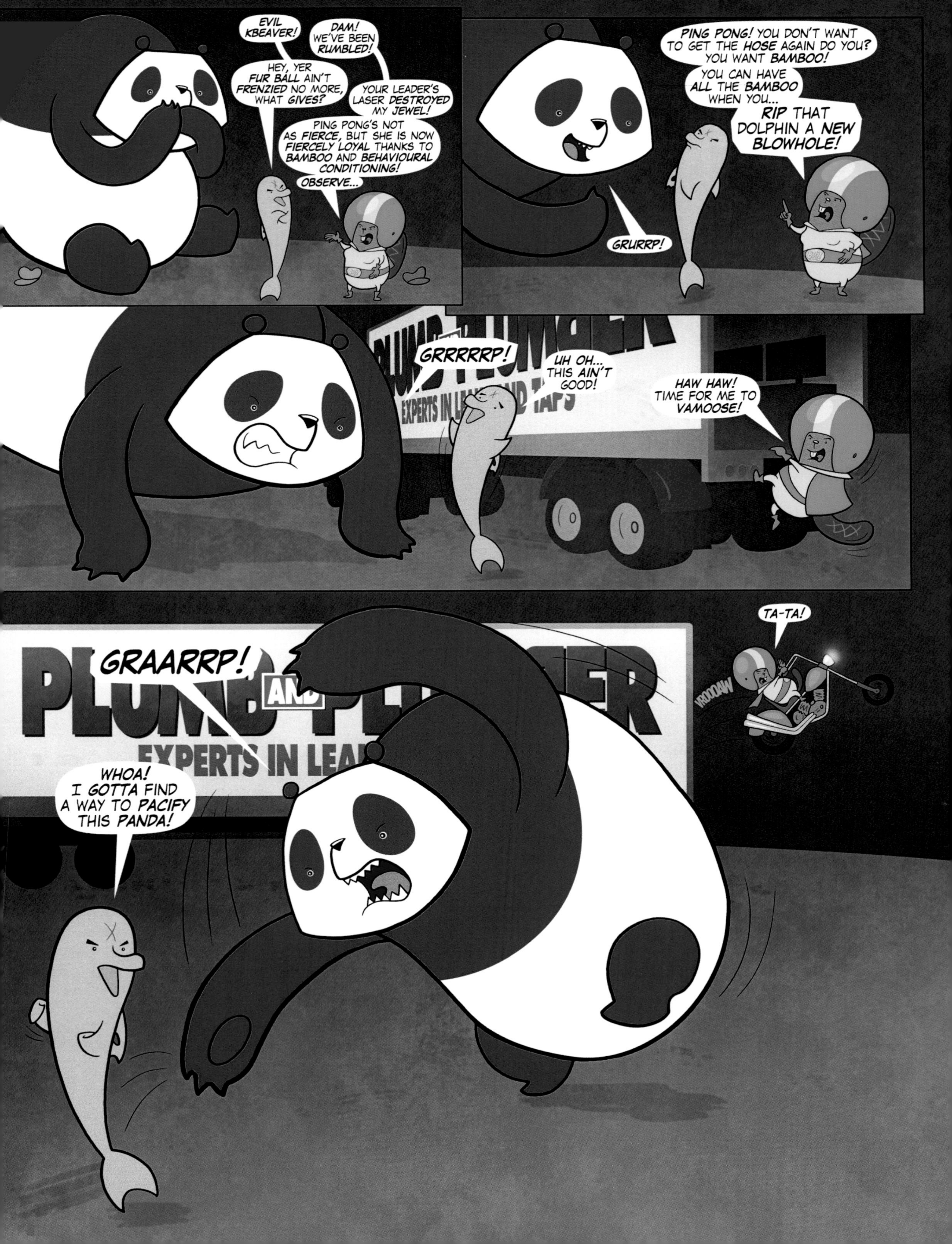
EVIL KBEAVER!
DAM! WE'VE BEEN RUMBLED!
HEY, YER FUR BALL AIN'T FRENZIED NO MORE, WHAT GIVES?
YOUR LEADER'S LASER DESTROYED MY JEWEL!
PING PONG'S NOT AS FIERCE, BUT SHE IS NOW FIERCELY LOYAL THANKS TO BAMBOO AND BEHAVIOURAL CONDITIONING!
OBSERVE...
PING PONG! YOU DON'T WANT TO GET THE HOSE AGAIN DO YOU? YOU WANT BAMBOO!
YOU CAN HAVE ALL THE BAMBOO WHEN YOU...
RIP THAT DOLPHIN A NEW BLOWHOLE!
GRURRP!
GRRRRRP!
UH OH... THIS AIN'T GOOD!
HAW HAW! TIME FOR ME TO VAMOOSE!
GRAARRP!
PLUMB AND PL
EXPERTS IN LEA
TA-TA!
VROOOAW
WHOA! I GOTTA FIND A WAY TO PACIFY THIS PANDA!

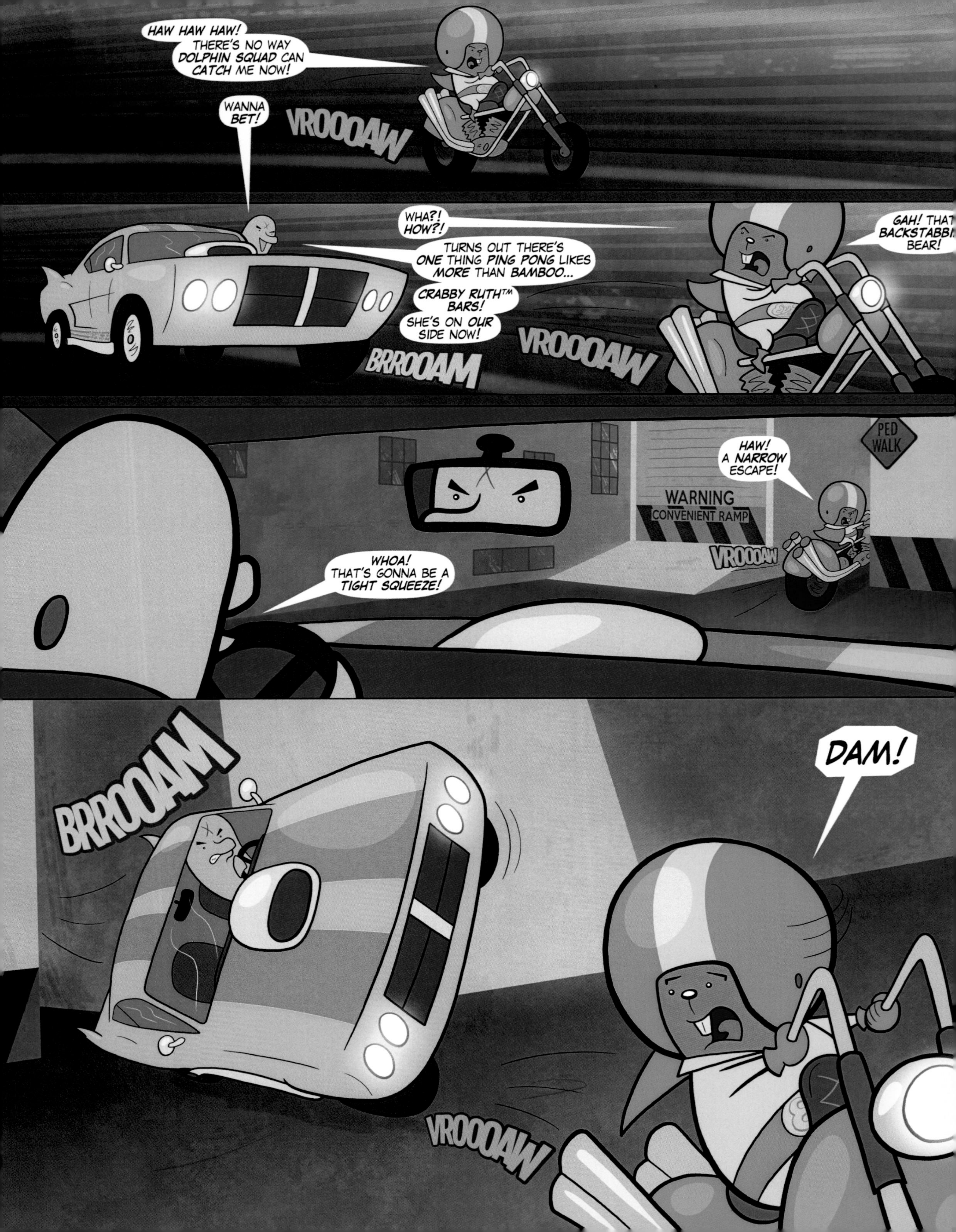

HAW HAW HAW!
THERE'S NO WAY DOLPHIN SQUAD CAN CATCH ME NOW!
WANNA BET!
VROOOAW
WHA?! HOW?!
TURNS OUT THERE'S ONE THING PING PONG LIKES MORE THAN BAMBOO...
CRABBY RUTH™ BARS!
SHE'S ON OUR SIDE NOW!
GAH! THAT BACKSTABBI BEAR!
BRROOAM
VROOOAW
PED WALK
HAW! A NARROW ESCAPE!
WARNING
CONVENIENT RAMP
VROOOAW
WHOA! THAT'S GONNA BE A TIGHT SQUEEZE!
BRROOAM
DAM!
VROOOAW

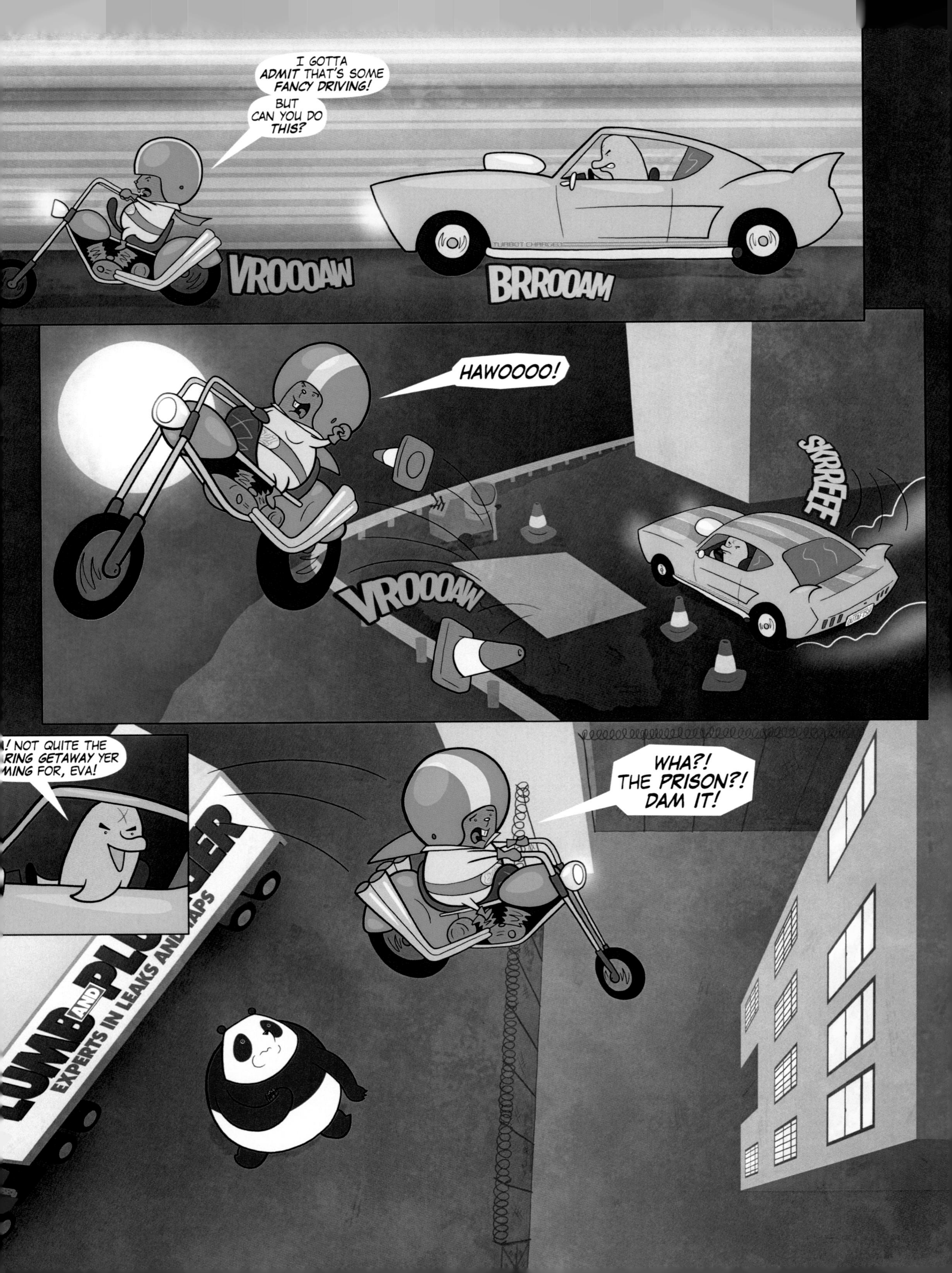

I GOTTA ADMIT THAT'S SOME FANCY DRIVING!
BUT CAN YOU DO THIS?
VROOOAW
TURBOT CHARGED
BRROOAM
HAWOOOO!
SKRREEE
VROOOAW
! NOT QUITE THE RING GETAWAY YER MING FOR, EVA!
WHA?! THE PRISON?! DAM IT!
EXPERTS IN LEAKS AND

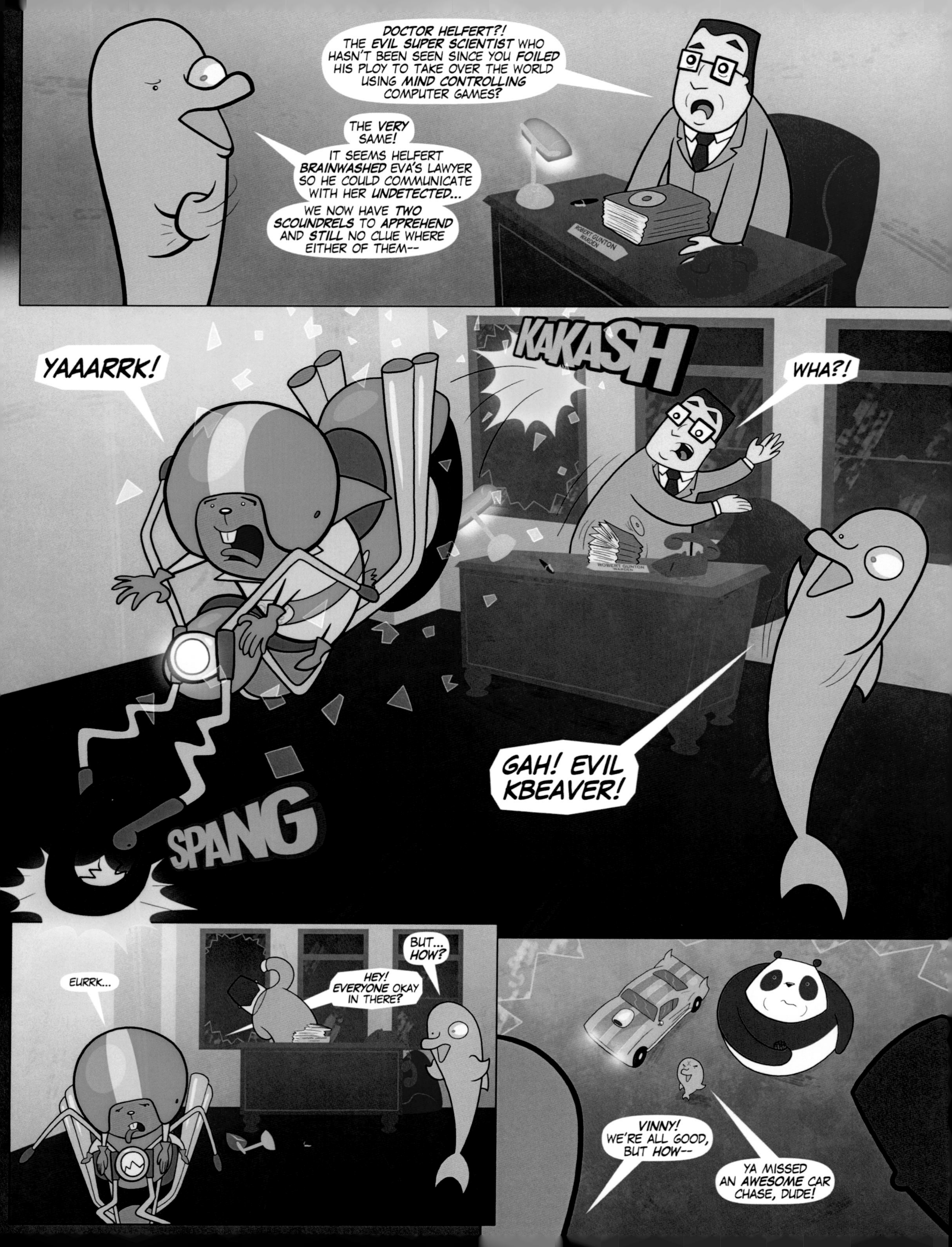
DOCTOR HELFERT?! THE EVIL SUPER SCIENTIST WHO HASN'T BEEN SEEN SINCE YOU FOILED HIS PLOY TO TAKE OVER THE WORLD USING MIND CONTROLLING COMPUTER GAMES?
THE VERY SAME!
IT SEEMS HELFERT BRAINWASHED EVA'S LAWYER SO HE COULD COMMUNICATE WITH HER UNDETECTED...
WE NOW HAVE TWO SCOUNDRELS TO APPREHEND AND STILL NO CLUE WHERE EITHER OF THEM--
ROBERT GUNTON WARDEN
YAAARRK!
KAKASH
WHA?!
GAH! EVIL KBEAVER!
SPANG
EURRK...
HEY! EVERYONE OKAY IN THERE?
BUT... HOW?
VINNY! WE'RE ALL GOOD, BUT HOW--
YA MISSED AN AWESOME CAR CHASE, DUDE!

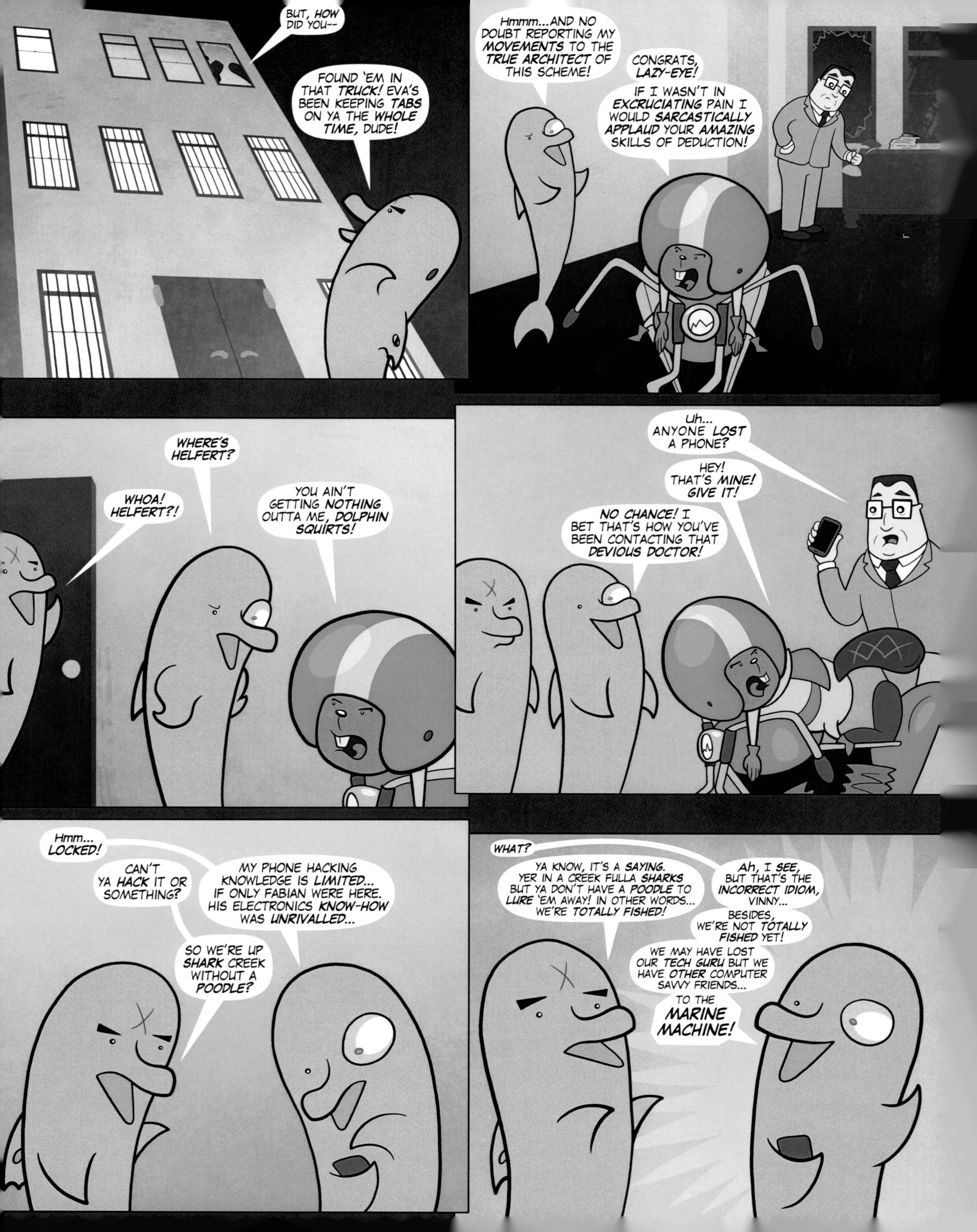
BUT, HOW DID YOU--
FOUND 'EM IN THAT TRUCK! EVA'S BEEN KEEPING TABS ON YA THE WHOLE TIME, DUDE!
Hmmm...AND NO DOUBT REPORTING MY MOVEMENTS TO THE TRUE ARCHITECT OF THIS SCHEME!
CONGRATS, LAZY-EYE!
IF I WASN'T IN EXCRUCIATING PAIN I WOULD SARCASTICALLY APPLAUD YOUR AMAZING SKILLS OF DEDUCTION!
WHERE'S HELFERT?
WHOA! HELFERT?!
YOU AIN'T GETTING NOTHING OUTTA ME, DOLPHIN SQUIRTS!
Uh... ANYONE LOST A PHONE?
HEY! THAT'S MINE! GIVE IT!
NO CHANCE! I BET THAT'S HOW YOU'VE BEEN CONTACTING THAT DEVIOUS DOCTOR!
Hmm... LOCKED!
CAN'T YA HACK IT OR SOMETHING?
MY PHONE HACKING KNOWLEDGE IS LIMITED... IF ONLY FABIAN WERE HERE. HIS ELECTRONICS KNOW-HOW WAS UNRIVALLED...
SO WE'RE UP SHARK CREEK WITHOUT A POODLE?
WHAT?
YA KNOW, IT'S A SAYING. YER IN A CREEK FULLA SHARKS BUT YA DON'T HAVE A POODLE TO LURE 'EM AWAY! IN OTHER WORDS... WE'RE TOTALLY FISHED!
Ah, I SEE, BUT THAT'S THE INCORRECT IDIOM, VINNY...
BESIDES, WE'RE NOT TOTALLY FISHED YET!
WE MAY HAVE LOST OUR TECH GURU BUT WE HAVE OTHER COMPUTER SAVVY FRIENDS...
TO THE MARINE MACHINE!

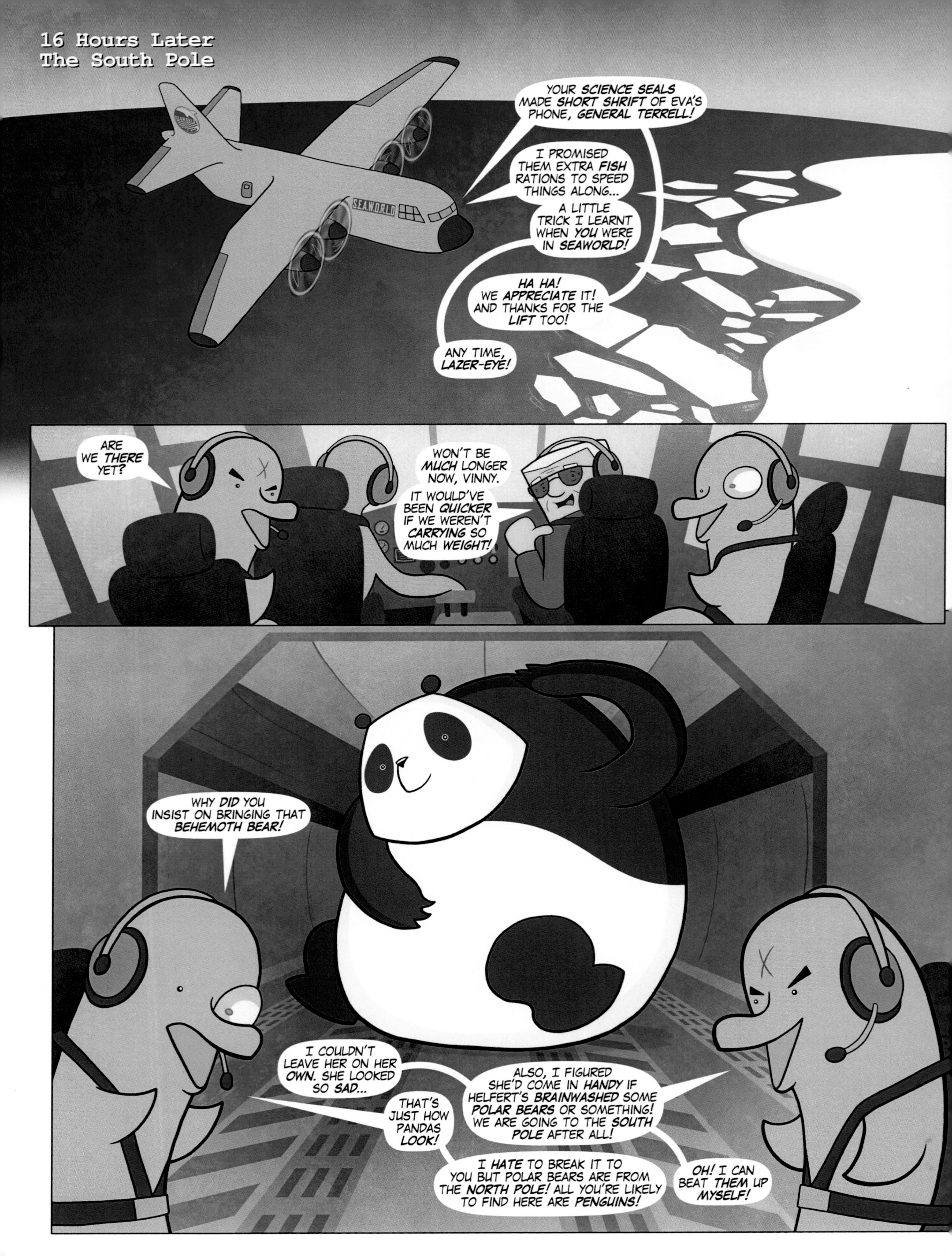
16 Hours Later
The South Pole
S.E.A.W.O.R.L.D
YOUR SCIENCE SEALS MADE SHORT SHRIFT OF EVA'S PHONE, GENERAL TERRELL!
I PROMISED THEM EXTRA FISH RATIONS TO SPEED THINGS ALONG...
A LITTLE TRICK I LEARNT WHEN YOU WERE IN SEAWORLD!
HA HA! WE APPRECIATE IT! AND THANKS FOR THE LIFT TOO!
ANY TIME, LAZER-EYE!
ARE WE THERE YET?
WON'T BE MUCH LONGER NOW, VINNY.
IT WOULD'VE BEEN QUICKER IF WE WEREN'T CARRYING SO MUCH WEIGHT!
WHY DID YOU INSIST ON BRINGING THAT BEHEMOTH BEAR!
I COULDN'T LEAVE HER ON HER OWN. SHE LOOKED SO SAD...
ALSO, I FIGURED SHE'D COME IN HANDY IF HELFERT'S BRAINWASHED SOME POLAR BEARS OR SOMETHING! WE ARE GOING TO THE SOUTH POLE AFTER ALL!
THAT'S JUST HOW PANDAS LOOK!
I HATE TO BREAK IT TO YOU BUT POLAR BEARS ARE FROM THE NORTH POLE! ALL YOU'RE LIKELY TO FIND HERE ARE PENGUINS!
OH! I CAN BEAT THEM UP MYSELF!

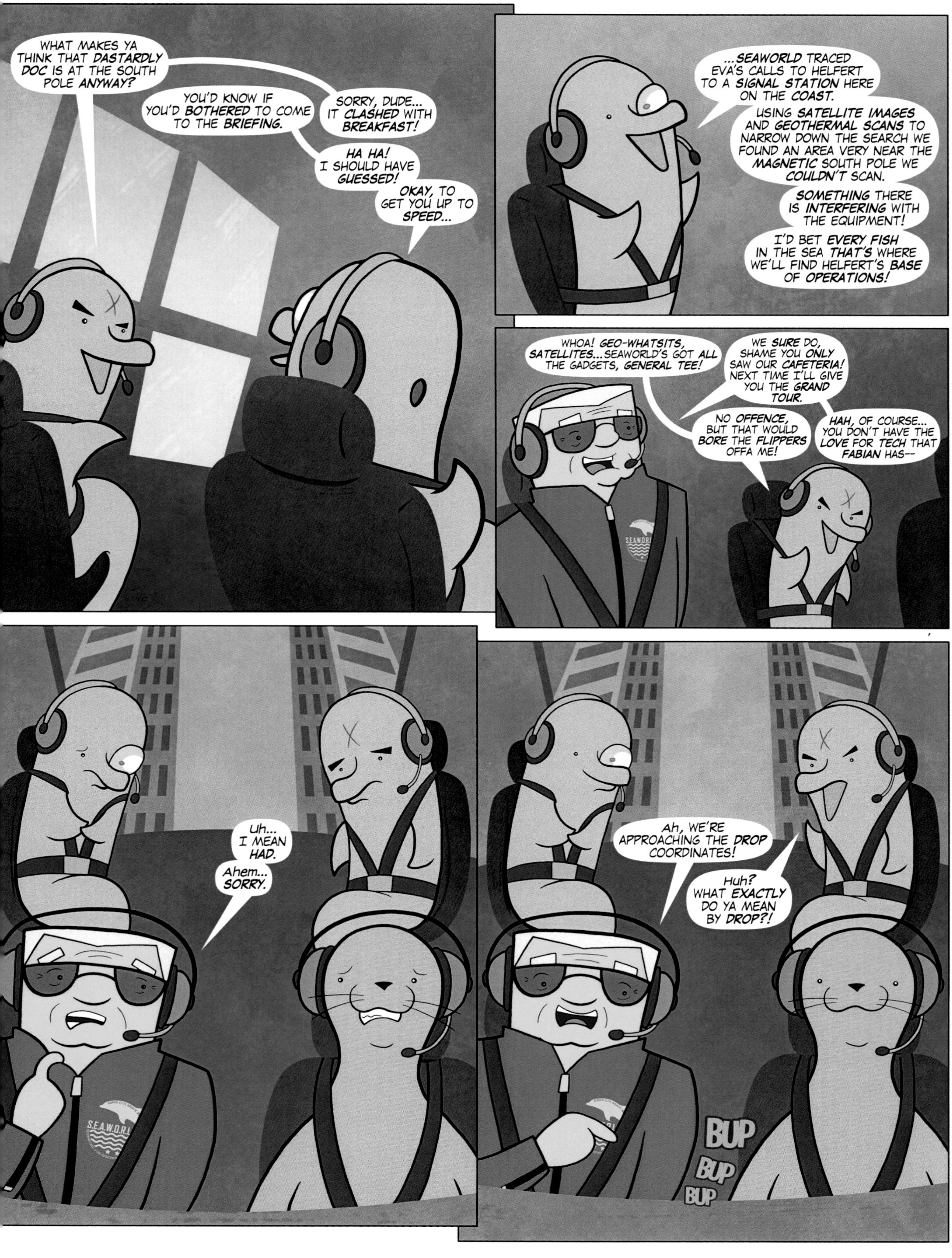
WHAT MAKES YA THINK THAT DASTARDLY DOC IS AT THE SOUTH POLE ANYWAY?
YOU'D KNOW IF YOU'D BOTHERED TO COME TO THE BRIEFING.
SORRY, DUDE... IT CLASHED WITH BREAKFAST!
HA HA! I SHOULD HAVE GUESSED!
OKAY, TO GET YOU UP TO SPEED...
...SEAWORLD TRACED EVA'S CALLS TO HELFERT TO A SIGNAL STATION HERE ON THE COAST.
USING SATELLITE IMAGES AND GEOTHERMAL SCANS TO NARROW DOWN THE SEARCH WE FOUND AN AREA VERY NEAR THE MAGNETIC SOUTH POLE WE COULDN'T SCAN.
SOMETHING THERE IS INTERFERING WITH THE EQUIPMENT!
I'D BET EVERY FISH IN THE SEA THAT'S WHERE WE'LL FIND HELFERT'S BASE OF OPERATIONS!
WHOA! GEO-WHATSITS, SATELLITES...SEAWORLD'S GOT ALL THE GADGETS, GENERAL TEE!
WE SURE DO, SHAME YOU ONLY SAW OUR CAFETERIA! NEXT TIME I'LL GIVE YOU THE GRAND TOUR.
NO OFFENCE, BUT THAT WOULD BORE THE FLIPPERS OFFA ME!
HAH, OF COURSE... YOU DON'T HAVE THE LOVE FOR TECH THAT FABIAN HAS--
Uh... I MEAN HAD.
Ahem... SORRY.
Ah, WE'RE APPROACHING THE DROP COORDINATES!
Huh? WHAT EXACTLY DO YA MEAN BY DROP?!
BUP
BUP
BUP

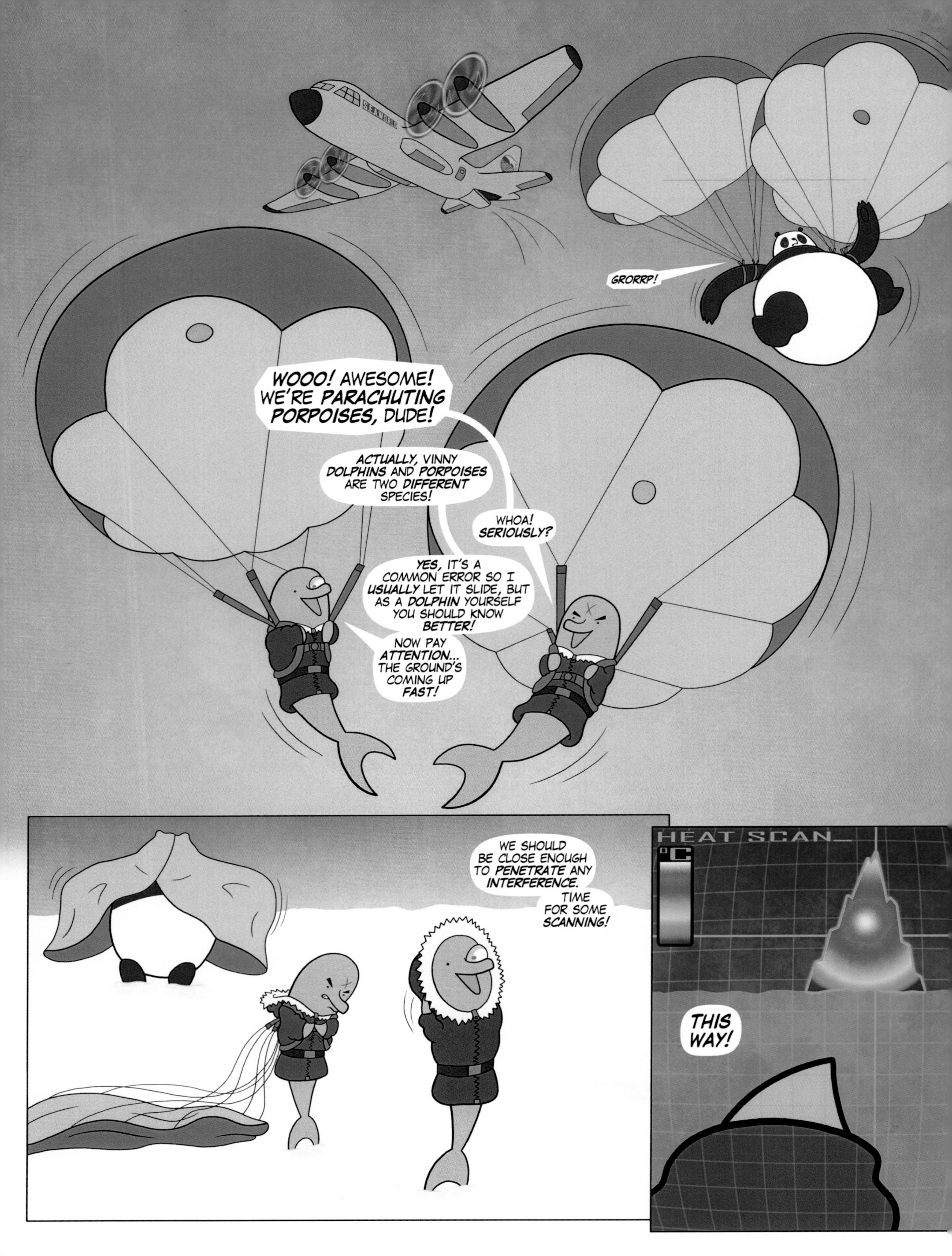
GRORRP!
WOOO! AWESOME! WE'RE PARACHUTING PORPOISES, DUDE!
ACTUALLY, VINNY DOLPHINS AND PORPOISES ARE TWO DIFFERENT SPECIES!
WHOA! SERIOUSLY?
YES, IT'S A COMMON ERROR SO I USUALLY LET IT SLIDE, BUT AS A DOLPHIN YOURSELF YOU SHOULD KNOW BETTER!
NOW PAY ATTENTION... THE GROUND'S COMING UP FAST!
WE SHOULD BE CLOSE ENOUGH TO PENETRATE ANY INTERFERENCE.
TIME FOR SOME SCANNING!
HEAT SCAN_
°C
THIS WAY!

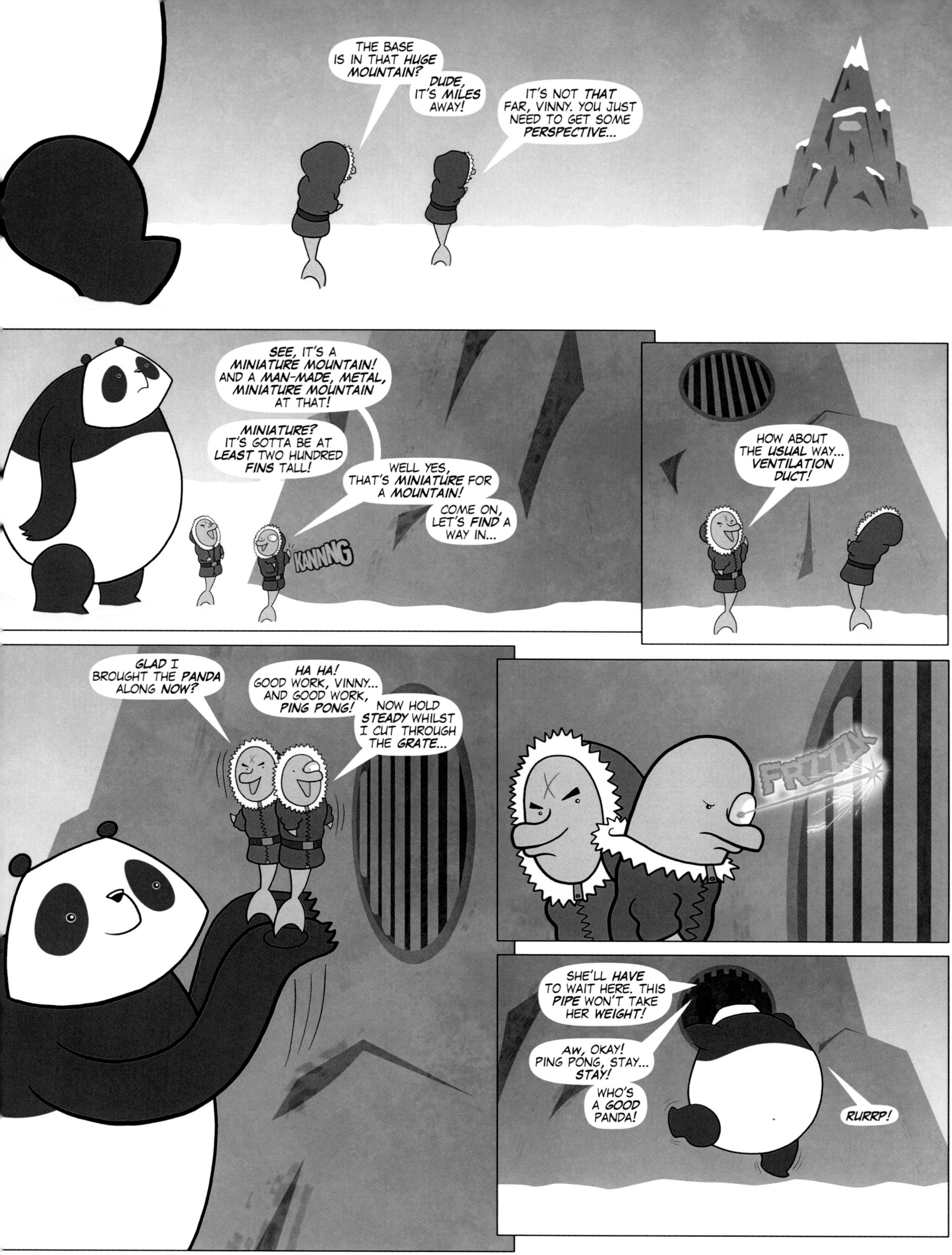
THE BASE IS IN THAT HUGE MOUNTAIN?
DUDE, IT'S MILES AWAY!
IT'S NOT THAT FAR, VINNY. YOU JUST NEED TO GET SOME PERSPECTIVE...
SEE, IT'S A MINIATURE MOUNTAIN! AND A MAN-MADE, METAL, MINIATURE MOUNTAIN AT THAT!
MINIATURE? IT'S GOTTA BE AT LEAST TWO HUNDRED FINS TALL!
WELL YES, THAT'S MINIATURE FOR A MOUNTAIN!
COME ON, LET'S FIND A WAY IN...
KANNNG
HOW ABOUT THE USUAL WAY... VENTILATION DUCT!
GLAD I BROUGHT THE PANDA ALONG NOW?
HA HA! GOOD WORK, VINNY... AND GOOD WORK, PING PONG!
NOW HOLD STEADY WHILST I CUT THROUGH THE GRATE...
FRZZTCK
SHE'LL HAVE TO WAIT HERE. THIS PIPE WON'T TAKE HER WEIGHT!
AW, OKAY! PING PONG, STAY... STAY!
WHO'S A GOOD PANDA!
RURRP!

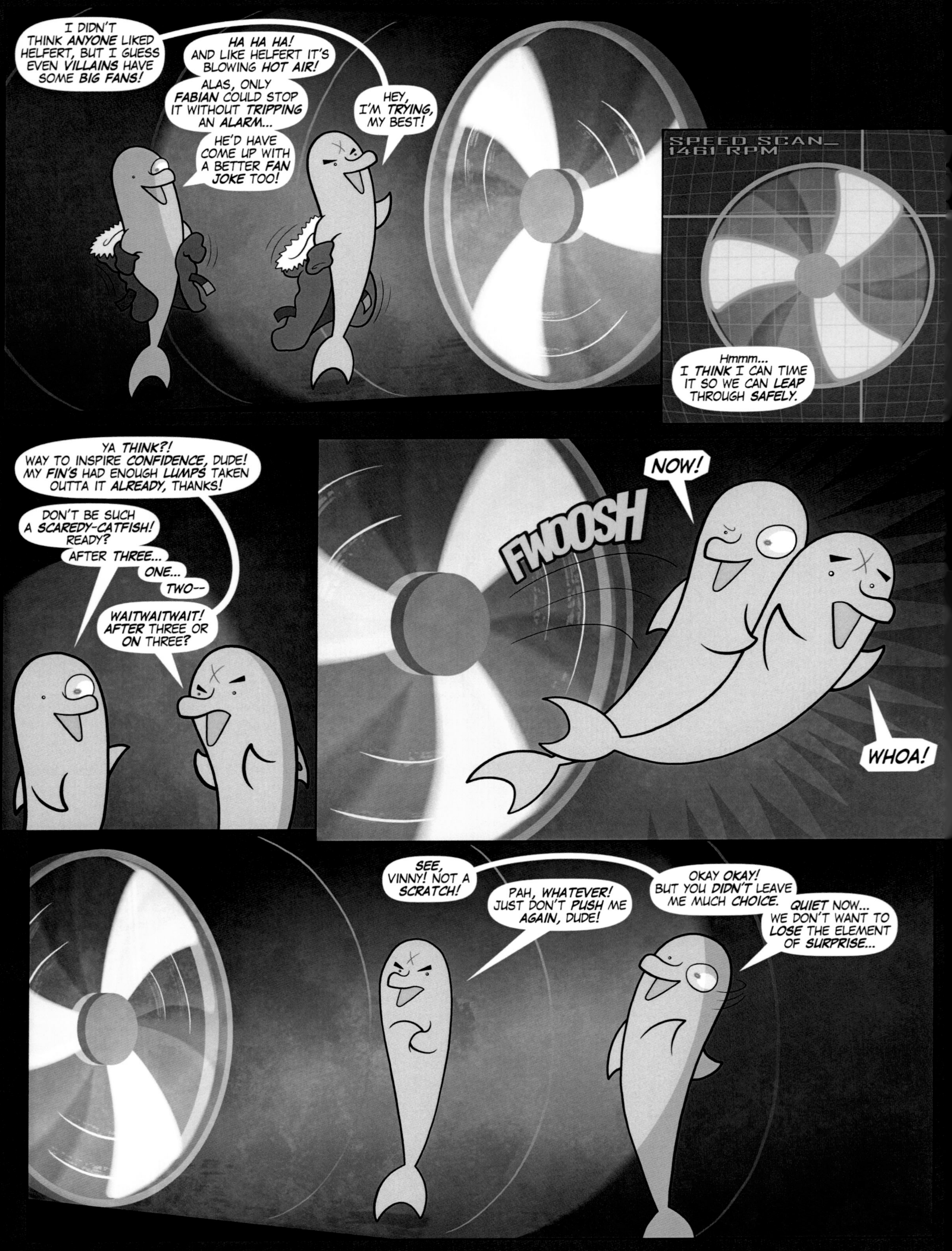
I DIDN'T THINK ANYONE LIKED HELFERT, BUT I GUESS EVEN VILLAINS HAVE SOME BIG FANS!
HA HA HA! AND LIKE HELFERT IT'S BLOWING HOT AIR!
HEY, I'M TRYING, MY BEST!
ALAS, ONLY FABIAN COULD STOP IT WITHOUT TRIPPING AN ALARM...
HE'D HAVE COME UP WITH A BETTER FAN JOKE TOO!
SPEED SCAN_
1461 RPM
Hmmm... I THINK I CAN TIME IT SO WE CAN LEAP THROUGH SAFELY.
YA THINK?! WAY TO INSPIRE CONFIDENCE, DUDE! MY FIN'S HAD ENOUGH LUMPS TAKEN OUTTA IT ALREADY, THANKS!
DON'T BE SUCH A SCAREDY-CATFISH! READY?
AFTER THREE...
ONE...
TWO--
WAITWAITWAIT! AFTER THREE OR ON THREE?
NOW!
FWOOSH
WHOA!
SEE, VINNY! NOT A SCRATCH!
OKAY OKAY! BUT YOU DIDN'T LEAVE ME MUCH CHOICE.
PAH, WHATEVER! JUST DON'T PUSH ME AGAIN, DUDE!
QUIET NOW... WE DON'T WANT TO LOSE THE ELEMENT OF SURPRISE...

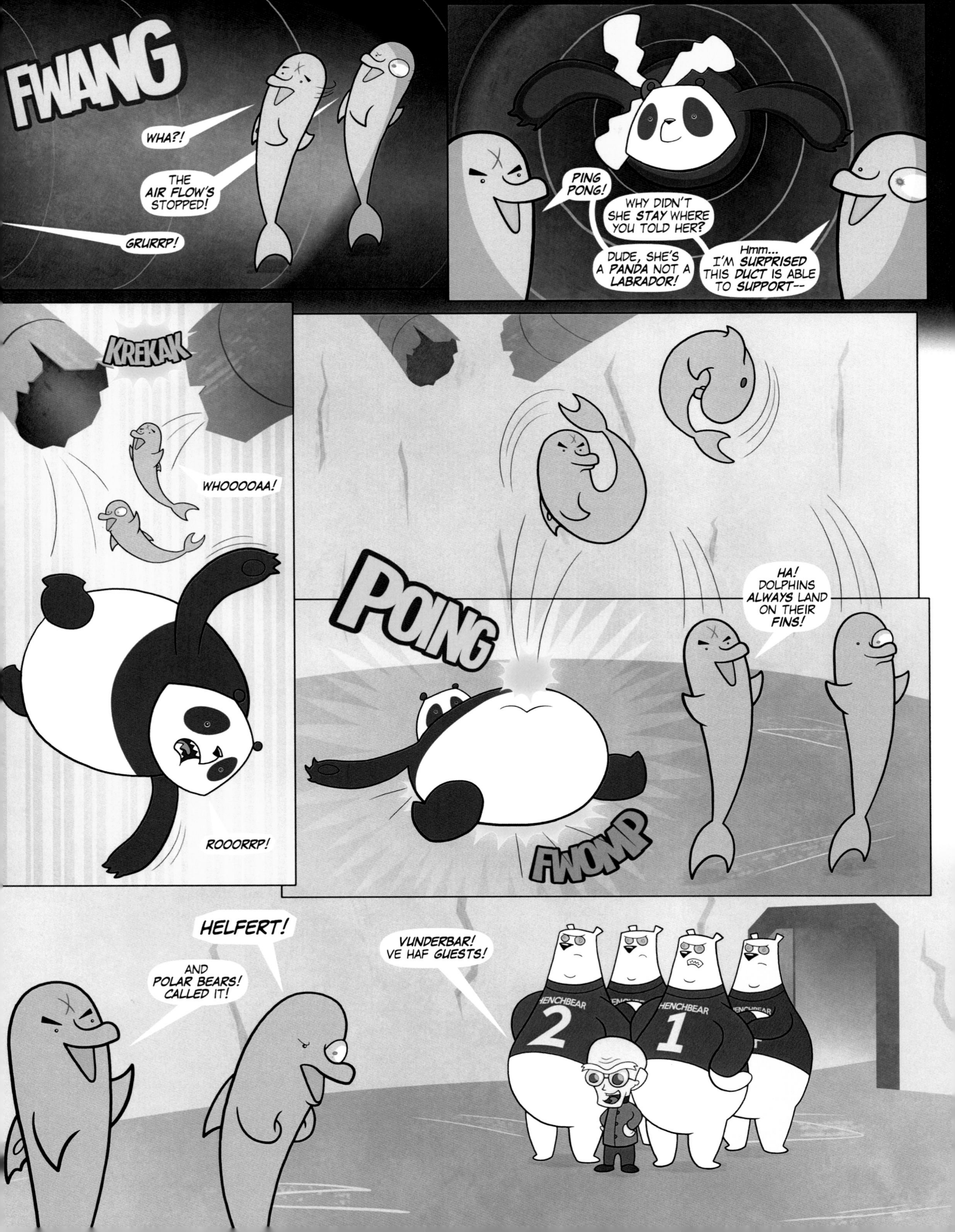

FWANG
WHA?!
THE AIR FLOW'S STOPPED!
GRURRP!
PING PONG!
WHY DIDN'T SHE STAY WHERE YOU TOLD HER?
DUDE, SHE'S A PANDA NOT A LABRADOR!
Hmm... I'M SURPRISED THIS DUCT IS ABLE TO SUPPORT--
KREKAK
WHOOOOAA!
ROOORRP!
POING
HA! DOLPHINS ALWAYS LAND ON THEIR FINS!
FWOMP
HELFERT!
AND POLAR BEARS! CALLED IT!
VUNDERBAR! VE HAF GUESTS!
HENCHBEAR 2
HENCHBEAR 1

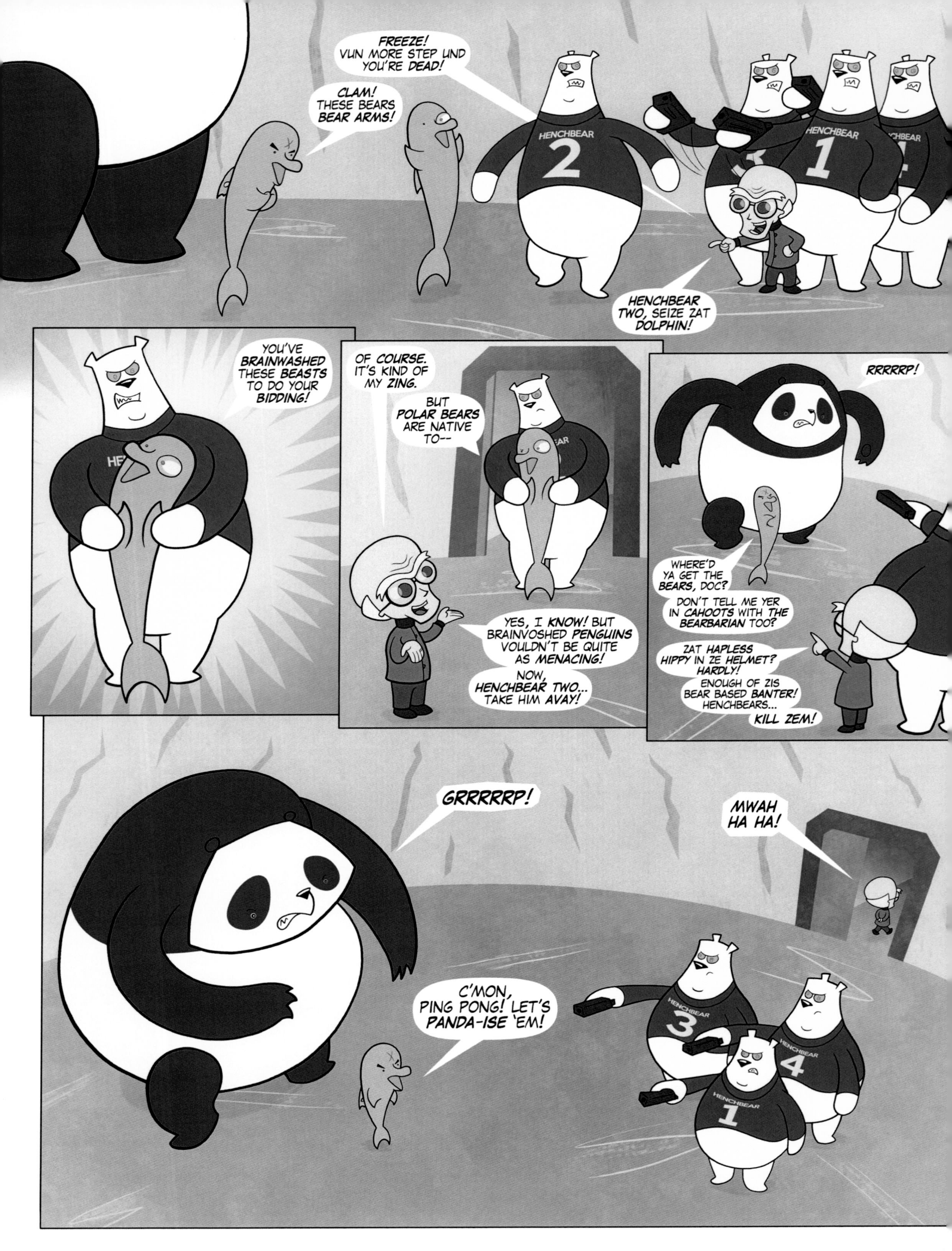

FREEZE! VUN MORE STEP UND YOU'RE DEAD!
CLAM! THESE BEARS BEAR ARMS!
HENCHBEAR
2
HENCHBEAR
1
HENCHBEAR TWO, SEIZE ZAT DOLPHIN!
YOU'VE BRAINWASHED THESE BEASTS TO DO YOUR BIDDING!
OF COURSE. IT'S KIND OF MY ZING.
BUT POLAR BEARS ARE NATIVE TO--
YES, I KNOW! BUT BRAINVOSHED PENGUINS VOULDN'T BE QUITE AS MENACING!
NOW, HENCHBEAR TWO... TAKE HIM AVAY!
RRRRRP!
WHERE'D YA GET THE BEARS, DOC?
DON'T TELL ME YER IN CAHOOTS WITH THE BEARBARIAN TOO?
ZAT HAPLESS HIPPY IN ZE HELMET? HARDLY!
ENOUGH OF ZIS BEAR BASED BANTER! HENCHBEARS... KILL ZEM!
GRRRRRP!
MWAH HA HA!
C'MON, PING PONG! LET'S PANDA-ISE 'EM!
HENCHBEAR
3
HENCHBEAR
4
HENCHBEAR
1

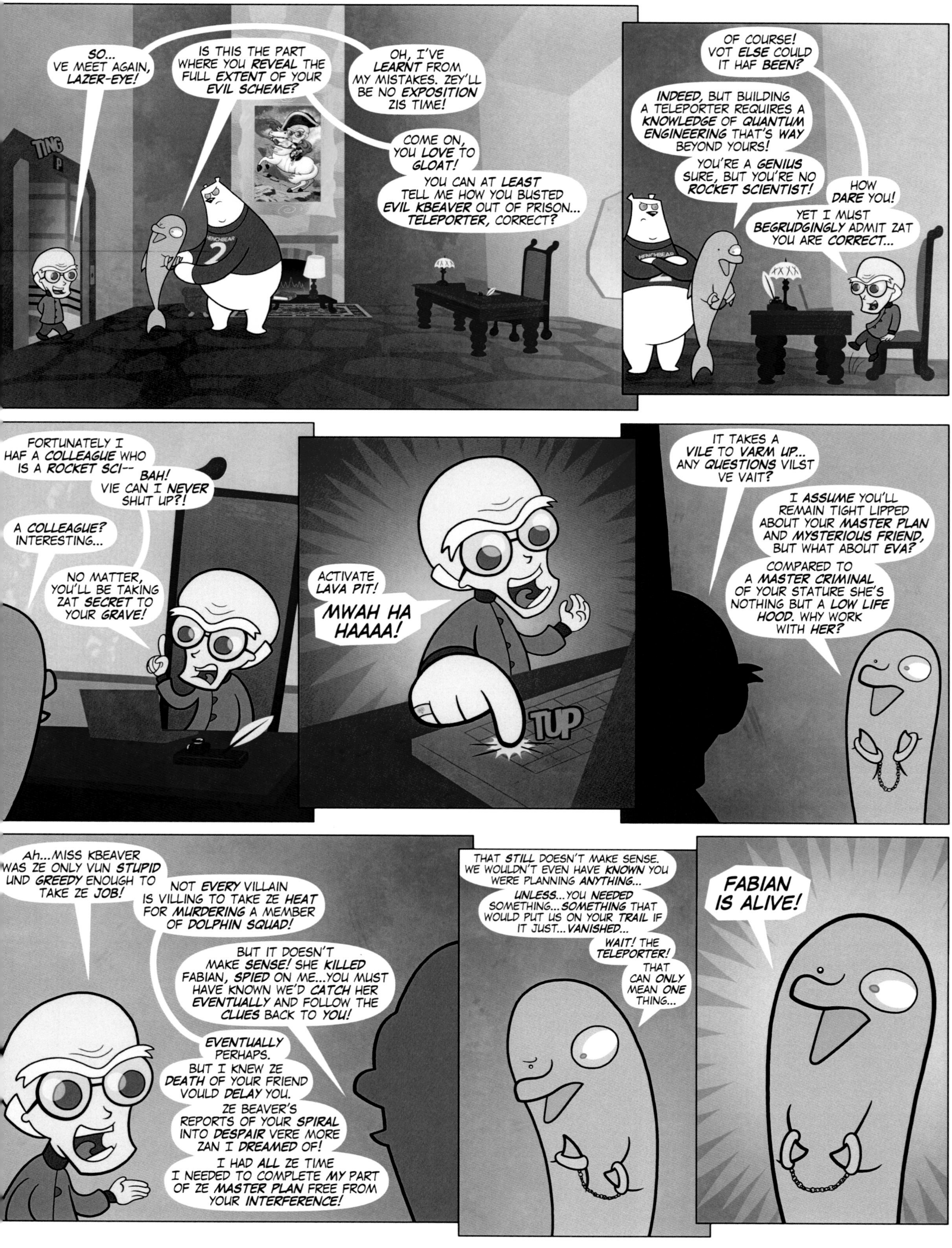
SO... VE MEET AGAIN, LAZER-EYE!
TING
IS THIS THE PART WHERE YOU REVEAL THE FULL EXTENT OF YOUR EVIL SCHEME?
OH, I'VE LEARNT FROM MY MISTAKES. ZEY'LL BE NO EXPOSITION ZIS TIME!
COME ON, YOU LOVE TO GLOAT!
YOU CAN AT LEAST TELL ME HOW YOU BUSTED EVIL KBEAVER OUT OF PRISON... TELEPORTER, CORRECT?
OF COURSE! VOT ELSE COULD IT HAF BEEN?
INDEED, BUT BUILDING A TELEPORTER REQUIRES A KNOWLEDGE OF QUANTUM ENGINEERING THAT'S WAY BEYOND YOURS!
YOU'RE A GENIUS SURE, BUT YOU'RE NO ROCKET SCIENTIST!
HOW DARE YOU!
YET I MUST BEGRUDGINGLY ADMIT ZAT YOU ARE CORRECT...
FORTUNATELY I HAF A COLLEAGUE WHO IS A ROCKET SCI--
BAH! VIE CAN I NEVER SHUT UP?!
A COLLEAGUE? INTERESTING...
NO MATTER, YOU'LL BE TAKING ZAT SECRET TO YOUR GRAVE!
ACTIVATE LAVA PIT!
MWAH HA HAAAA!
TUP
IT TAKES A VILE TO VARM UP... ANY QUESTIONS VILST VE VAIT?
I ASSUME YOU'LL REMAIN TIGHT LIPPED ABOUT YOUR MASTER PLAN AND MYSTERIOUS FRIEND, BUT WHAT ABOUT EVA?
COMPARED TO A MASTER CRIMINAL OF YOUR STATURE SHE'S NOTHING BUT A LOW LIFE HOOD. WHY WORK WITH HER?
Ah...MISS KBEAVER WAS ZE ONLY VUN STUPID UND GREEDY ENOUGH TO TAKE ZE JOB!
NOT EVERY VILLAIN IS VILLING TO TAKE ZE HEAT FOR MURDERING A MEMBER OF DOLPHIN SQUAD!
BUT IT DOESN'T MAKE SENSE! SHE KILLED FABIAN, SPIED ON ME...YOU MUST HAVE KNOWN WE'D CATCH HER EVENTUALLY AND FOLLOW THE CLUES BACK TO YOU!
EVENTUALLY PERHAPS.
BUT I KNEW ZE DEATH OF YOUR FRIEND VOULD DELAY YOU.
ZE BEAVER'S REPORTS OF YOUR SPIRAL INTO DESPAIR VERE MORE ZAN I DREAMED OF!
I HAD ALL ZE TIME I NEEDED TO COMPLETE MY PART OF ZE MASTER PLAN FREE FROM YOUR INTERFERENCE!
THAT STILL DOESN'T MAKE SENSE. WE WOULDN'T EVEN HAVE KNOWN YOU WERE PLANNING ANYTHING...
UNLESS...YOU NEEDED SOMETHING...SOMETHING THAT WOULD PUT US ON YOUR TRAIL IF IT JUST...VANISHED...
WAIT! THE TELEPORTER!
THAT CAN ONLY MEAN ONE THING...
FABIAN IS ALIVE!

MWAH HA HA! SO YOU FINALLY REALISE VOT A *FOOL* YOU HAF BEEN!

I GET QUITE ZE *KICK* SEEING ZAT *SUPPOSEDLY SUPER SMART CEREBRUM* OF YOURS IN ACTION!

YES, YOUR *PINK FRIEND* IS ALIVE... FOR ZE *TIME BEING* AT LEAST!

BUT WE SAW FABIAN GET *ATOMISED!*

OF COURSE... BECAUSE HE *VOS* ATOMISED! ZAT'S HOW TELEPORTING *VERKS!*

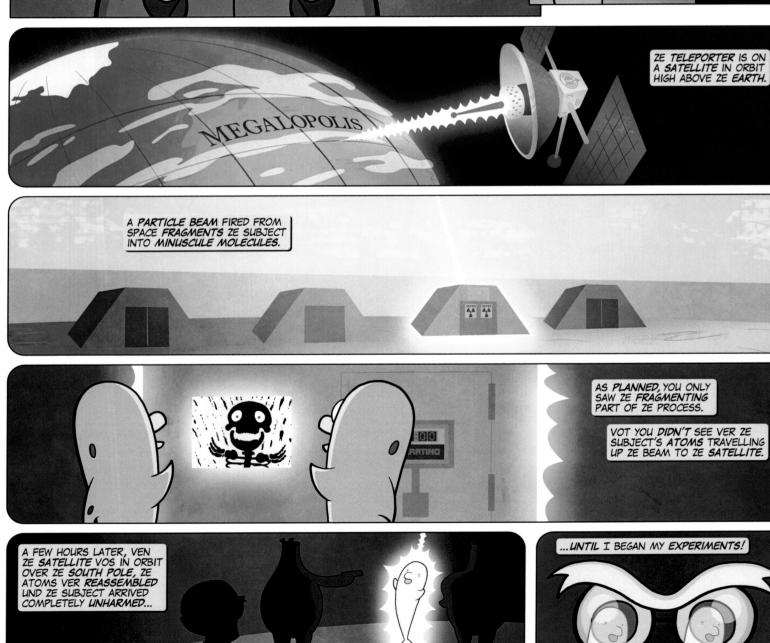

ZE *TELEPORTER* IS ON A *SATELLITE* IN ORBIT HIGH ABOVE ZE *EARTH.*

MEGALOPOLIS

A *PARTICLE BEAM* FIRED FROM SPACE *FRAGMENTS* ZE SUBJECT INTO *MINUSCULE MOLECULES.*

AS *PLANNED,* YOU ONLY SAW ZE *FRAGMENTING* PART OF ZE PROCESS.

VOT YOU *DIDN'T* SEE VER ZE SUBJECT'S *ATOMS* TRAVELLING UP ZE BEAM TO ZE *SATELLITE.*

A FEW HOURS LATER, VEN ZE *SATELLITE* VOS IN ORBIT OVER ZE *SOUTH POLE,* ZE ATOMS VER *REASSEMBLED* UND ZE SUBJECT ARRIVED COMPLETELY *UNHARMED...*

...UNTIL I BEGAN MY *EXPERIMENTS!*

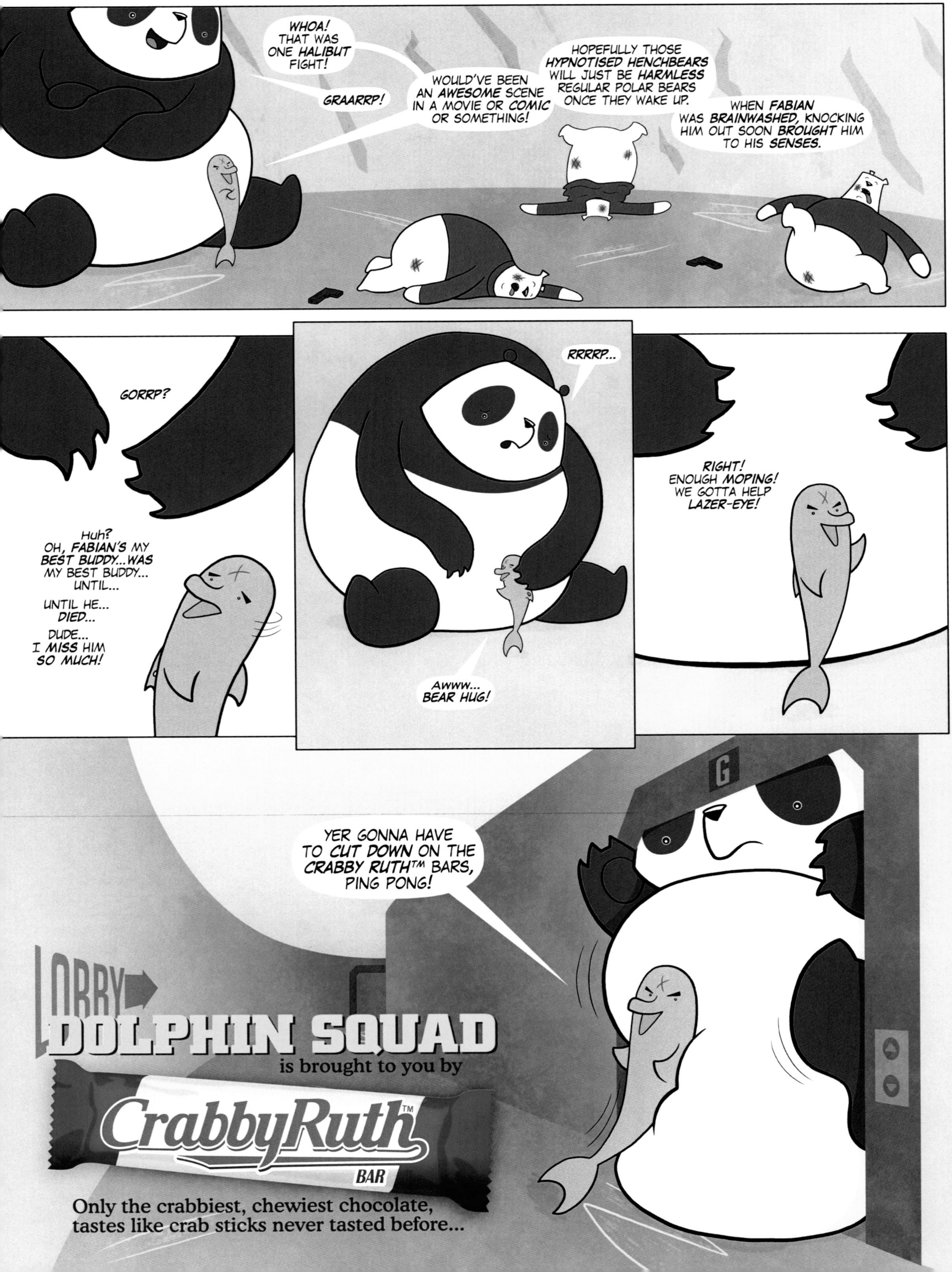
WHOA! THAT WAS ONE HALIBUT FIGHT!
GRAARRP!
WOULD'VE BEEN AN AWESOME SCENE IN A MOVIE OR COMIC OR SOMETHING!
HOPEFULLY THOSE HYPNOTISED HENCHBEARS WILL JUST BE HARMLESS REGULAR POLAR BEARS ONCE THEY WAKE UP.
WHEN FABIAN WAS BRAINWASHED, KNOCKING HIM OUT SOON BROUGHT HIM TO HIS SENSES.
GORRP?
Huh? OH, FABIAN'S MY BEST BUDDY...WAS MY BEST BUDDY... UNTIL...
UNTIL HE... DIED...
DUDE... I MISS HIM SO MUCH!
RRRRP...
AWWW... BEAR HUG!
RIGHT! ENOUGH MOPING! WE GOTTA HELP LAZER-EYE!
G
YER GONNA HAVE TO CUT DOWN ON THE CRABBY RUTH™ BARS, PING PONG!
LOBBY
DOLPHIN SQUAD
is brought to you by
CrabbyRuth™
BAR
Only the crabbiest, chewiest chocolate, tastes like crab sticks never tasted before...

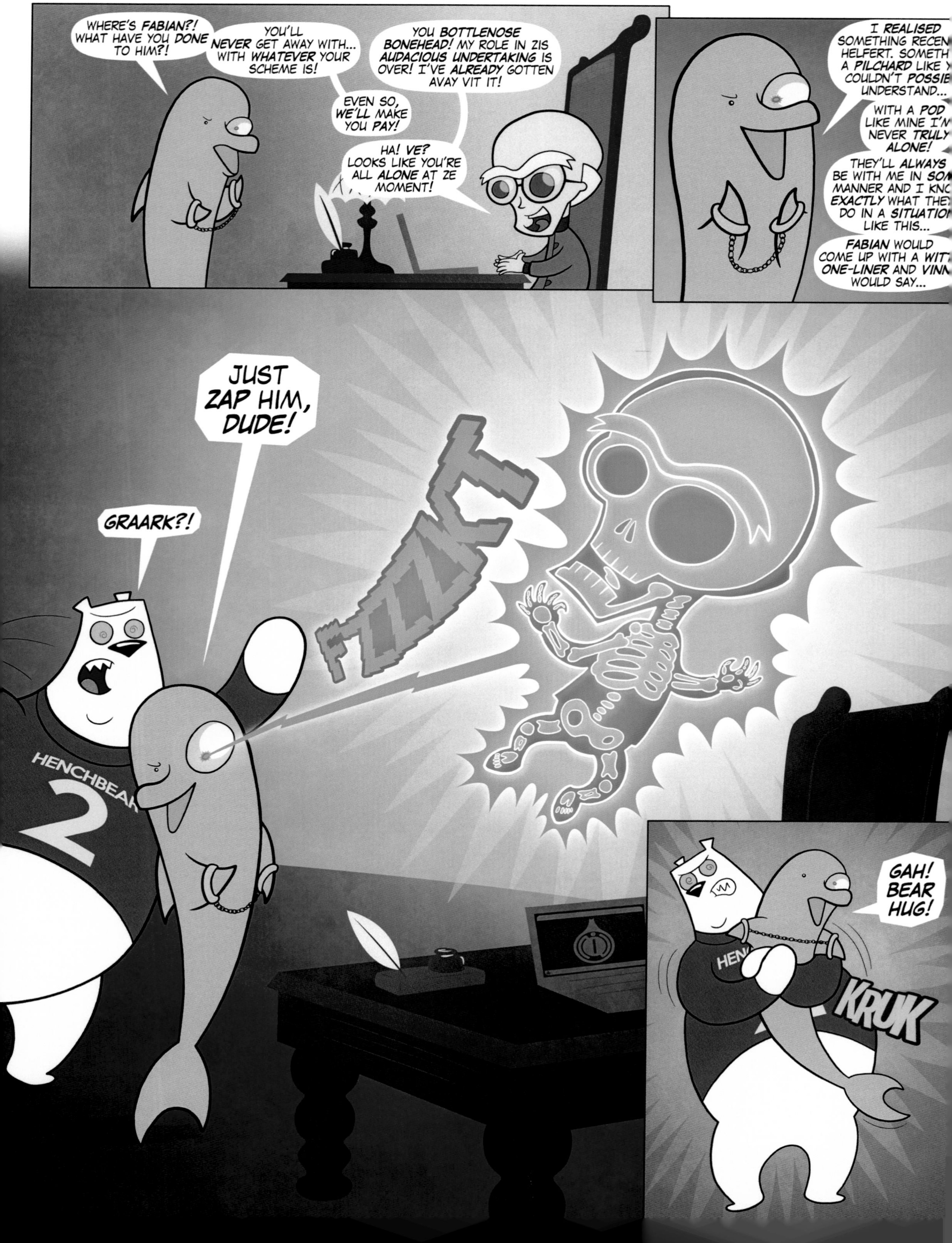
WHERE'S FABIAN?! WHAT HAVE YOU DONE TO HIM?!
YOU'LL NEVER GET AWAY WITH... WITH WHATEVER YOUR SCHEME IS!
YOU BOTTLENOSE BONEHEAD! MY ROLE IN ZIS AUDACIOUS UNDERTAKING IS OVER! I'VE ALREADY GOTTEN AVAY VIT IT!
EVEN SO, WE'LL MAKE YOU PAY!
HA! VE? LOOKS LIKE YOU'RE ALL ALONE AT ZE MOMENT!
I REALISED SOMETHING RECEN HELFERT. SOMETH A PILCHARD LIKE Y COULDN'T POSSIB UNDERSTAND...
WITH A POD LIKE MINE I'M NEVER TRULY ALONE!
THEY'LL ALWAYS BE WITH ME IN SOM MANNER AND I KNO EXACTLY WHAT THEY DO IN A SITUATION LIKE THIS...
FABIAN WOULD COME UP WITH A WIT ONE-LINER AND VINN WOULD SAY...
JUST ZAP HIM, DUDE!
GRAARK?!
FZZZKT
HENCHBEAR 2
GAH! BEAR HUG!
KRUK

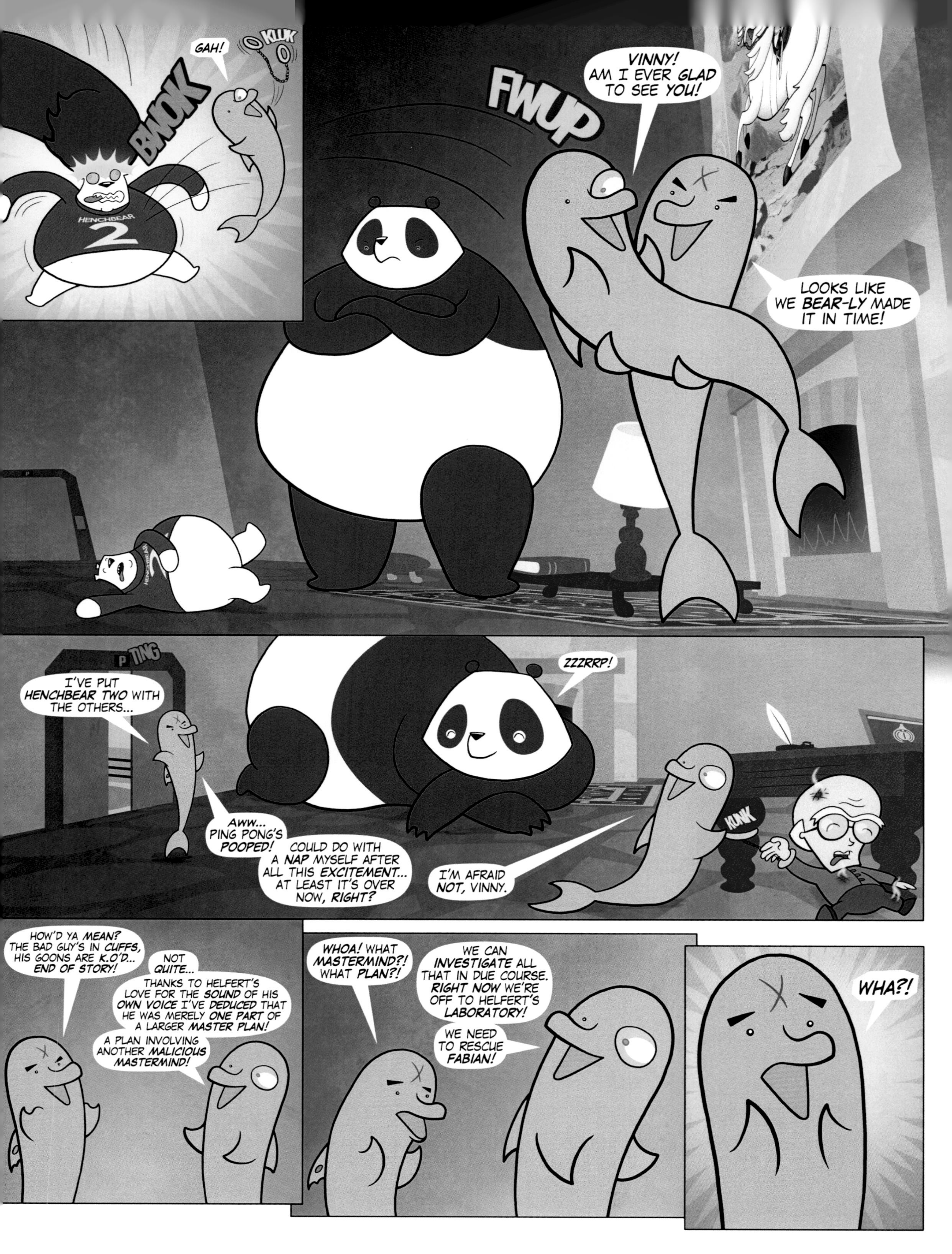
BWOK
GAH!
KLUNK
FWUP
VINNY! AM I EVER GLAD TO SEE YOU!
LOOKS LIKE WE BEAR-LY MADE IT IN TIME!
HENCHBEAR 2
TING
I'VE PUT HENCHBEAR TWO WITH THE OTHERS...
ZZZRRP!
AWW... PING PONG'S POOPED!
COULD DO WITH A NAP MYSELF AFTER ALL THIS EXCITEMENT... AT LEAST IT'S OVER NOW, RIGHT?
KUNK
I'M AFRAID NOT, VINNY.
HOW'D YA MEAN? THE BAD GUY'S IN CUFFS, HIS GOONS ARE K.O'D... END OF STORY!
NOT QUITE...
THANKS TO HELFERT'S LOVE FOR THE SOUND OF HIS OWN VOICE I'VE DEDUCED THAT HE WAS MERELY ONE PART OF A LARGER MASTER PLAN!
A PLAN INVOLVING ANOTHER MALICIOUS MASTERMIND!
WHOA! WHAT MASTERMIND?! WHAT PLAN?!
WE CAN INVESTIGATE ALL THAT IN DUE COURSE. RIGHT NOW WE'RE OFF TO HELFERT'S LABORATORY!
WE NEED TO RESCUE FABIAN!
WHA?!

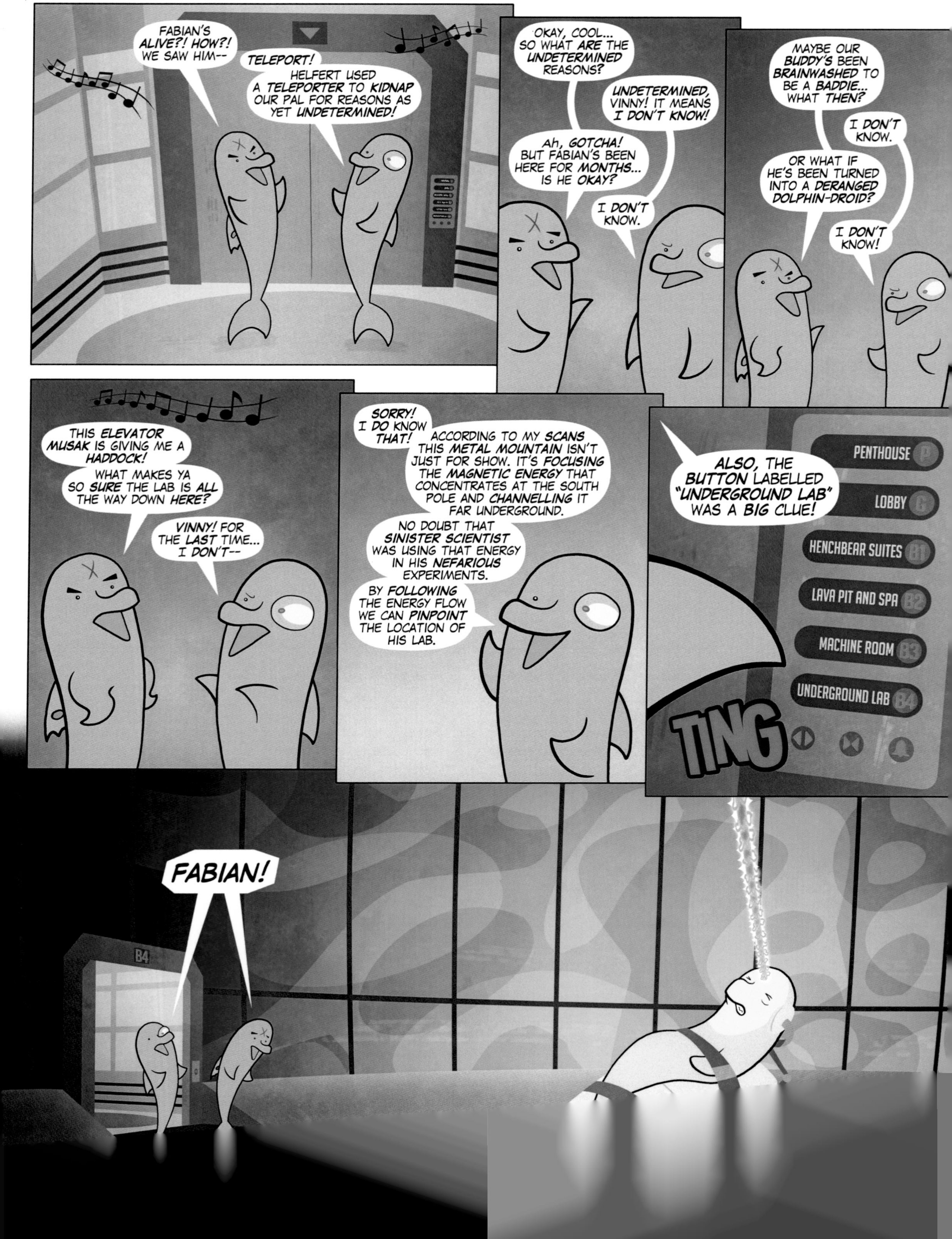
FABIAN'S ALIVE?! HOW?! WE SAW HIM--
TELEPORT! HELFERT USED A TELEPORTER TO KIDNAP OUR PAL FOR REASONS AS YET UNDETERMINED!
OKAY, COOL... SO WHAT ARE THE UNDETERMINED REASONS?
UNDETERMINED, VINNY! IT MEANS I DON'T KNOW!
Ah, GOTCHA! BUT FABIAN'S BEEN HERE FOR MONTHS... IS HE OKAY?
I DON'T KNOW.
MAYBE OUR BUDDY'S BEEN BRAINWASHED TO BE A BADDIE... WHAT THEN?
I DON'T KNOW.
OR WHAT IF HE'S BEEN TURNED INTO A DERANGED DOLPHIN-DROID?
I DON'T KNOW!
THIS ELEVATOR MUSAK IS GIVING ME A HADDOCK!
WHAT MAKES YA SO SURE THE LAB IS ALL THE WAY DOWN HERE?
VINNY! FOR THE LAST TIME... I DON'T--
SORRY! I DO KNOW THAT!
ACCORDING TO MY SCANS THIS METAL MOUNTAIN ISN'T JUST FOR SHOW. IT'S FOCUSING THE MAGNETIC ENERGY THAT CONCENTRATES AT THE SOUTH POLE AND CHANNELLING IT FAR UNDERGROUND.
NO DOUBT THAT SINISTER SCIENTIST WAS USING THAT ENERGY IN HIS NEFARIOUS EXPERIMENTS.
BY FOLLOWING THE ENERGY FLOW WE CAN PINPOINT THE LOCATION OF HIS LAB.
ALSO, THE BUTTON LABELLED "UNDERGROUND LAB" WAS A BIG CLUE!
PENTHOUSE P
LOBBY G
HENCHBEAR SUITES B1
LAVA PIT AND SPA B2
MACHINE ROOM B3
UNDERGROUND LAB B4
TING
FABIAN!
B4

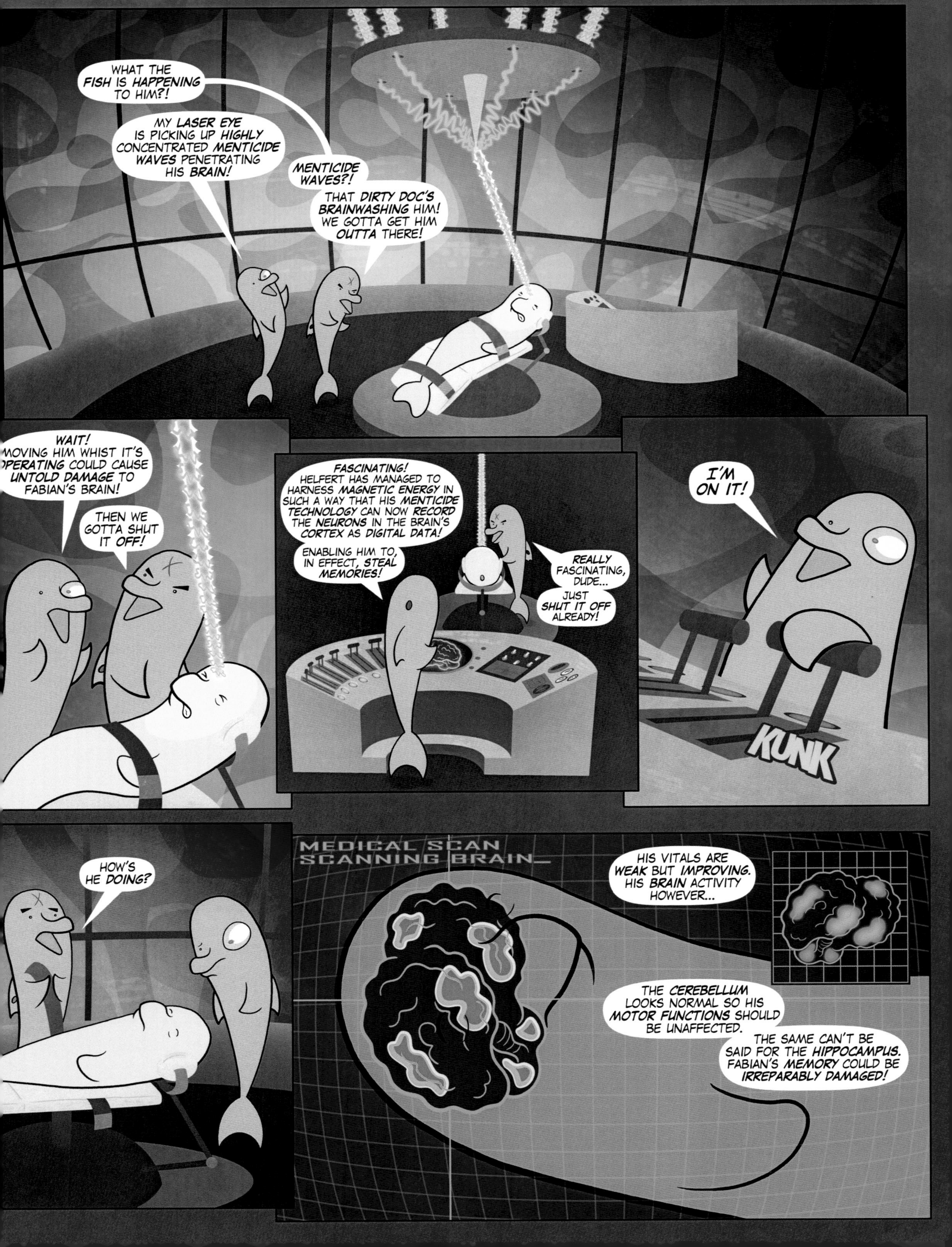

WHAT THE FISH IS HAPPENING TO HIM?!
MY LASER EYE IS PICKING UP HIGHLY CONCENTRATED MENTICIDE WAVES PENETRATING HIS BRAIN!
MENTICIDE WAVES?!
THAT DIRTY DOC'S BRAINWASHING HIM! WE GOTTA GET HIM OUTTA THERE!
WAIT! MOVING HIM WHIST IT'S OPERATING COULD CAUSE UNTOLD DAMAGE TO FABIAN'S BRAIN!
THEN WE GOTTA SHUT IT OFF!
FASCINATING! HELFERT HAS MANAGED TO HARNESS MAGNETIC ENERGY IN SUCH A WAY THAT HIS MENTICIDE TECHNOLOGY CAN NOW RECORD THE NEURONS IN THE BRAIN'S CORTEX AS DIGITAL DATA!
ENABLING HIM TO, IN EFFECT, STEAL MEMORIES!
REALLY FASCINATING, DUDE...
JUST SHUT IT OFF ALREADY!
I'M ON IT!
KUNK
HOW'S HE DOING?
MEDICAL SCAN
SCANNING BRAIN_
HIS VITALS ARE WEAK BUT IMPROVING. HIS BRAIN ACTIVITY HOWEVER...
THE CEREBELLUM LOOKS NORMAL SO HIS MOTOR FUNCTIONS SHOULD BE UNAFFECTED.
THE SAME CAN'T BE SAID FOR THE HIPPOCAMPUS. FABIAN'S MEMORY COULD BE IRREPARABLY DAMAGED!

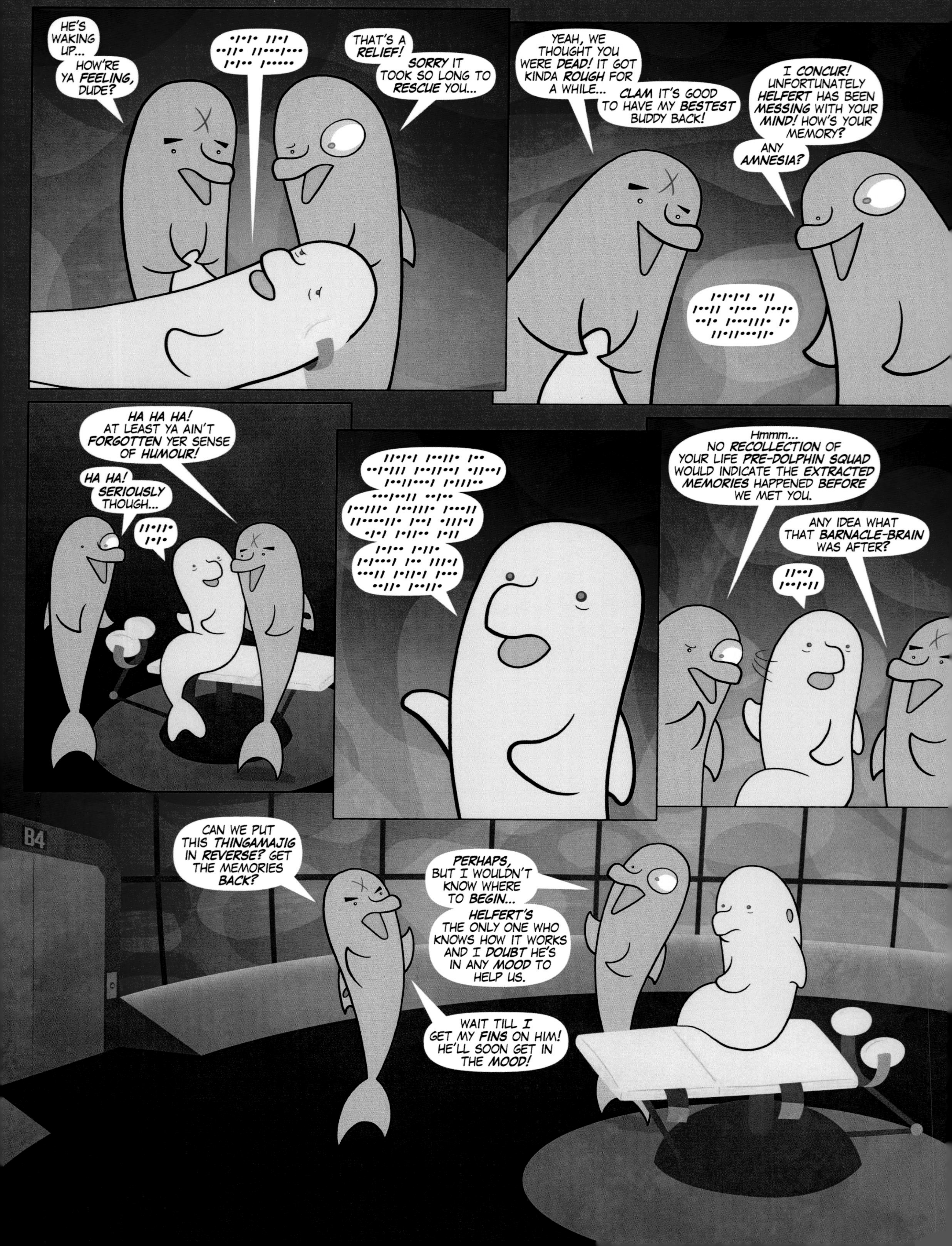

HE'S WAKING UP... HOW'RE YA FEELING, DUDE?
THAT'S A RELIEF! SORRY IT TOOK SO LONG TO RESCUE YOU...
YEAH, WE THOUGHT YOU WERE DEAD! IT GOT KINDA ROUGH FOR A WHILE...
CLAM IT'S GOOD TO HAVE MY BESTEST BUDDY BACK!
I CONCUR! UNFORTUNATELY HELFERT HAS BEEN MESSING WITH YOUR MIND! HOW'S YOUR MEMORY?
ANY AMNESIA?
HA HA HA! AT LEAST YA AIN'T FORGOTTEN YER SENSE OF HUMOUR!
HA HA! SERIOUSLY THOUGH...
Hmmm... NO RECOLLECTION OF YOUR LIFE PRE-DOLPHIN SQUAD WOULD INDICATE THE EXTRACTED MEMORIES HAPPENED BEFORE WE MET YOU.
ANY IDEA WHAT THAT BARNACLE-BRAIN WAS AFTER?
B4
CAN WE PUT THIS THINGAMAJIG IN REVERSE? GET THE MEMORIES BACK?
PERHAPS, BUT I WOULDN'T KNOW WHERE TO BEGIN...
HELFERT'S THE ONLY ONE WHO KNOWS HOW IT WORKS AND I DOUBT HE'S IN ANY MOOD TO HELP US.
WAIT TILL I GET MY FINS ON HIM! HE'LL SOON GET IN THE MOOD!

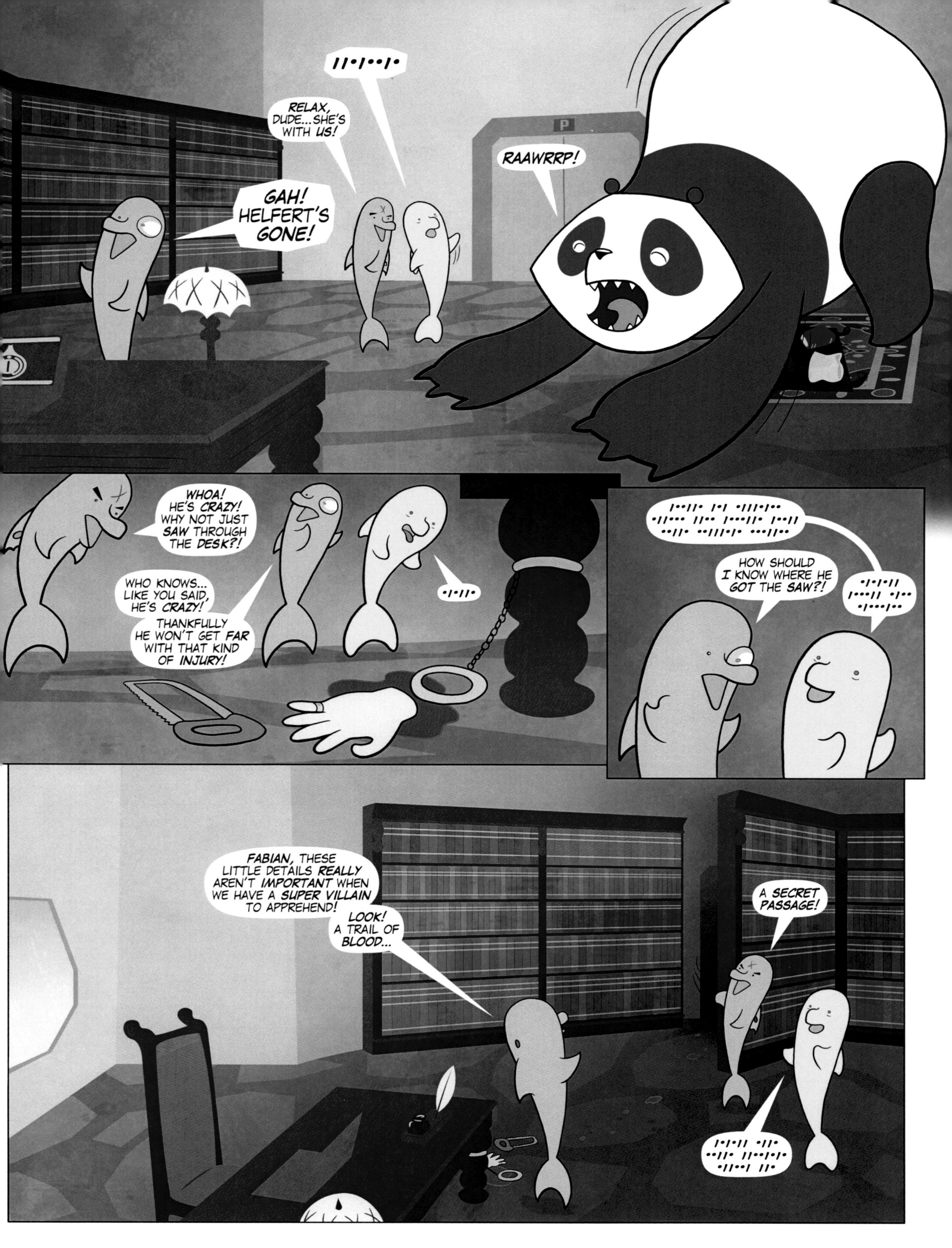
GAH! HELFERT'S GONE!
RELAX, DUDE...SHE'S WITH US!
RAAWRRP!
WHOA! HE'S CRAZY! WHY NOT JUST SAW THROUGH THE DESK?!
WHO KNOWS... LIKE YOU SAID, HE'S CRAZY! THANKFULLY HE WON'T GET FAR WITH THAT KIND OF INJURY!
HOW SHOULD I KNOW WHERE HE GOT THE SAW?!
FABIAN, THESE LITTLE DETAILS REALLY AREN'T IMPORTANT WHEN WE HAVE A SUPER VILLAIN TO APPREHEND!
LOOK! A TRAIL OF BLOOD...
A SECRET PASSAGE!

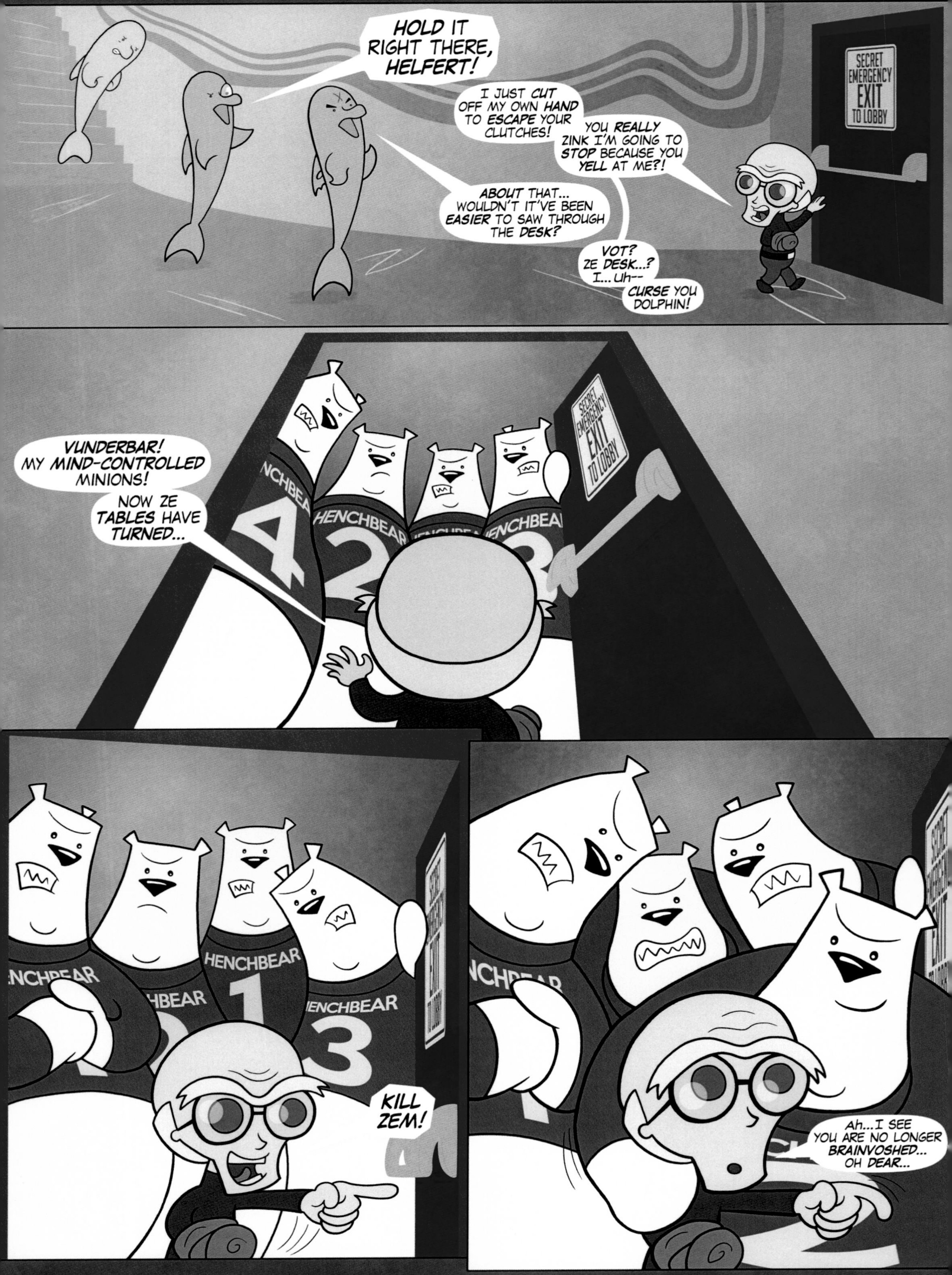
SECRET EMERGENCY EXIT TO LOBBY
HOLD IT RIGHT THERE, HELFERT!
I JUST CUT OFF MY OWN HAND TO ESCAPE YOUR CLUTCHES!
YOU REALLY ZINK I'M GOING TO STOP BECAUSE YOU YELL AT ME?!
ABOUT THAT... WOULDN'T IT'VE BEEN EASIER TO SAW THROUGH THE DESK?
VOT? ZE DESK...? I... uh--
CURSE YOU DOLPHIN!
VUNDERBAR! MY MIND-CONTROLLED MINIONS!
NOW ZE TABLES HAVE TURNED...
HENCHBEAR 4
HENCHBEAR 2
HENCHBEAR 3
HENCHBEAR 1
KILL ZEM!
Ah... I SEE YOU ARE NO LONGER BRAINVOSHED... OH DEAR...

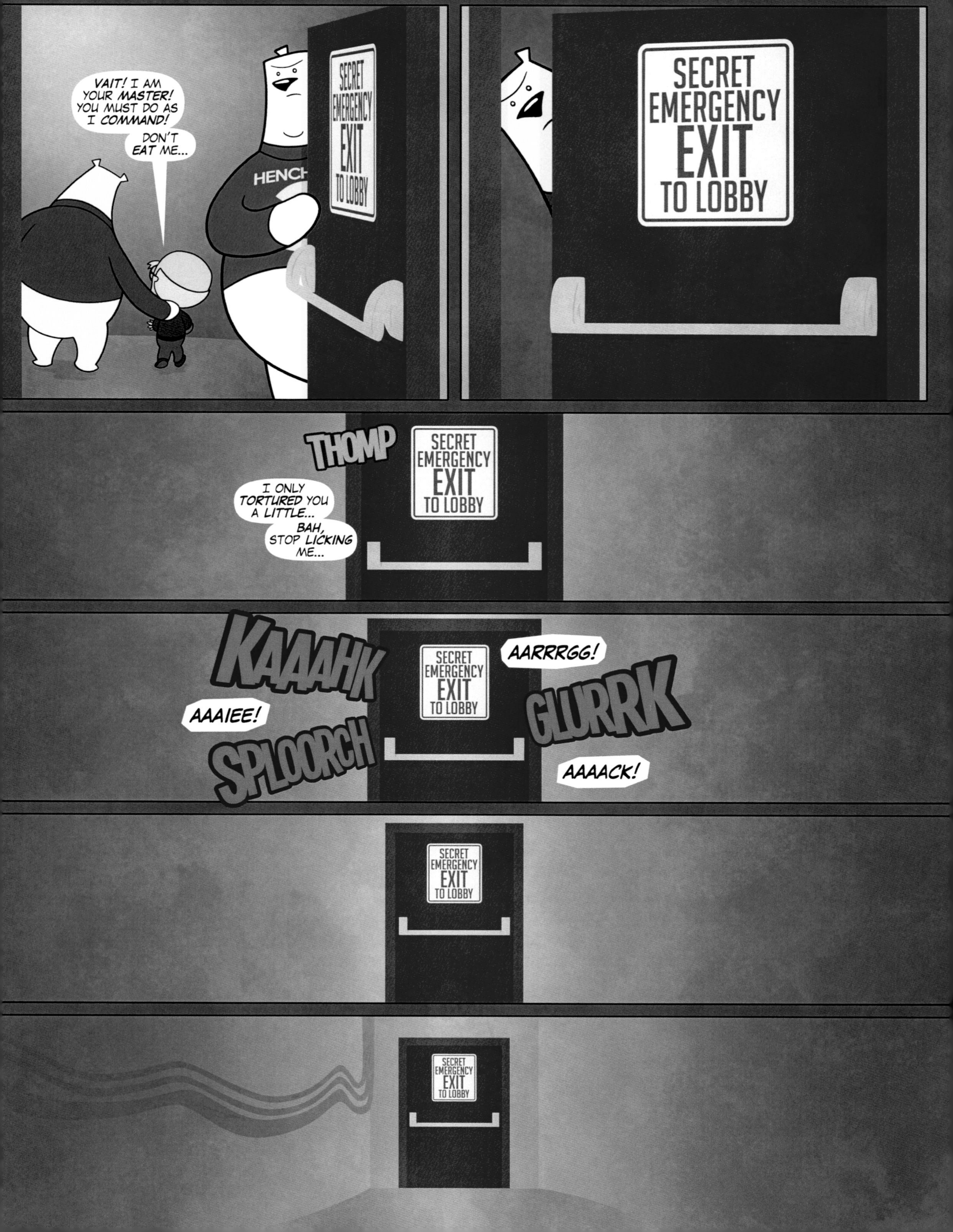

VAIT! I AM YOUR MASTER! YOU MUST DO AS I COMMAND!
DON'T EAT ME...
HENCH
SECRET EMERGENCY EXIT TO LOBBY
SECRET EMERGENCY EXIT TO LOBBY
THOMP
SECRET EMERGENCY EXIT TO LOBBY
I ONLY TORTURED YOU A LITTLE...
BAH, STOP LICKING ME...
KAAAHK
SECRET EMERGENCY EXIT TO LOBBY
AARRRGG!
AAAIEE!
GLURRK
SPLOORCH
AAAACK!
SECRET EMERGENCY EXIT TO LOBBY
SECRET EMERGENCY EXIT TO LOBBY

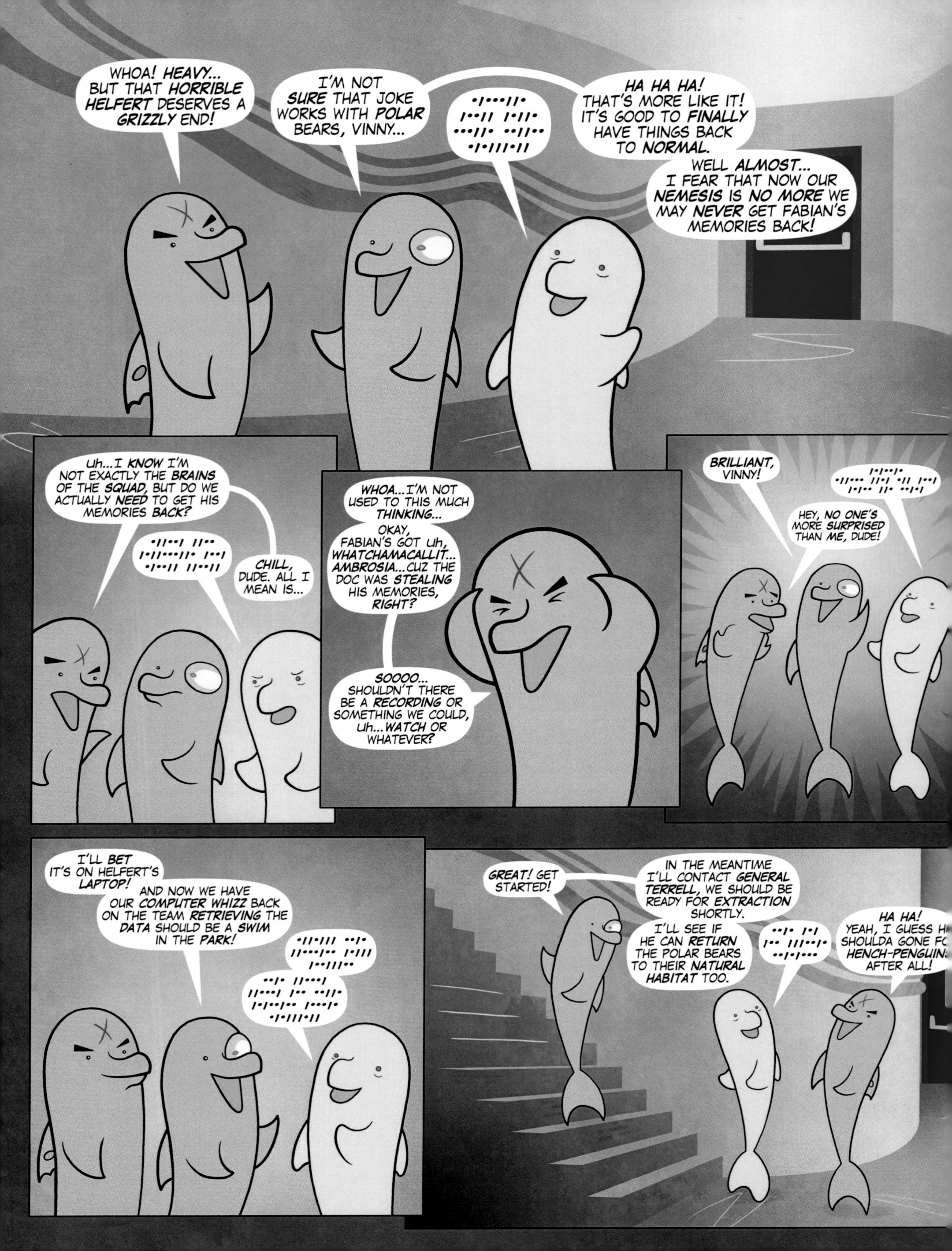

WHOA! HEAVY... BUT THAT HORRIBLE HELFERT DESERVES A GRIZZLY END!
I'M NOT SURE THAT JOKE WORKS WITH POLAR BEARS, VINNY...
HA HA HA! THAT'S MORE LIKE IT! IT'S GOOD TO FINALLY HAVE THINGS BACK TO NORMAL.
WELL ALMOST... I FEAR THAT NOW OUR NEMESIS IS NO MORE WE MAY NEVER GET FABIAN'S MEMORIES BACK!
Uh...I KNOW I'M NOT EXACTLY THE BRAINS OF THE SQUAD, BUT DO WE ACTUALLY NEED TO GET HIS MEMORIES BACK?
CHILL, DUDE. ALL I MEAN IS...
WHOA...I'M NOT USED TO THIS MUCH THINKING...
OKAY, FABIAN'S GOT Uh, WHATCHAMACALLIT... AMBROSIA...CUZ THE DOC WAS STEALING HIS MEMORIES, RIGHT?
SOOOO... SHOULDN'T THERE BE A RECORDING OR SOMETHING WE COULD, Uh...WATCH OR WHATEVER?
BRILLIANT, VINNY!
HEY, NO ONE'S MORE SURPRISED THAN ME, DUDE!
I'LL BET IT'S ON HELFERT'S LAPTOP!
AND NOW WE HAVE OUR COMPUTER WHIZZ BACK ON THE TEAM RETRIEVING THE DATA SHOULD BE A SWIM IN THE PARK!
GREAT! GET STARTED!
IN THE MEANTIME I'LL CONTACT GENERAL TERRELL, WE SHOULD BE READY FOR EXTRACTION SHORTLY.
I'LL SEE IF HE CAN RETURN THE POLAR BEARS TO THEIR NATURAL HABITAT TOO.
HA HA! YEAH, I GUESS H SHOULDA GONE FO HENCH-PENGUIN AFTER ALL!

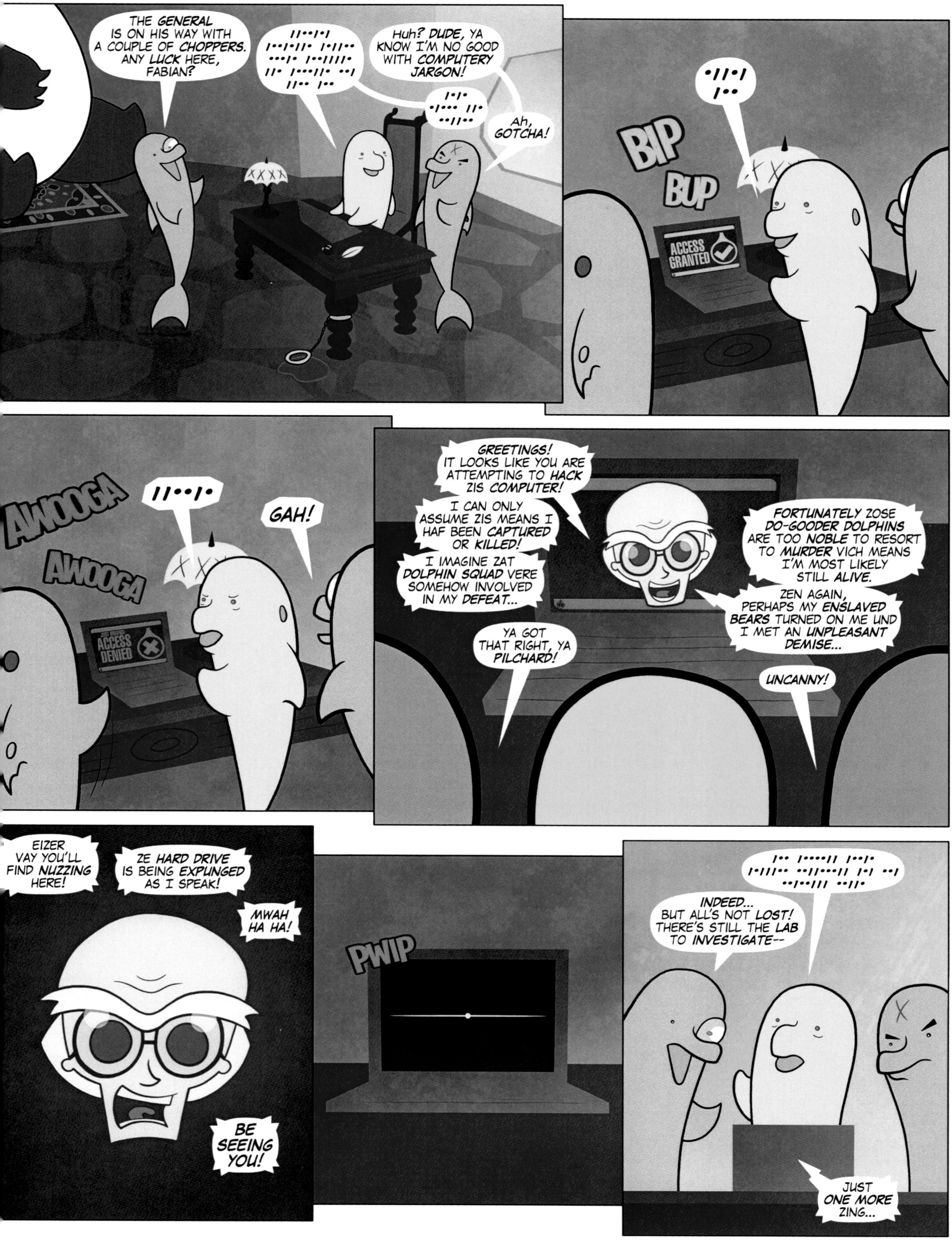

THE GENERAL IS ON HIS WAY WITH A COUPLE OF CHOPPERS. ANY LUCK HERE, FABIAN?
Huh? DUDE, YA KNOW I'M NO GOOD WITH COMPUTERY JARGON!
Ah, GOTCHA!
BIP
BUP
ACCESS GRANTED
AWOOGA
AWOOGA
GAH!
ACCESS DENIED
GREETINGS! IT LOOKS LIKE YOU ARE ATTEMPTING TO HACK ZIS COMPUTER!
I CAN ONLY ASSUME ZIS MEANS I HAF BEEN CAPTURED OR KILLED!
I IMAGINE ZAT DOLPHIN SQUAD VERE SOMEHOW INVOLVED IN MY DEFEAT...
FORTUNATELY ZOSE DO-GOODER DOLPHINS ARE TOO NOBLE TO RESORT TO MURDER VICH MEANS I'M MOST LIKELY STILL ALIVE.
ZEN AGAIN, PERHAPS MY ENSLAVED BEARS TURNED ON ME UND I MET AN UNPLEASANT DEMISE...
YA GOT THAT RIGHT, YA PILCHARD!
UNCANNY!
EIZER VAY YOU'LL FIND NUZZING HERE!
ZE HARD DRIVE IS BEING EXPUNGED AS I SPEAK!
MWAH HA HA!
BE SEEING YOU!
PWIP
INDEED... BUT ALL'S NOT LOST! THERE'S STILL THE LAB TO INVESTIGATE--
JUST ONE MORE ZING...

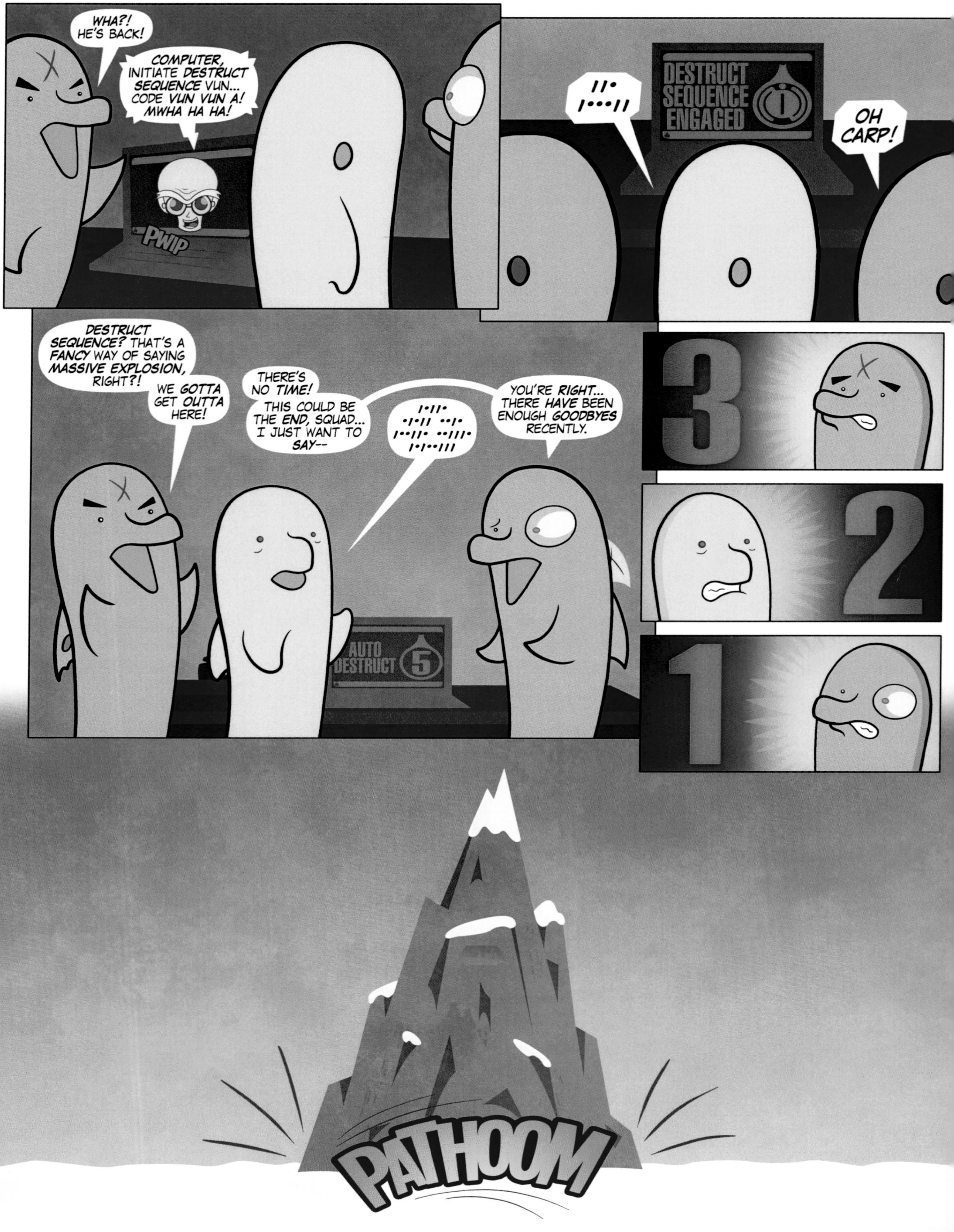
WHA?! HE'S BACK!
COMPUTER, INITIATE DESTRUCT SEQUENCE VUN... CODE VUN VUN A! MWHA HA HA!
PWIP
DESTRUCT SEQUENCE ENGAGED
!!• !•••!!
OH CARP!
DESTRUCT SEQUENCE? THAT'S A FANCY WAY OF SAYING MASSIVE EXPLOSION, RIGHT?!
WE GOTTA GET OUTTA HERE!
THERE'S NO TIME!
THIS COULD BE THE END, SQUAD... I JUST WANT TO SAY--
!•!!• •!•!! ••!• !••!!• ••!!!• !•!••!!!
YOU'RE RIGHT... THERE HAVE BEEN ENOUGH GOODBYES RECENTLY.
AUTO DESTRUCT 5
3
2
1
PATHOOM

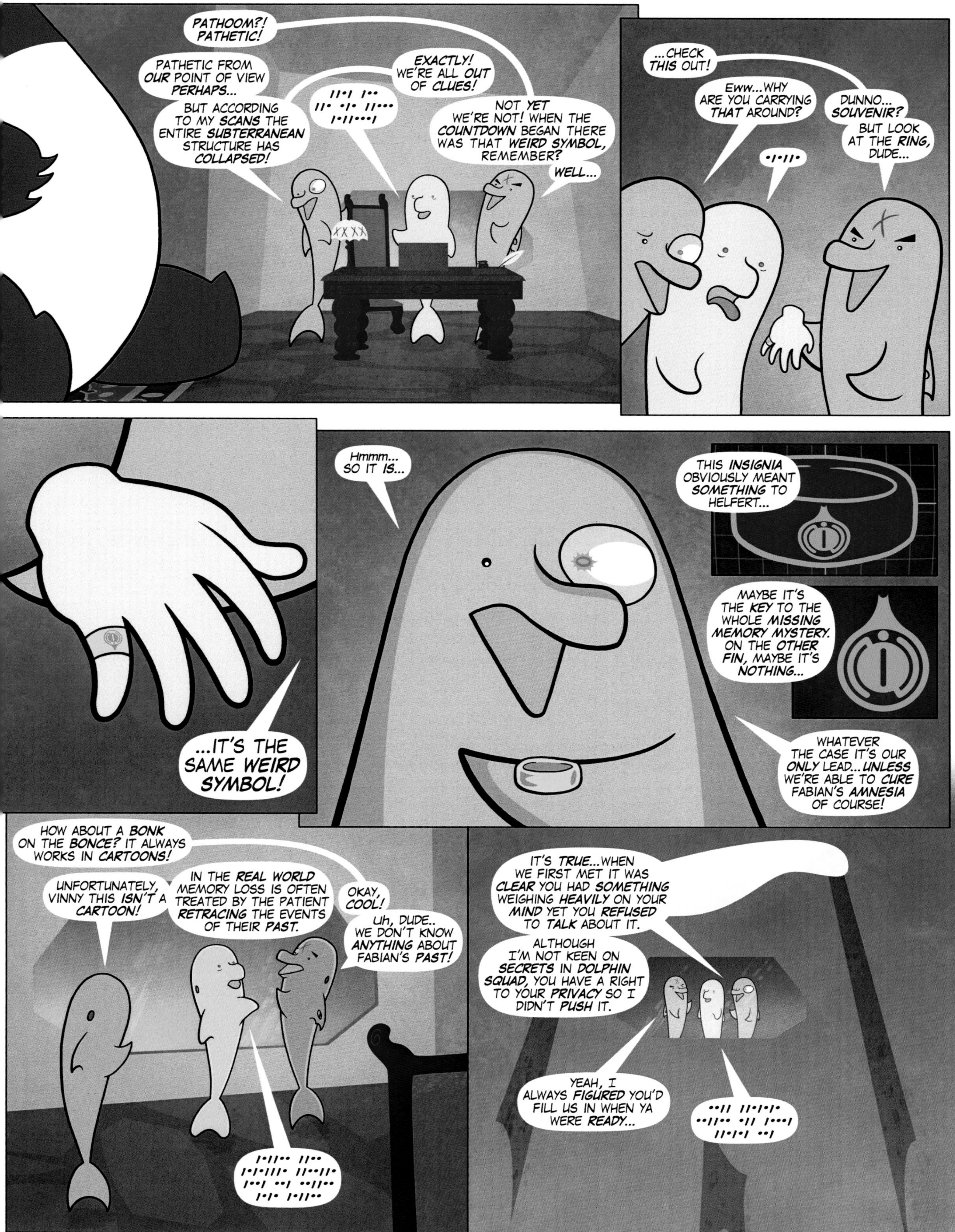

PATHOOM?! PATHETIC!
PATHETIC FROM OUR POINT OF VIEW PERHAPS...
BUT ACCORDING TO MY SCANS THE ENTIRE SUBTERRANEAN STRUCTURE HAS COLLAPSED!
EXACTLY! WE'RE ALL OUT OF CLUES!
NOT YET WE'RE NOT! WHEN THE COUNTDOWN BEGAN THERE WAS THAT WEIRD SYMBOL, REMEMBER?
WELL...
...CHECK THIS OUT!
EWW...WHY ARE YOU CARRYING THAT AROUND?
DUNNO... SOUVENIR?
BUT LOOK AT THE RING, DUDE...
...IT'S THE SAME WEIRD SYMBOL!
Hmmm... SO IT IS...
THIS INSIGNIA OBVIOUSLY MEANT SOMETHING TO HELFERT...
MAYBE IT'S THE KEY TO THE WHOLE MISSING MEMORY MYSTERY. ON THE OTHER FIN, MAYBE IT'S NOTHING...
WHATEVER THE CASE IT'S OUR ONLY LEAD...UNLESS WE'RE ABLE TO CURE FABIAN'S AMNESIA OF COURSE!
HOW ABOUT A BONK ON THE BONCE? IT ALWAYS WORKS IN CARTOONS!
UNFORTUNATELY, VINNY THIS ISN'T A CARTOON!
IN THE REAL WORLD MEMORY LOSS IS OFTEN TREATED BY THE PATIENT RETRACING THE EVENTS OF THEIR PAST.
OKAY, COOL!
Uh, DUDE.. WE DON'T KNOW ANYTHING ABOUT FABIAN'S PAST!
IT'S TRUE...WHEN WE FIRST MET IT WAS CLEAR YOU HAD SOMETHING WEIGHING HEAVILY ON YOUR MIND YET YOU REFUSED TO TALK ABOUT IT.
ALTHOUGH I'M NOT KEEN ON SECRETS IN DOLPHIN SQUAD, YOU HAVE A RIGHT TO YOUR PRIVACY SO I DIDN'T PUSH IT.
YEAH, I ALWAYS FIGURED YOU'D FILL US IN WHEN YA WERE READY...

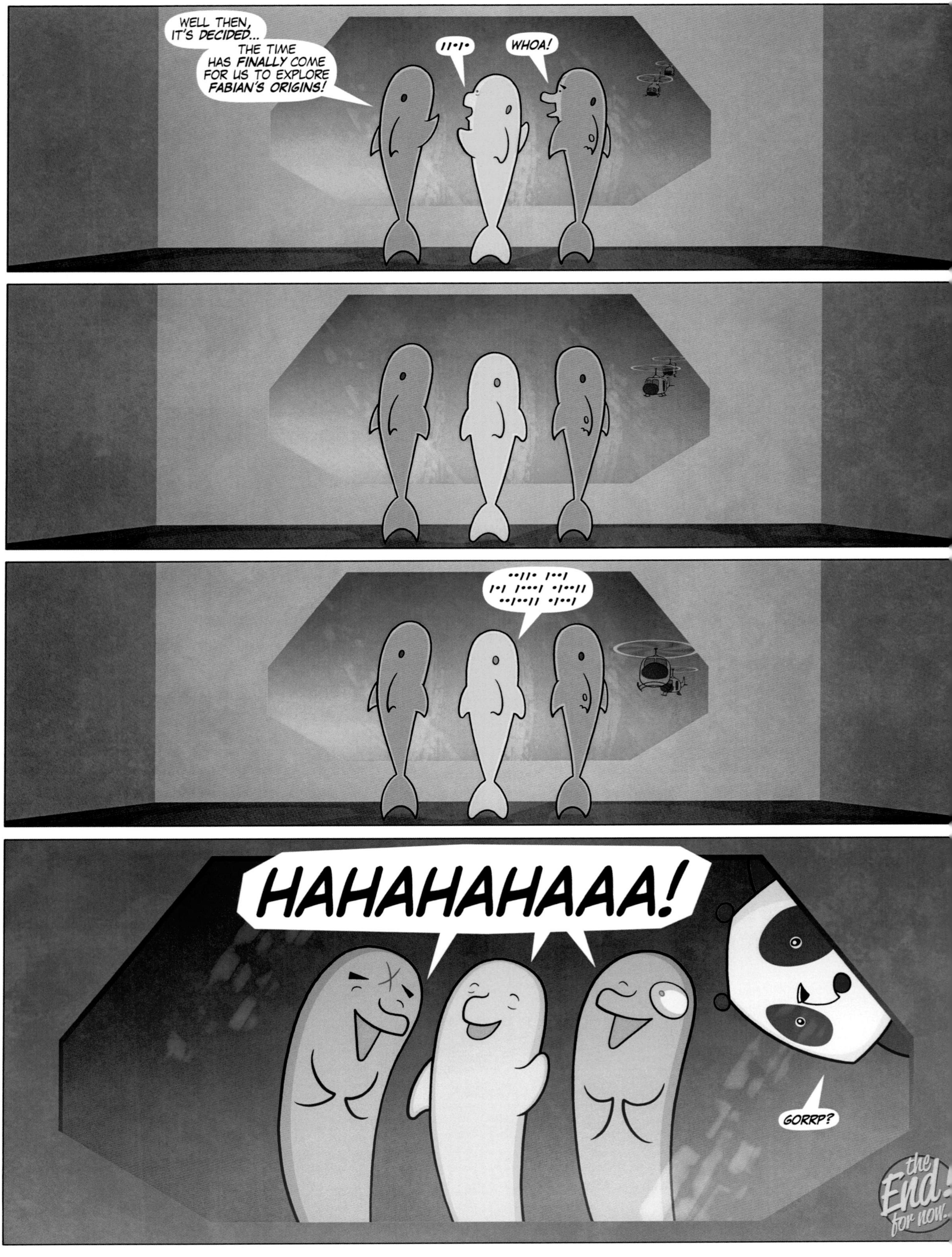
WELL THEN, IT'S DECIDED... THE TIME HAS FINALLY COME FOR US TO EXPLORE FABIAN'S ORIGINS!
WHOA!
HAHAHAHAAA!
GORRP?
the End! for now.

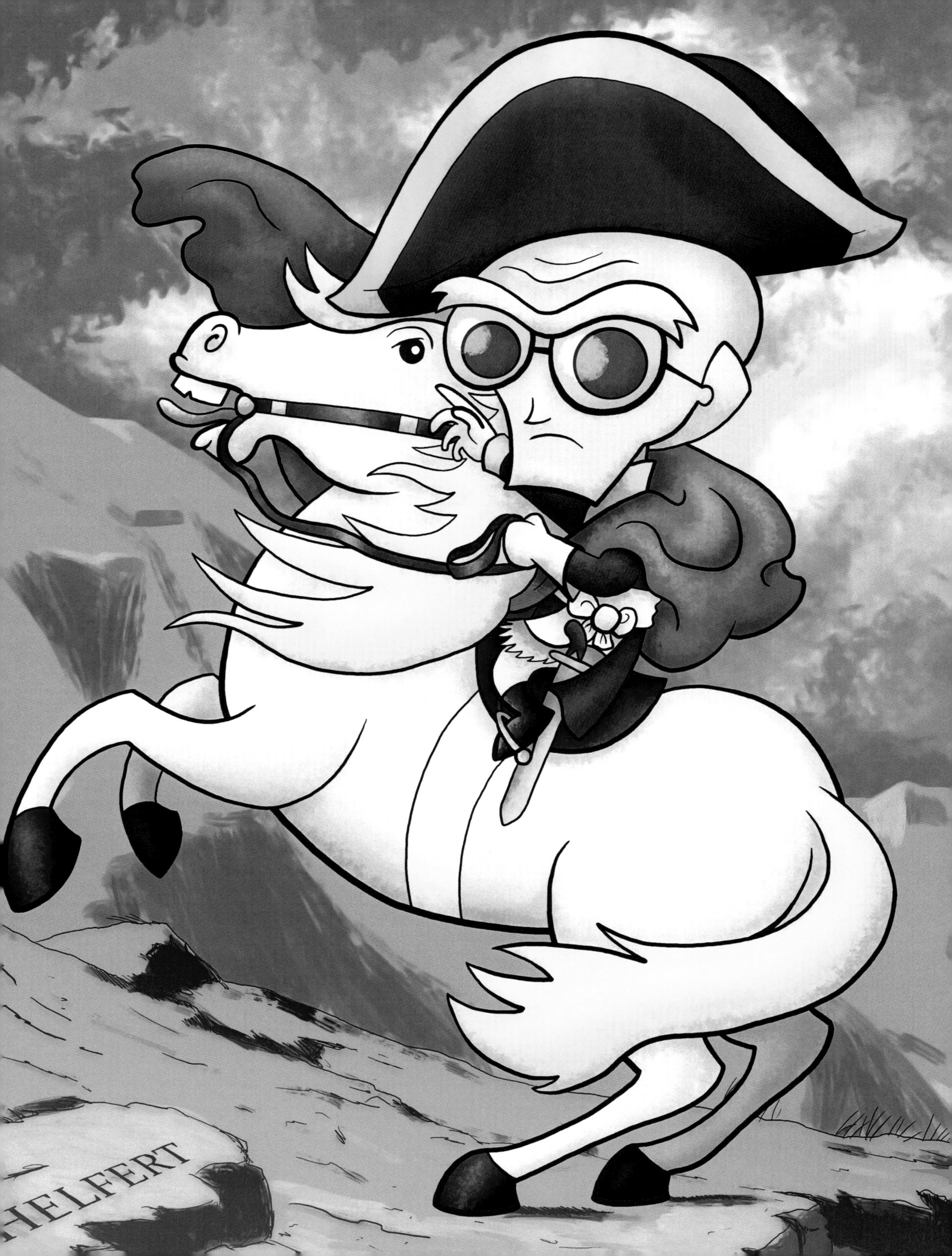
HELFERT

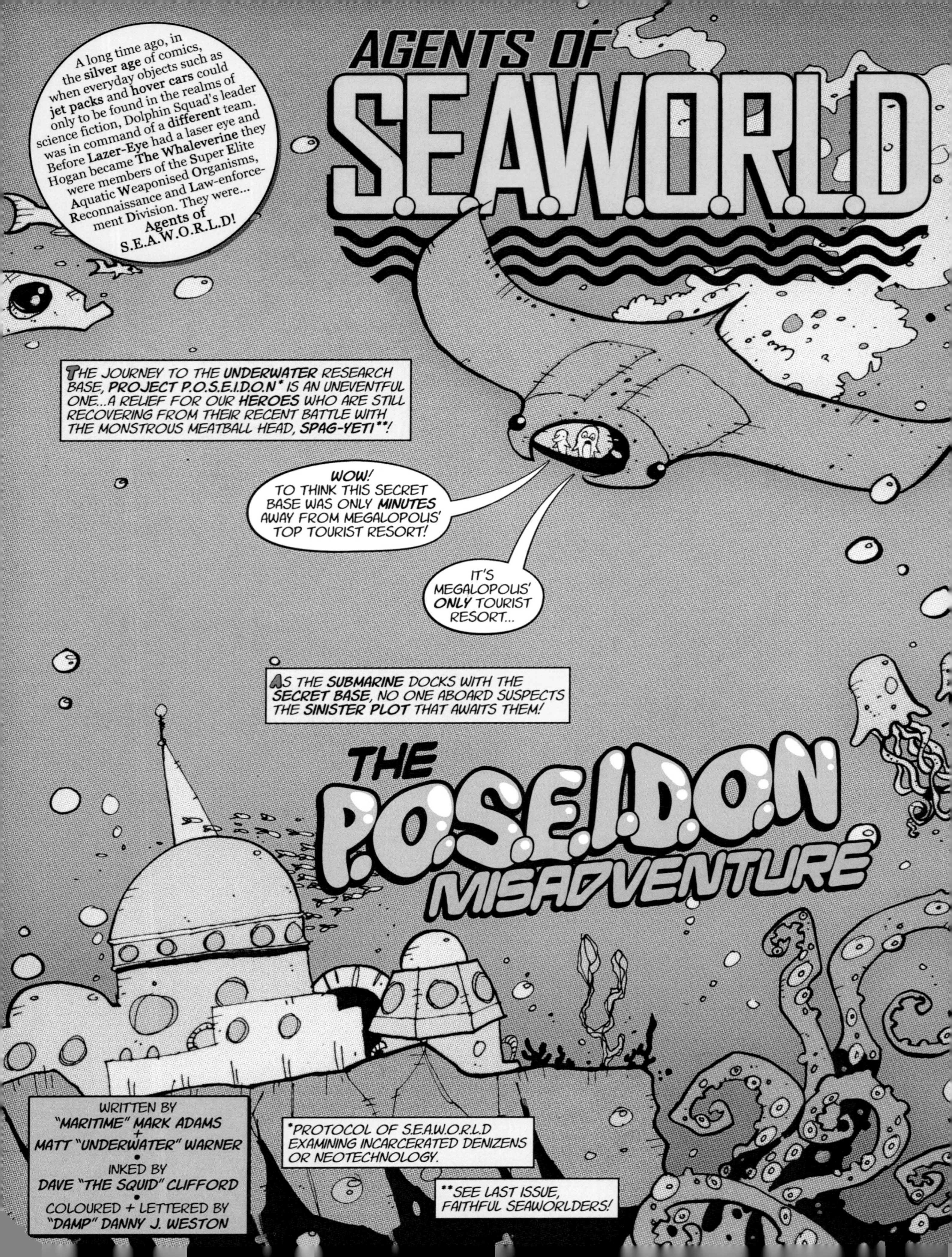

A long time ago, in the silver age of comics, when everyday objects such as jet packs and hover cars could only to be found in the realms of science fiction, Dolphin Squad's leader was in command of a different team. Before Lazer-Eye had a laser eye and Hogan became The Whaleverine they were members of the Super Elite Aquatic Weaponised Organisms, Reconnaissance and Law-enforcement Division. They were... Agents of S.E.A.W.O.R.L.D!
AGENTS OF
S.E.A.W.O.R.L.D
THE JOURNEY TO THE UNDERWATER RESEARCH BASE, PROJECT P.O.S.E.I.D.O.N* IS AN UNEVENTFUL ONE...A RELIEF FOR OUR HEROES WHO ARE STILL RECOVERING FROM THEIR RECENT BATTLE WITH THE MONSTROUS MEATBALL HEAD, SPAG-YETI**!
WOW! TO THINK THIS SECRET BASE WAS ONLY MINUTES AWAY FROM MEGALOPOUS' TOP TOURIST RESORT!
IT'S MEGALOPOUS' ONLY TOURIST RESORT...
AS THE SUBMARINE DOCKS WITH THE SECRET BASE, NO ONE ABOARD SUSPECTS THE SINISTER PLOT THAT AWAITS THEM!
THE P.O.S.E.I.D.O.N MISADVENTURE
WRITTEN BY "MARITIME" MARK ADAMS + MATT "UNDERWATER" WARNER • INKED BY DAVE "THE SQUID" CLIFFORD • COLOURED + LETTERED BY "DAMP" DANNY J. WESTON
*PROTOCOL OF S.E.A.W.O.R.L.D EXAMINING INCARCERATED DENIZENS OR NEOTECHNOLOGY.
**SEE LAST ISSUE, FAITHFUL SEAWORLDERS!

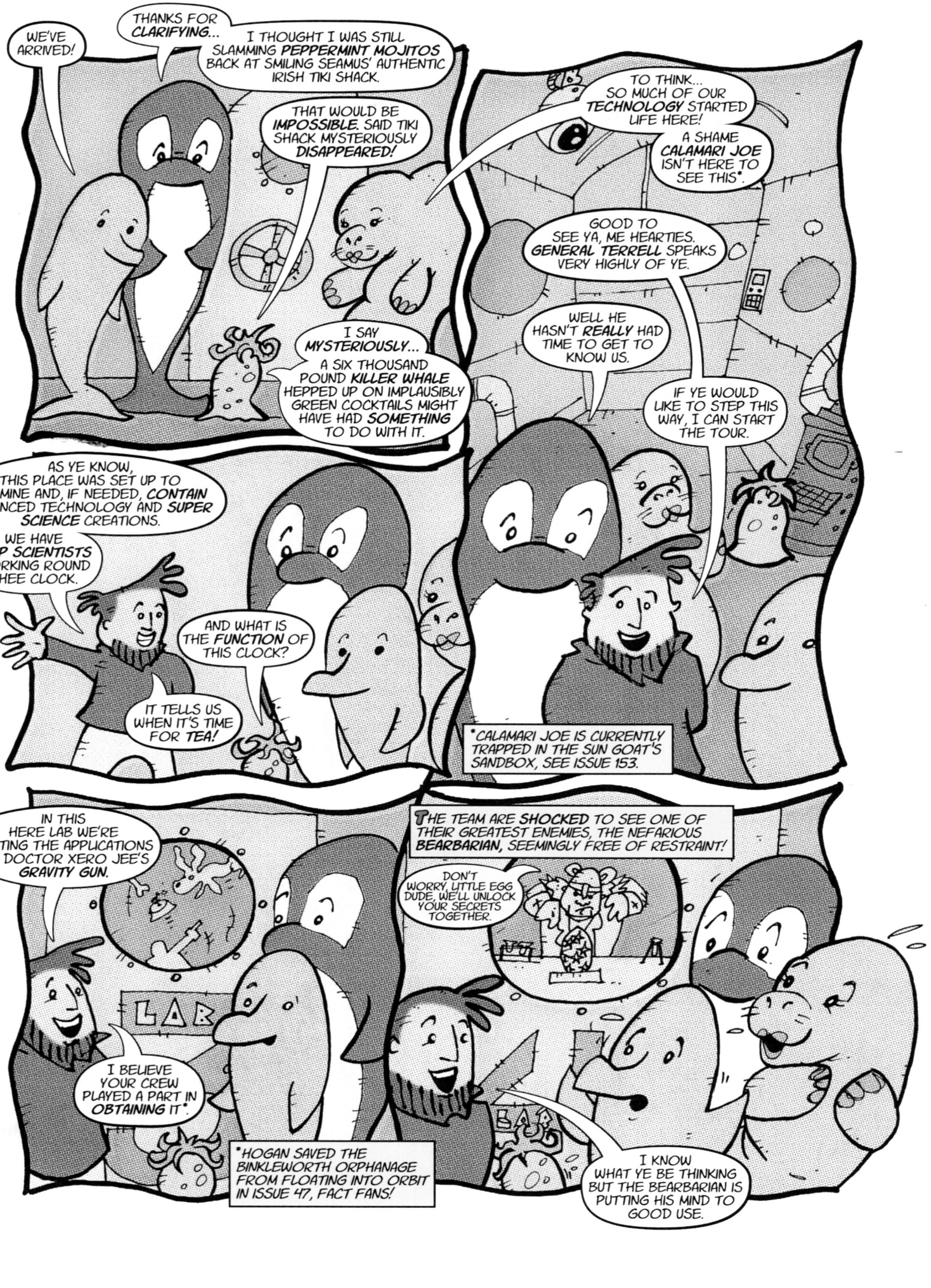
WE'VE ARRIVED!
THANKS FOR CLARIFYING...
I THOUGHT I WAS STILL SLAMMING PEPPERMINT MOJITOS BACK AT SMILING SEAMUS' AUTHENTIC IRISH TIKI SHACK.
THAT WOULD BE IMPOSSIBLE. SAID TIKI SHACK MYSTERIOUSLY DISAPPEARED!
I SAY MYSTERIOUSLY...
A SIX THOUSAND POUND KILLER WHALE HEPPED UP ON IMPLAUSIBLY GREEN COCKTAILS MIGHT HAVE HAD SOMETHING TO DO WITH IT.
TO THINK... SO MUCH OF OUR TECHNOLOGY STARTED LIFE HERE!
A SHAME CALAMARI JOE ISN'T HERE TO SEE THIS*.
GOOD TO SEE YA, ME HEARTIES. GENERAL TERRELL SPEAKS VERY HIGHLY OF YE.
WELL HE HASN'T REALLY HAD TIME TO GET TO KNOW US.
IF YE WOULD LIKE TO STEP THIS WAY, I CAN START THE TOUR.
*CALAMARI JOE IS CURRENTLY TRAPPED IN THE SUN GOAT'S SANDBOX, SEE ISSUE 153.
AS YE KNOW, THIS PLACE WAS SET UP TO EXAMINE AND, IF NEEDED, CONTAIN ADVANCED TECHNOLOGY AND SUPER SCIENCE CREATIONS.
WE HAVE TOP SCIENTISTS WORKING ROUND THEE CLOCK.
AND WHAT IS THE FUNCTION OF THIS CLOCK?
IT TELLS US WHEN IT'S TIME FOR TEA!
IN THIS HERE LAB WE'RE TESTING THE APPLICATIONS OF DOCTOR XERO JEE'S GRAVITY GUN.
LAB
I BELIEVE YOUR CREW PLAYED A PART IN OBTAINING IT*.
*HOGAN SAVED THE BINKLEWORTH ORPHANAGE FROM FLOATING INTO ORBIT IN ISSUE 47, FACT FANS!
THE TEAM ARE SHOCKED TO SEE ONE OF THEIR GREATEST ENEMIES, THE NEFARIOUS BEARBARIAN, SEEMINGLY FREE OF RESTRAINT!
DON'T WORRY, LITTLE EGG DUDE, WE'LL UNLOCK YOUR SECRETS TOGETHER.
I KNOW WHAT YE BE THINKING BUT THE BEARBARIAN IS PUTTING HIS MIND TO GOOD USE.

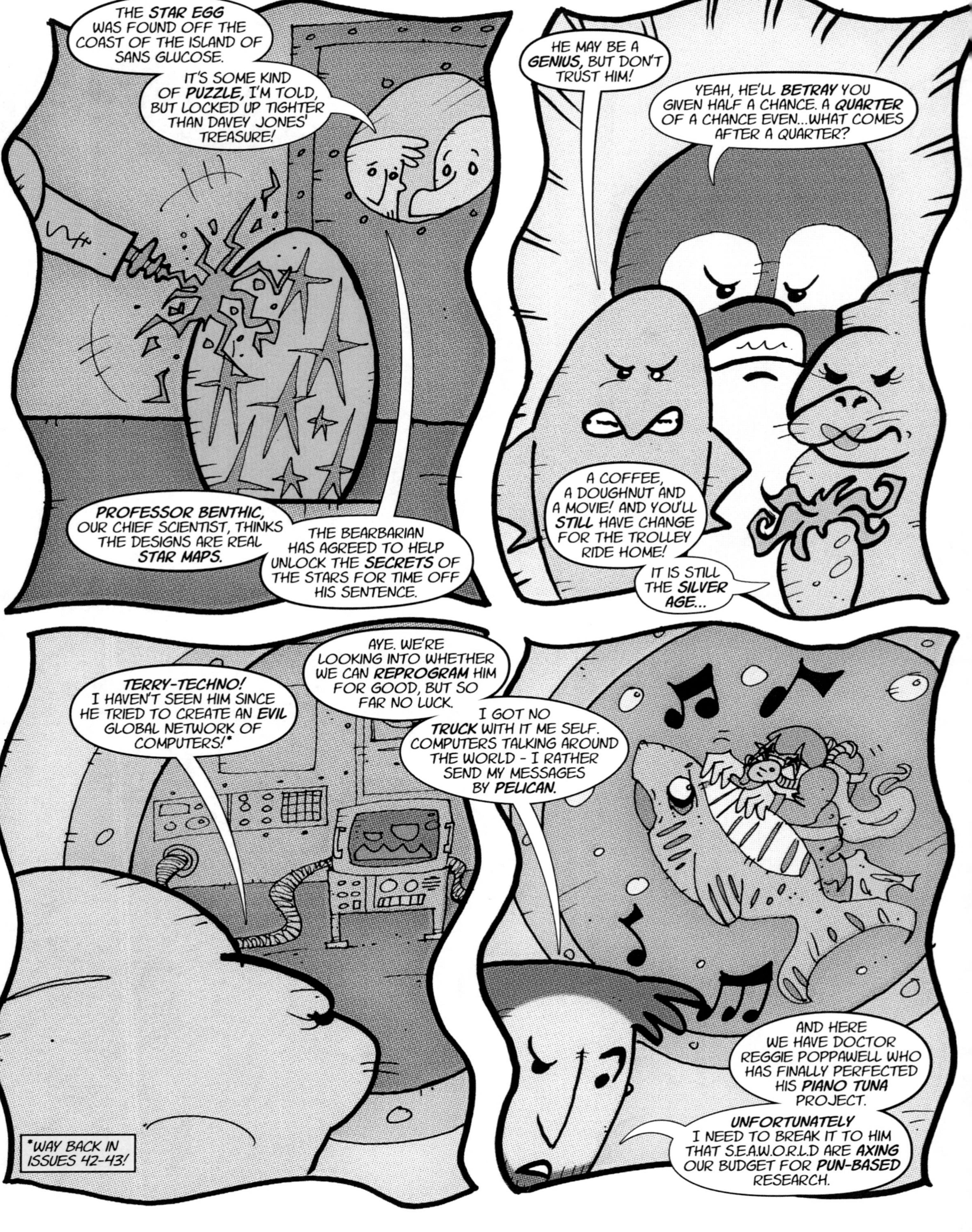
THE STAR EGG WAS FOUND OFF THE COAST OF THE ISLAND OF SANS GLUCOSE.
IT'S SOME KIND OF PUZZLE, I'M TOLD, BUT LOCKED UP TIGHTER THAN DAVEY JONES' TREASURE!
PROFESSOR BENTHIC, OUR CHIEF SCIENTIST, THINKS THE DESIGNS ARE REAL STAR MAPS.
THE BEARBARIAN HAS AGREED TO HELP UNLOCK THE SECRETS OF THE STARS FOR TIME OFF HIS SENTENCE.
HE MAY BE A GENIUS, BUT DON'T TRUST HIM!
YEAH, HE'LL BETRAY YOU GIVEN HALF A CHANCE. A QUARTER OF A CHANCE EVEN...WHAT COMES AFTER A QUARTER?
A COFFEE, A DOUGHNUT AND A MOVIE! AND YOU'LL STILL HAVE CHANGE FOR THE TROLLEY RIDE HOME!
IT IS STILL THE SILVER AGE...
TERRY-TECHNO! I HAVEN'T SEEN HIM SINCE HE TRIED TO CREATE AN EVIL GLOBAL NETWORK OF COMPUTERS!*
AYE. WE'RE LOOKING INTO WHETHER WE CAN REPROGRAM HIM FOR GOOD, BUT SO FAR NO LUCK.
I GOT NO TRUCK WITH IT ME SELF. COMPUTERS TALKING AROUND THE WORLD - I RATHER SEND MY MESSAGES BY PELICAN.
*WAY BACK IN ISSUES 42-43!
AND HERE WE HAVE DOCTOR REGGIE POPPAWELL WHO HAS FINALLY PERFECTED HIS PIANO TUNA PROJECT.
UNFORTUNATELY I NEED TO BREAK IT TO HIM THAT S.E.A.W.O.R.L.D ARE AXING OUR BUDGET FOR PUN-BASED RESEARCH.

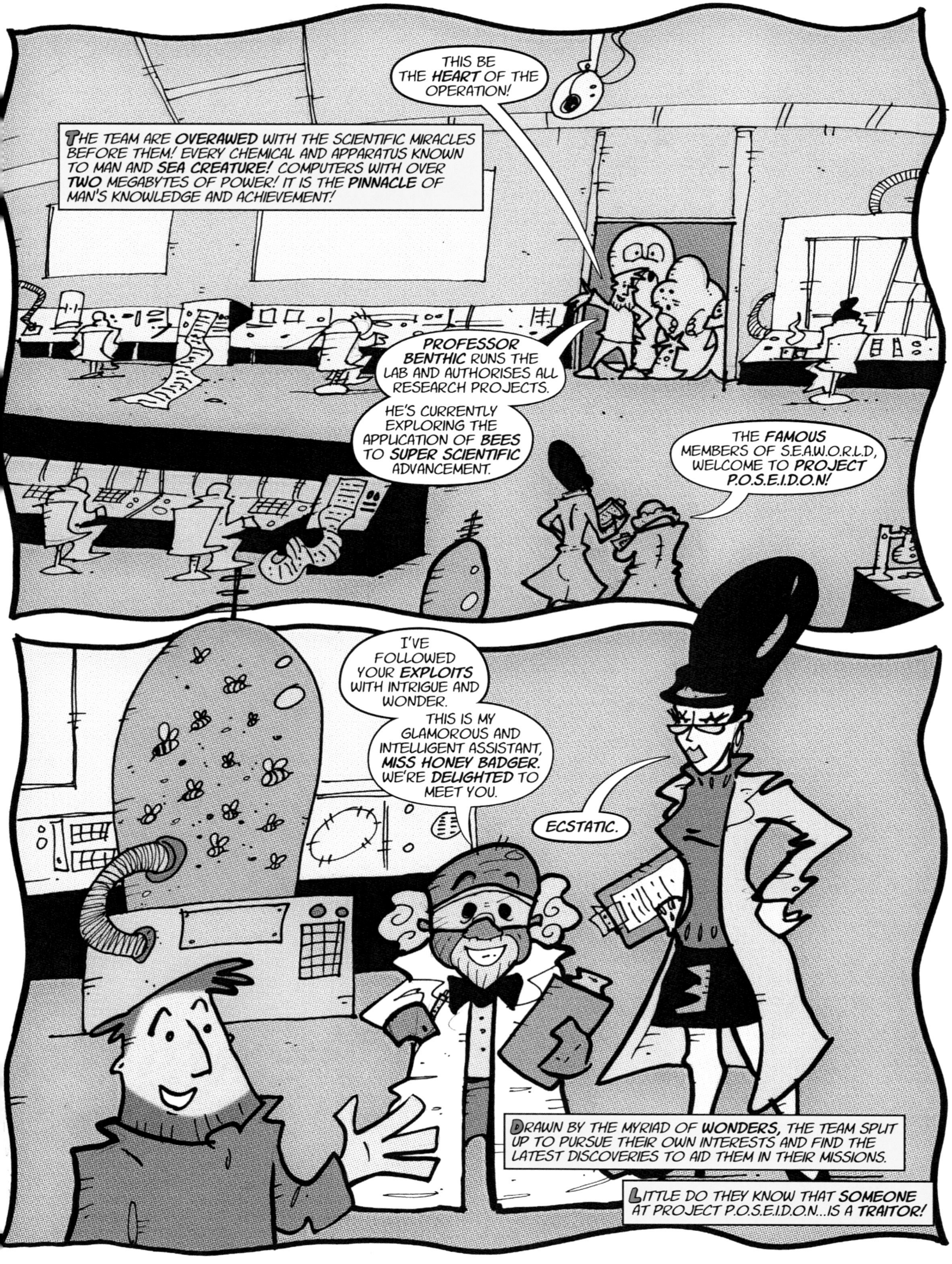

THE TEAM ARE OVERAWED WITH THE SCIENTIFIC MIRACLES BEFORE THEM! EVERY CHEMICAL AND APPARATUS KNOWN TO MAN AND SEA CREATURE! COMPUTERS WITH OVER TWO MEGABYTES OF POWER! IT IS THE PINNACLE OF MAN'S KNOWLEDGE AND ACHIEVEMENT!
THIS BE THE HEART OF THE OPERATION!
PROFESSOR BENTHIC RUNS THE LAB AND AUTHORISES ALL RESEARCH PROJECTS.
HE'S CURRENTLY EXPLORING THE APPLICATION OF BEES TO SUPER SCIENTIFIC ADVANCEMENT.
THE FAMOUS MEMBERS OF S.E.A.W.O.R.L.D, WELCOME TO PROJECT P.O.S.E.I.D.O.N!
I'VE FOLLOWED YOUR EXPLOITS WITH INTRIGUE AND WONDER.
THIS IS MY GLAMOROUS AND INTELLIGENT ASSISTANT, MISS HONEY BADGER. WE'RE DELIGHTED TO MEET YOU.
ECSTATIC.
DRAWN BY THE MYRIAD OF WONDERS, THE TEAM SPLIT UP TO PURSUE THEIR OWN INTERESTS AND FIND THE LATEST DISCOVERIES TO AID THEM IN THEIR MISSIONS.
LITTLE DO THEY KNOW THAT SOMEONE AT PROJECT P.O.S.E.I.D.O.N...IS A TRAITOR!

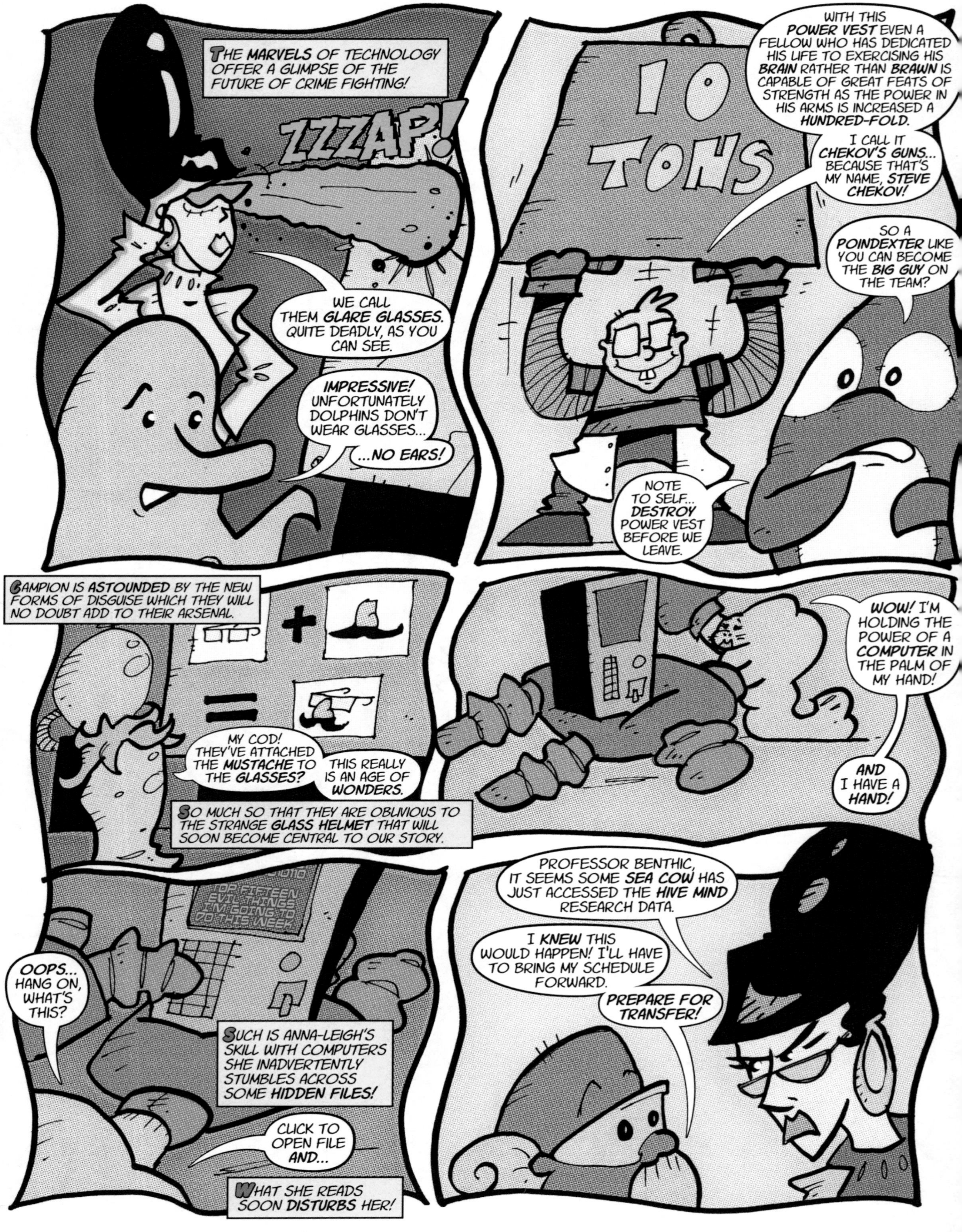

THE MARVELS OF TECHNOLOGY OFFER A GLIMPSE OF THE FUTURE OF CRIME FIGHTING!
ZZZAP!
WE CALL THEM GLARE GLASSES. QUITE DEADLY, AS YOU CAN SEE.
IMPRESSIVE! UNFORTUNATELY DOLPHINS DON'T WEAR GLASSES...
...NO EARS!
10 TONS
WITH THIS POWER VEST EVEN A FELLOW WHO HAS DEDICATED HIS LIFE TO EXERCISING HIS BRAIN RATHER THAN BRAWN IS CAPABLE OF GREAT FEATS OF STRENGTH AS THE POWER IN HIS ARMS IS INCREASED A HUNDRED-FOLD.
I CALL IT CHEKOV'S GUNS... BECAUSE THAT'S MY NAME, STEVE CHEKOV!
SO A POINDEXTER LIKE YOU CAN BECOME THE BIG GUY ON THE TEAM?
NOTE TO SELF... DESTROY POWER VEST BEFORE WE LEAVE.
CAMPION IS ASTOUNDED BY THE NEW FORMS OF DISGUISE WHICH THEY WILL NO DOUBT ADD TO THEIR ARSENAL.
MY COD! THEY'VE ATTACHED THE MUSTACHE TO THE GLASSES?
THIS REALLY IS AN AGE OF WONDERS.
SO MUCH SO THAT THEY ARE OBLIVIOUS TO THE STRANGE GLASS HELMET THAT WILL SOON BECOME CENTRAL TO OUR STORY.
WOW! I'M HOLDING THE POWER OF A COMPUTER IN THE PALM OF MY HAND!
AND I HAVE A HAND!
TOP FIFTEEN EVIL THINGS I'M GOING TO DO THIS WEEK.
OOPS... HANG ON, WHAT'S THIS?
SUCH IS ANNA-LEIGH'S SKILL WITH COMPUTERS SHE INADVERTENTLY STUMBLES ACROSS SOME HIDDEN FILES!
CLICK TO OPEN FILE AND...
WHAT SHE READS SOON DISTURBS HER!
PROFESSOR BENTHIC, IT SEEMS SOME SEA COW HAS JUST ACCESSED THE HIVE MIND RESEARCH DATA.
I KNEW THIS WOULD HAPPEN! I'LL HAVE TO BRING MY SCHEDULE FORWARD.
PREPARE FOR TRANSFER!

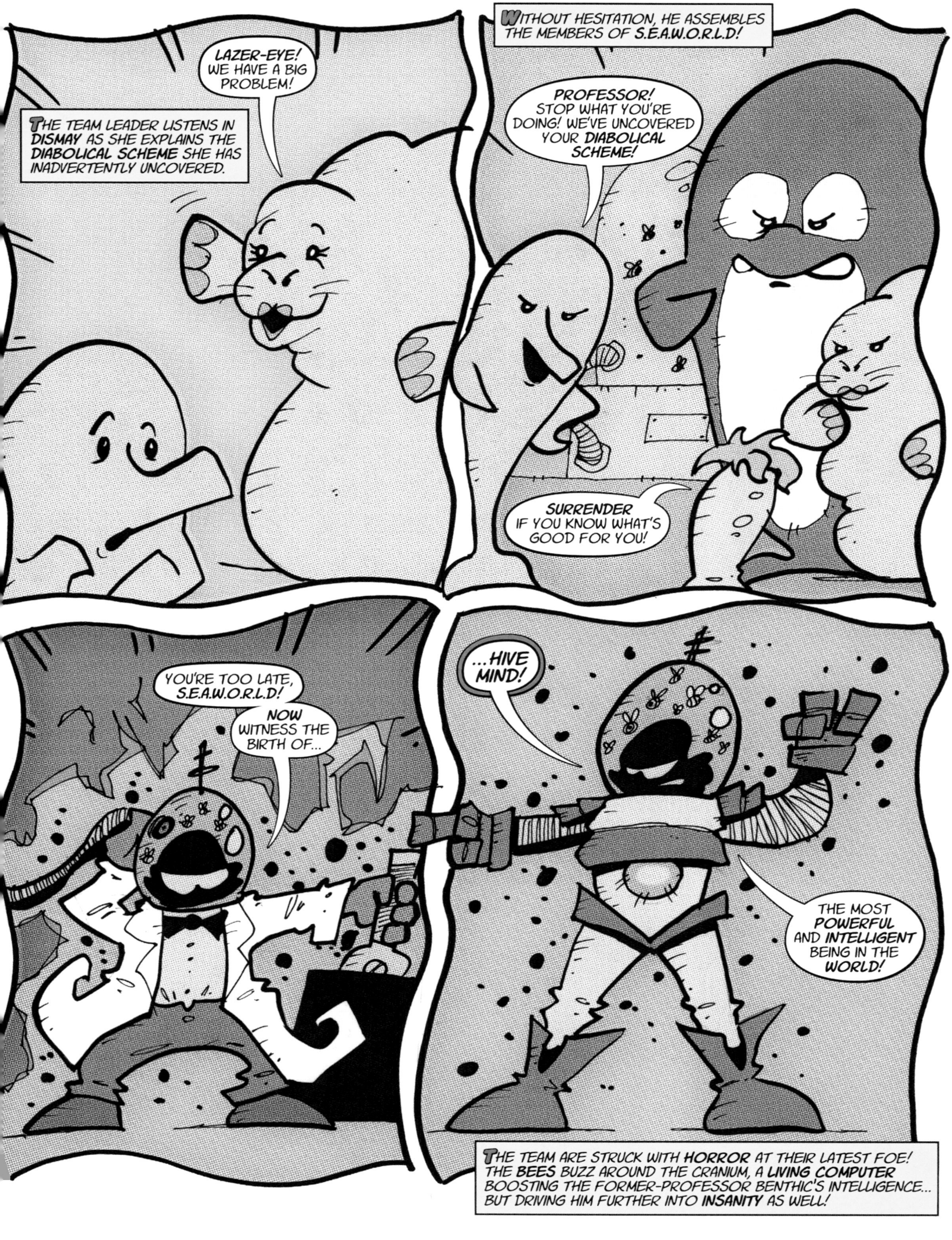
LAZER-EYE! WE HAVE A BIG PROBLEM!
THE TEAM LEADER LISTENS IN DISMAY AS SHE EXPLAINS THE DIABOLICAL SCHEME SHE HAS INADVERTENTLY UNCOVERED.
WITHOUT HESITATION, HE ASSEMBLES THE MEMBERS OF S.E.A.W.O.R.L.D!
PROFESSOR! STOP WHAT YOU'RE DOING! WE'VE UNCOVERED YOUR DIABOLICAL SCHEME!
SURRENDER IF YOU KNOW WHAT'S GOOD FOR YOU!
YOU'RE TOO LATE, S.E.A.W.O.R.L.D!
NOW WITNESS THE BIRTH OF...
...HIVE MIND!
THE MOST POWERFUL AND INTELLIGENT BEING IN THE WORLD!
THE TEAM ARE STRUCK WITH HORROR AT THEIR LATEST FOE! THE BEES BUZZ AROUND THE CRANIUM, A LIVING COMPUTER BOOSTING THE FORMER-PROFESSOR BENTHIC'S INTELLIGENCE... BUT DRIVING HIM FURTHER INTO INSANITY AS WELL!

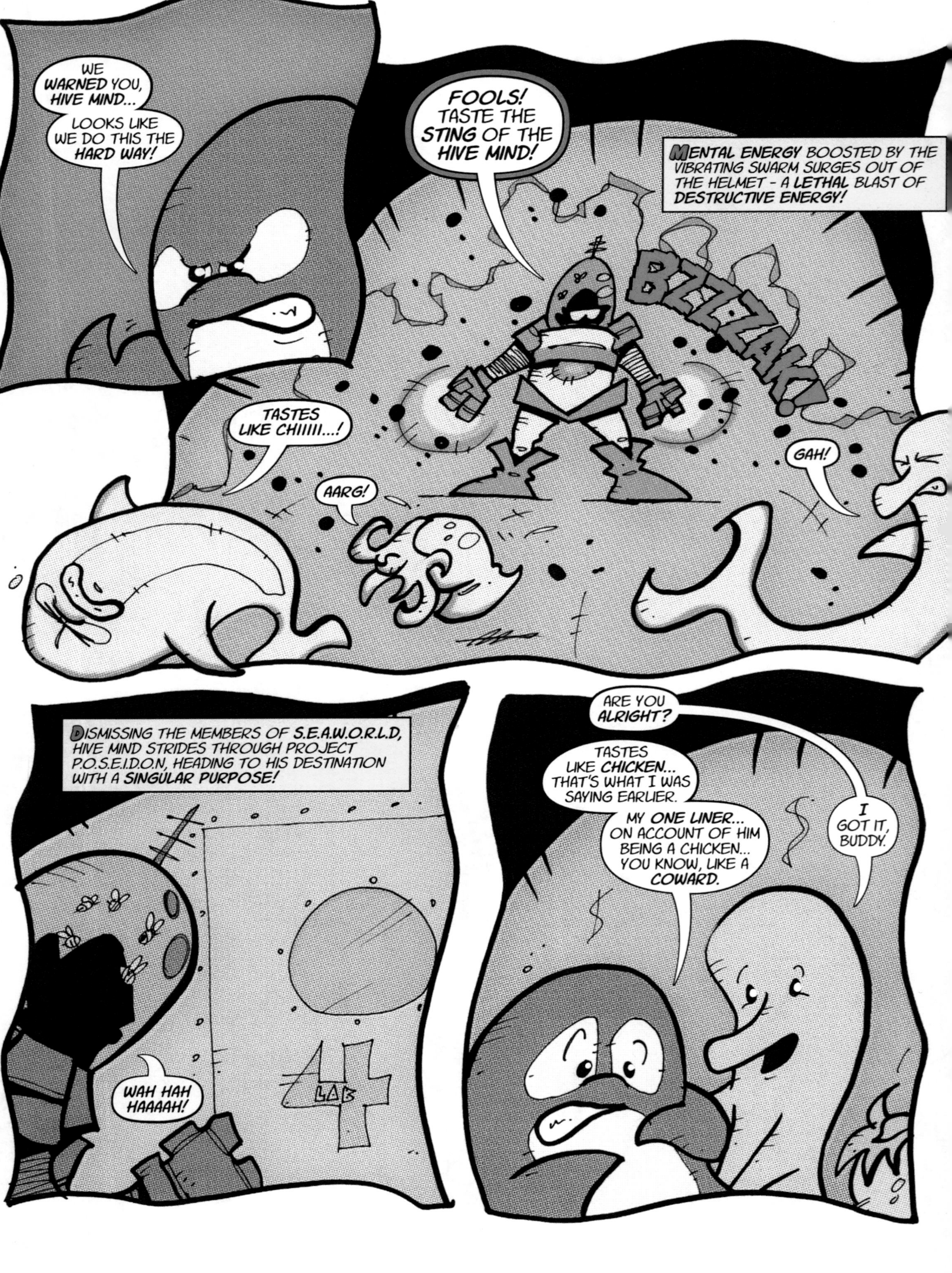
WE WARNED YOU, HIVE MIND...
LOOKS LIKE WE DO THIS THE HARD WAY!
FOOLS! TASTE THE STING OF THE HIVE MIND!
MENTAL ENERGY BOOSTED BY THE VIBRATING SWARM SURGES OUT OF THE HELMET - A LETHAL BLAST OF DESTRUCTIVE ENERGY!
BZZZAK!
TASTES LIKE CHIIIII...!
AARG!
GAH!
DISMISSING THE MEMBERS OF S.E.A.W.O.R.L.D, HIVE MIND STRIDES THROUGH PROJECT P.O.S.E.I.D.O.N, HEADING TO HIS DESTINATION WITH A SINGULAR PURPOSE!
WAH HAH HAAAAH!
LAB 4
ARE YOU ALRIGHT?
TASTES LIKE CHICKEN... THAT'S WHAT I WAS SAYING EARLIER.
MY ONE LINER... ON ACCOUNT OF HIM BEING A CHICKEN... YOU KNOW, LIKE A COWARD.
I GOT IT, BUDDY.

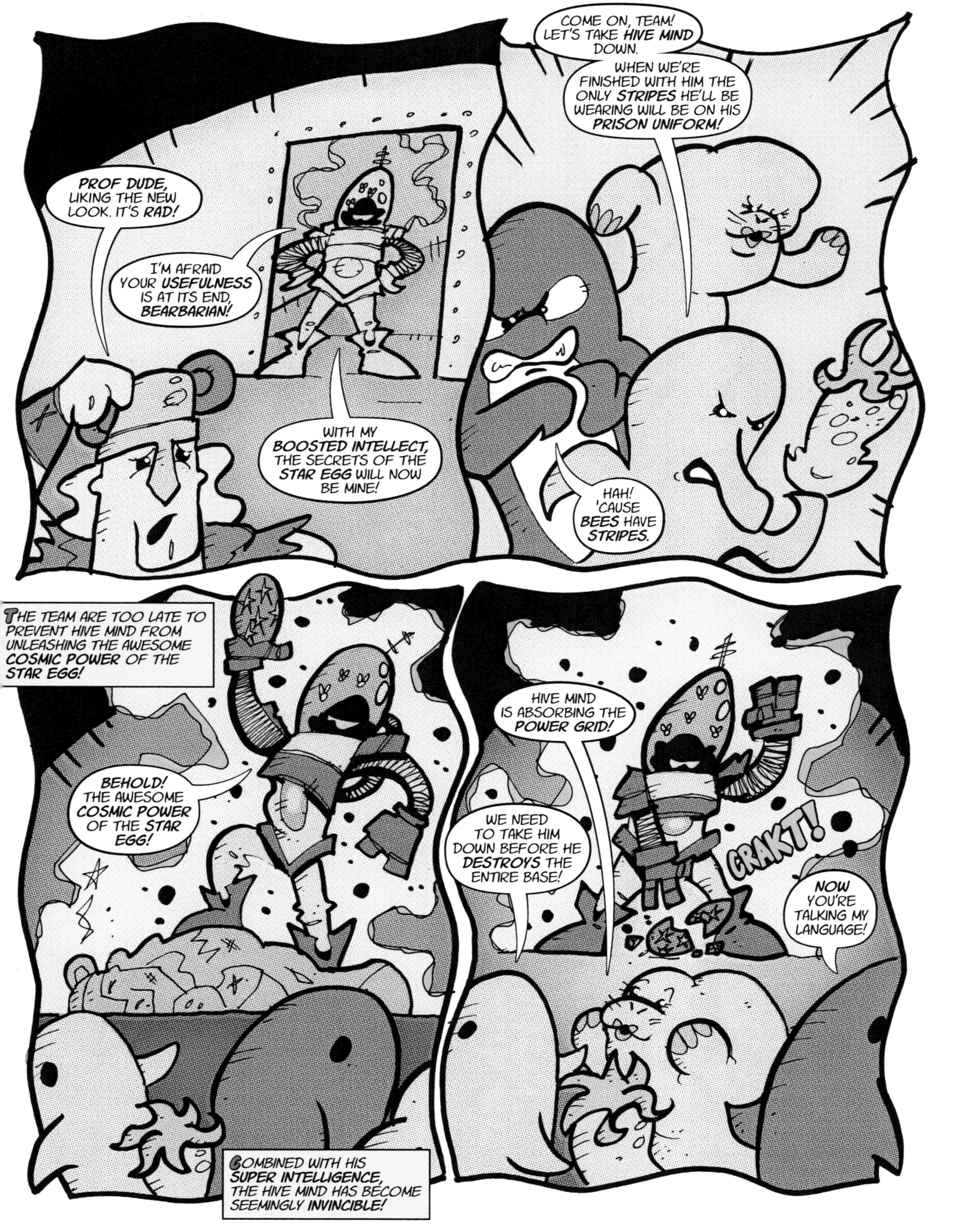
PROF DUDE, LIKING THE NEW LOOK. IT'S RAD!
I'M AFRAID YOUR USEFULNESS IS AT ITS END, BEARBARIAN!
WITH MY BOOSTED INTELLECT, THE SECRETS OF THE STAR EGG WILL NOW BE MINE!
COME ON, TEAM! LET'S TAKE HIVE MIND DOWN.
WHEN WE'RE FINISHED WITH HIM THE ONLY STRIPES HE'LL BE WEARING WILL BE ON HIS PRISON UNIFORM!
HAH! 'CAUSE BEES HAVE STRIPES.
THE TEAM ARE TOO LATE TO PREVENT HIVE MIND FROM UNLEASHING THE AWESOME COSMIC POWER OF THE STAR EGG!
BEHOLD! THE AWESOME COSMIC POWER OF THE STAR EGG!
COMBINED WITH HIS SUPER INTELLIGENCE, THE HIVE MIND HAS BECOME SEEMINGLY INVINCIBLE!
HIVE MIND IS ABSORBING THE POWER GRID!
WE NEED TO TAKE HIM DOWN BEFORE HE DESTROYS THE ENTIRE BASE!
CRAKT!
NOW YOU'RE TALKING MY LANGUAGE!

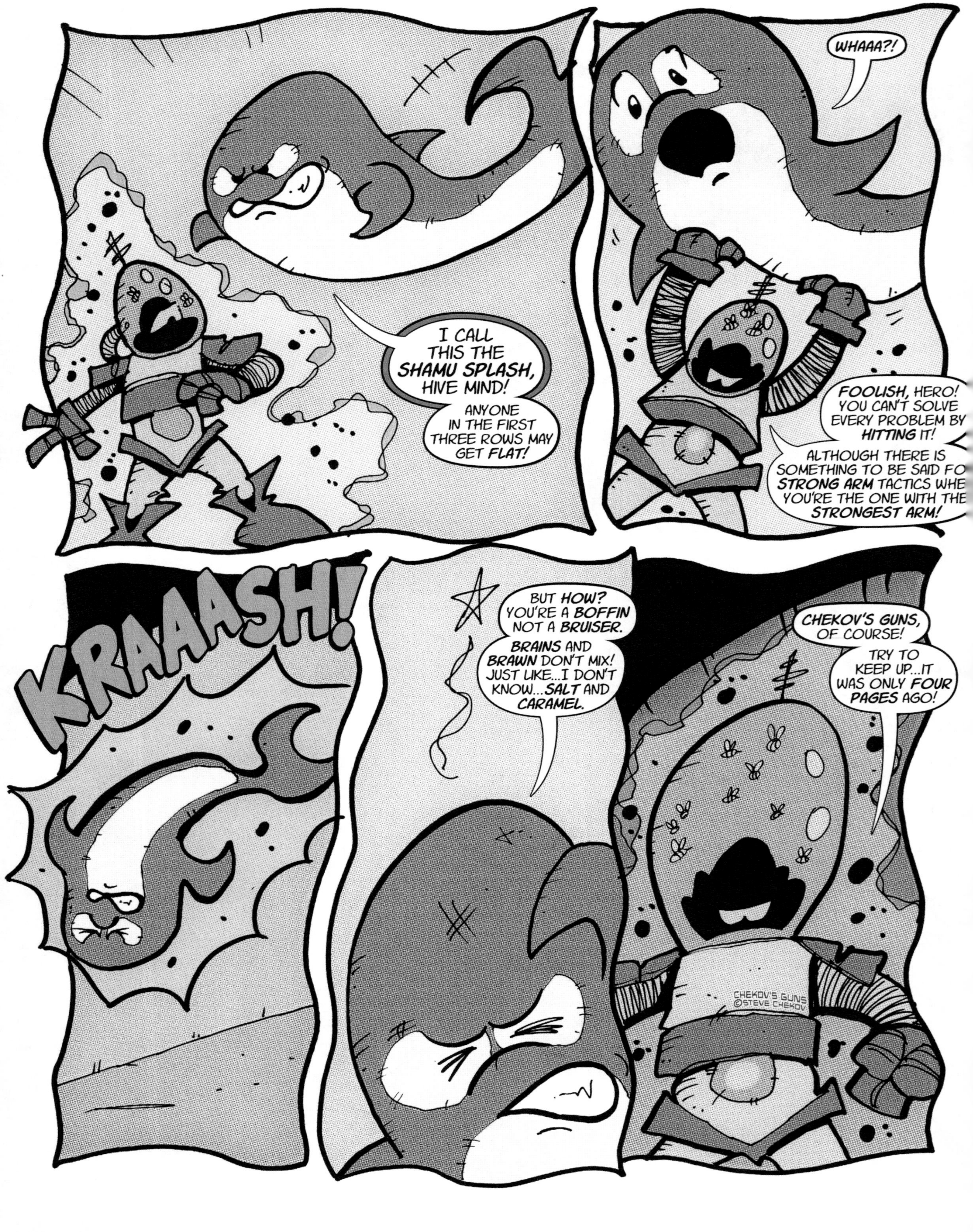
I CALL THIS THE SHAMU SPLASH, HIVE MIND!
ANYONE IN THE FIRST THREE ROWS MAY GET FLAT!
WHAAA?!
FOOLISH, HERO! YOU CAN'T SOLVE EVERY PROBLEM BY HITTING IT!
ALTHOUGH THERE IS SOMETHING TO BE SAID FO STRONG ARM TACTICS WHE YOU'RE THE ONE WITH THE STRONGEST ARM!
KRAAASH!
BUT HOW? YOU'RE A BOFFIN NOT A BRUISER.
BRAINS AND BRAWN DON'T MIX! JUST LIKE...I DON'T KNOW...SALT AND CARAMEL.
CHEKOV'S GUNS, OF COURSE!
TRY TO KEEP UP...IT WAS ONLY FOUR PAGES AGO!
CHEKOV'S GUNS ©STEVE CHEKOV

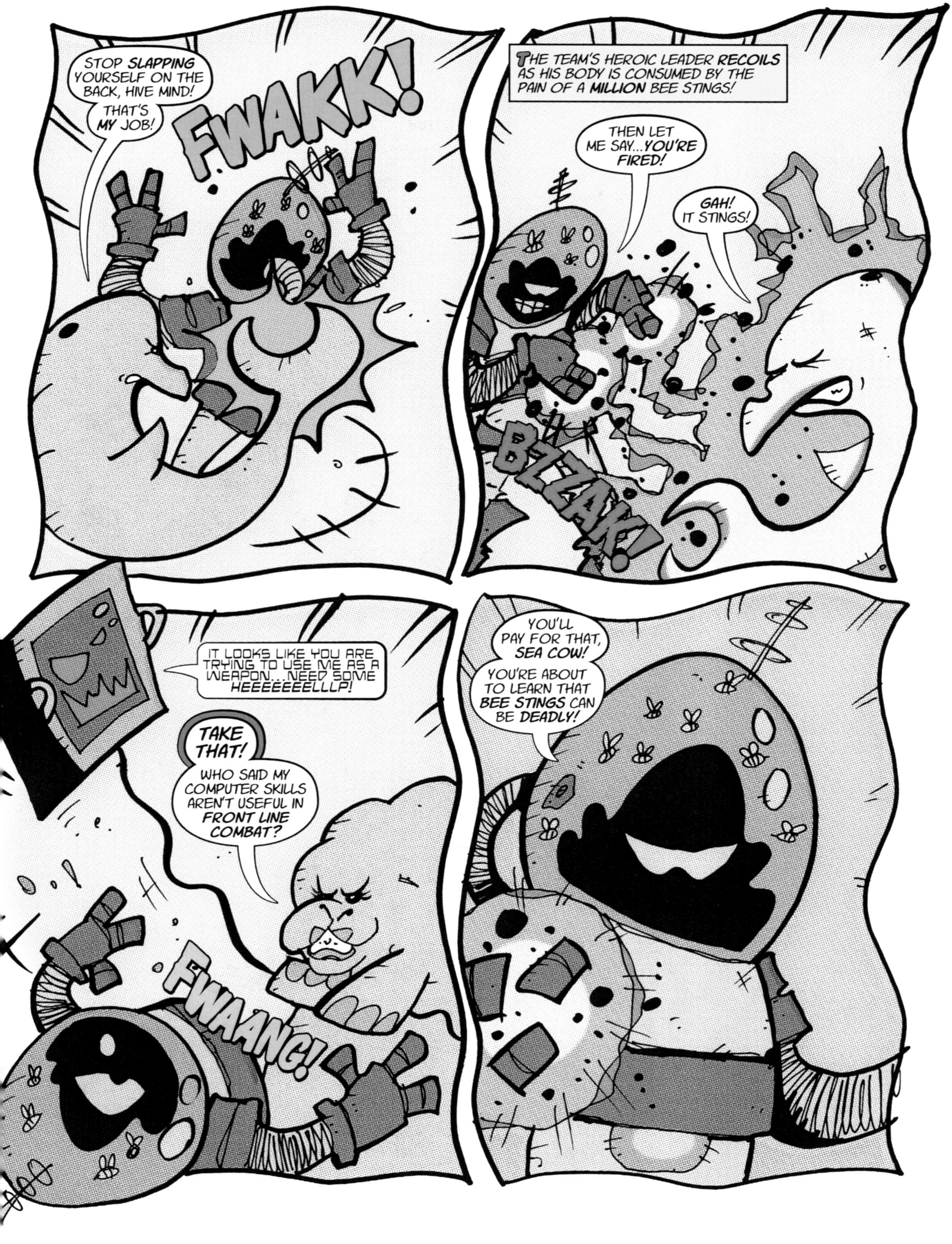
STOP SLAPPING YOURSELF ON THE BACK, HIVE MIND!
THAT'S MY JOB!
FWAKK!
THE TEAM'S HEROIC LEADER RECOILS AS HIS BODY IS CONSUMED BY THE PAIN OF A MILLION BEE STINGS!
THEN LET ME SAY...YOU'RE FIRED!
GAH! IT STINGS!
BZZAK!
IT LOOKS LIKE YOU ARE TRYING TO USE ME AS A WEAPON... NEED SOME HEEEEEEELLLP!
TAKE THAT!
WHO SAID MY COMPUTER SKILLS AREN'T USEFUL IN FRONT LINE COMBAT?
FWAANG!
YOU'LL PAY FOR THAT, SEA COW!
YOU'RE ABOUT TO LEARN THAT BEE STINGS CAN BE DEADLY!

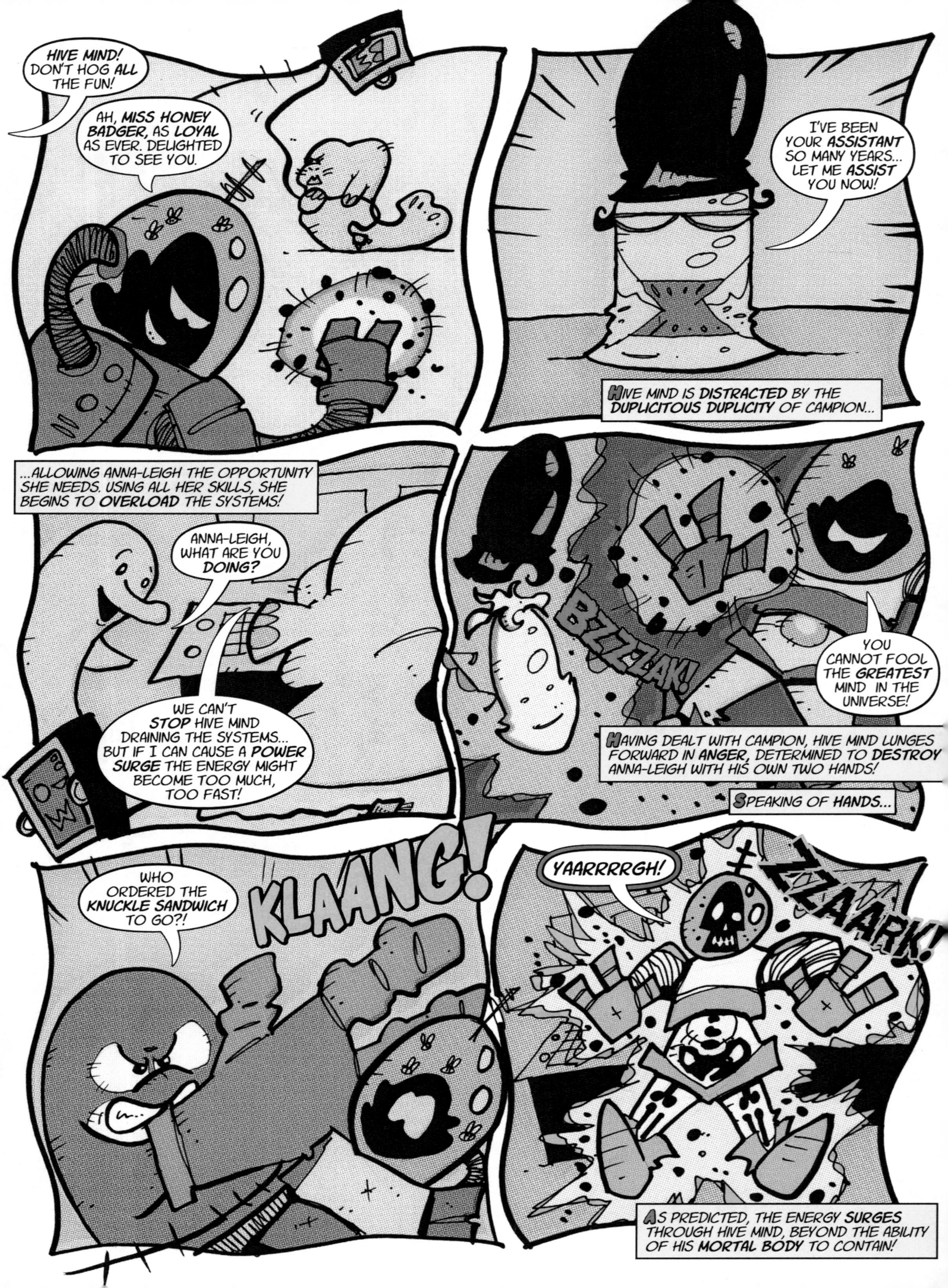
HIVE MIND! DON'T HOG ALL THE FUN!
AH, MISS HONEY BADGER, AS LOYAL AS EVER. DELIGHTED TO SEE YOU.
I'VE BEEN YOUR ASSISTANT SO MANY YEARS... LET ME ASSIST YOU NOW!
HIVE MIND IS DISTRACTED BY THE DUPLICITOUS DUPLICITY OF CAMPION...
...ALLOWING ANNA-LEIGH THE OPPORTUNITY SHE NEEDS. USING ALL HER SKILLS, SHE BEGINS TO OVERLOAD THE SYSTEMS!
ANNA-LEIGH, WHAT ARE YOU DOING?
WE CAN'T STOP HIVE MIND DRAINING THE SYSTEMS... BUT IF I CAN CAUSE A POWER SURGE THE ENERGY MIGHT BECOME TOO MUCH, TOO FAST!
BZZZAK!
YOU CANNOT FOOL THE GREATEST MIND IN THE UNIVERSE!
HAVING DEALT WITH CAMPION, HIVE MIND LUNGES FORWARD IN ANGER, DETERMINED TO DESTROY ANNA-LEIGH WITH HIS OWN TWO HANDS!
SPEAKING OF HANDS...
WHO ORDERED THE KNUCKLE SANDWICH TO GO?!
KLAANG!
YAARRRRGH!
ZZAARK!
AS PREDICTED, THE ENERGY SURGES THROUGH HIVE MIND, BEYOND THE ABILITY OF HIS MORTAL BODY TO CONTAIN!

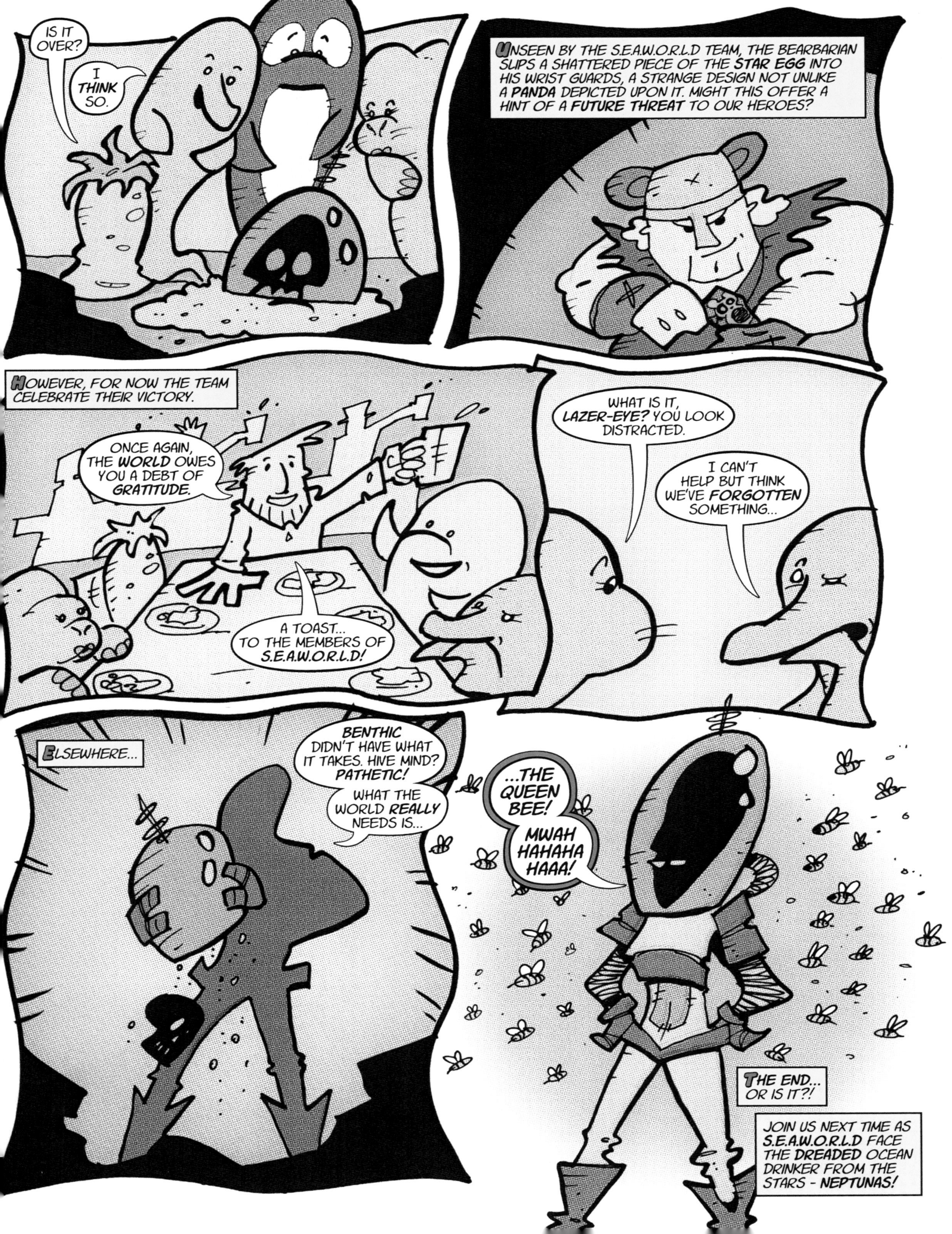
IS IT OVER?
I THINK SO.
UNSEEN BY THE S.E.A.W.O.R.L.D TEAM, THE BEARBARIAN SLIPS A SHATTERED PIECE OF THE STAR EGG INTO HIS WRIST GUARDS, A STRANGE DESIGN NOT UNLIKE A PANDA DEPICTED UPON IT. MIGHT THIS OFFER A HINT OF A FUTURE THREAT TO OUR HEROES?
HOWEVER, FOR NOW THE TEAM CELEBRATE THEIR VICTORY.
ONCE AGAIN, THE WORLD OWES YOU A DEBT OF GRATITUDE.
A TOAST... TO THE MEMBERS OF S.E.A.W.O.R.L.D!
WHAT IS IT, LAZER-EYE? YOU LOOK DISTRACTED.
I CAN'T HELP BUT THINK WE'VE FORGOTTEN SOMETHING...
ELSEWHERE...
BENTHIC DIDN'T HAVE WHAT IT TAKES. HIVE MIND? PATHETIC!
WHAT THE WORLD REALLY NEEDS IS...
...THE QUEEN BEE!
MWAH HAHAHA HAAA!
THE END... OR IS IT?!
JOIN US NEXT TIME AS S.E.A.W.O.R.L.D FACE THE DREADED OCEAN DRINKER FROM THE STARS - NEPTUNAS!

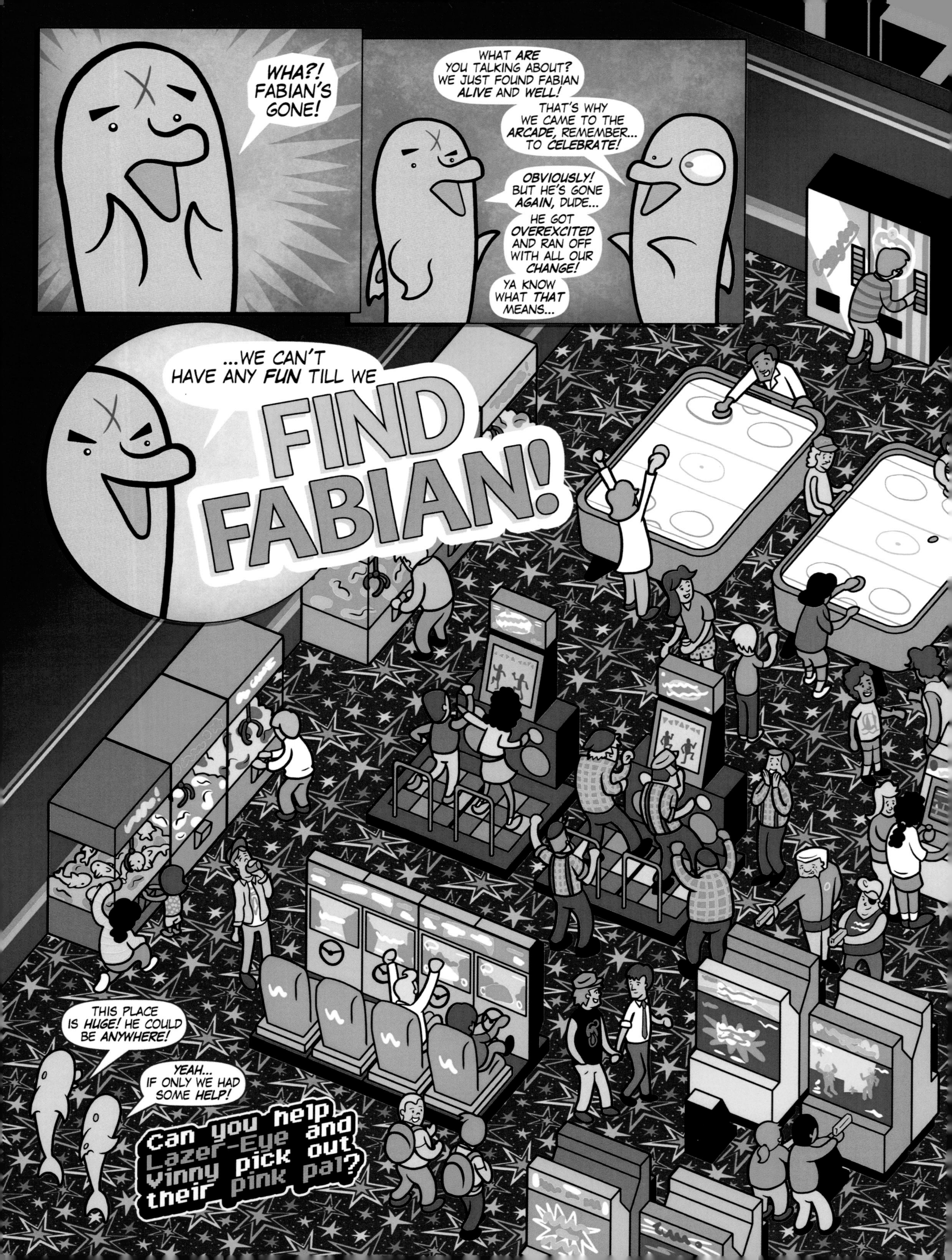

WHA?! FABIAN'S GONE!
WHAT ARE YOU TALKING ABOUT? WE JUST FOUND FABIAN ALIVE AND WELL!
THAT'S WHY WE CAME TO THE ARCADE, REMEMBER... TO CELEBRATE!
OBVIOUSLY! BUT HE'S GONE AGAIN, DUDE...
HE GOT OVEREXCITED AND RAN OFF WITH ALL OUR CHANGE!
YA KNOW WHAT THAT MEANS...
...WE CAN'T HAVE ANY FUN TILL WE
FIND FABIAN!
THIS PLACE IS HUGE! HE COULD BE ANYWHERE!
YEAH... IF ONLY WE HAD SOME HELP!
Can you help Lazer-Eye and Vinny pick out their pink pal?

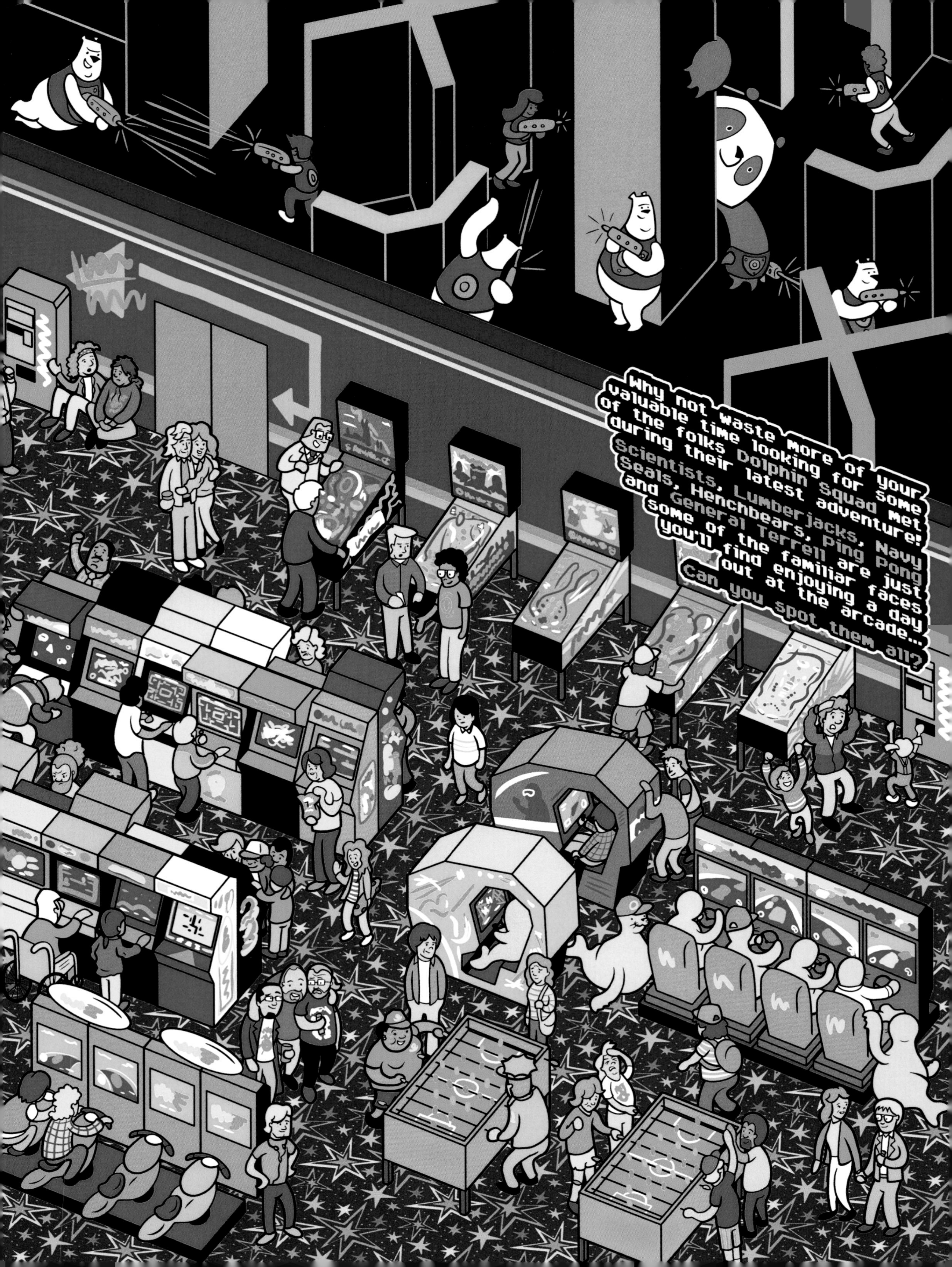

Why not waste more of your valuable time looking for some of the folks Dolphin Squad met during their latest adventure! Scientists, Lumberjacks, Navy Seals, Henchbears, Ping Pong and General Terrell are just some of the familiar faces you'll find enjoying a day out at the arcade... Can you spot them all?

DOLPHIN SQUAD WILL RETURN

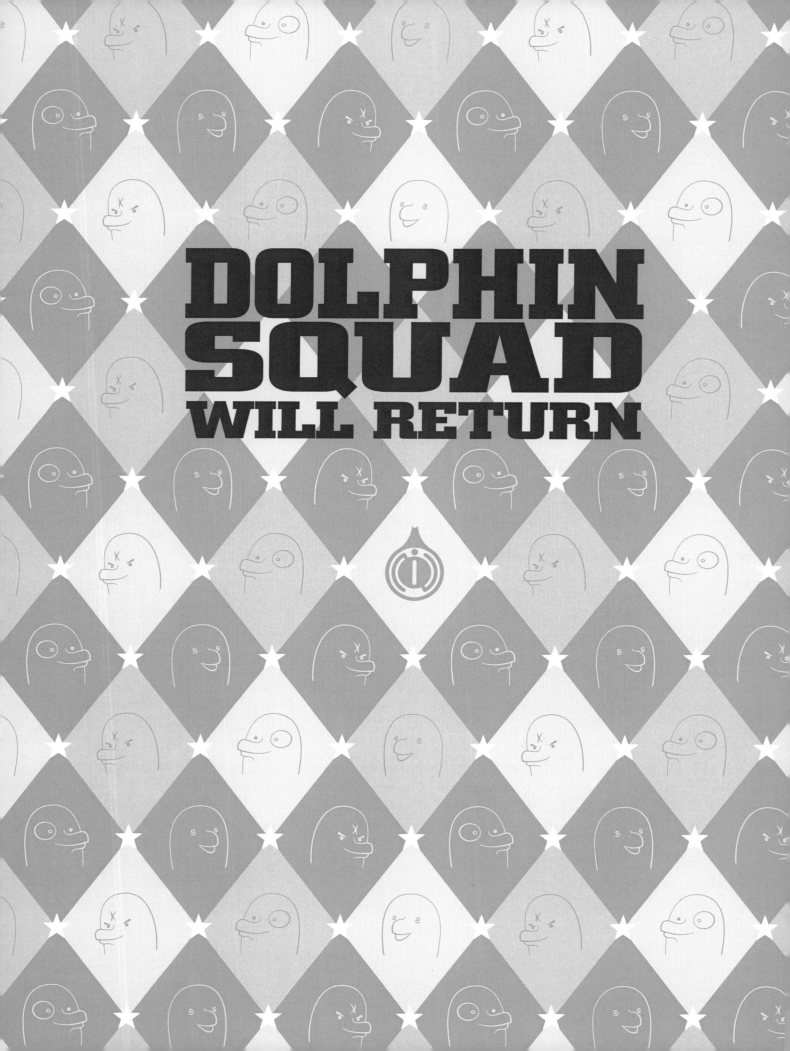